BROWN

BOY

BARELY

BLOSSOMS

BROWN

BOY

BARELY

BLOSSOMS

AFZAL HUDA

IGUANA

Publisher: Cheryl Hawley
Editor: Annie Tucker
Book cover design: Ivan Kurylenko
Illustration: Afzal Huda

ISBN 978-1-77180-607-7 (paperback)
ISBN 978-1-77180-608-4 (epub)

This is an original print edition of *Brown Boy Barely Blossoms*.

For Immi & Nush

AUTHOR NOTE

Some terms are defined in the footnotes. I've translated them based on common usage in many languages of the Indian subcontinent.

CHAPTER ONE

At the end of summer and the beginning of fall, burgundy maple leaves twirled for the first time; cranberries, apples, and plums blossomed; and Ashiq Amlani arrived at the Vancouver International Airport holding his crisp, blue Canadian passport. He stepped off the plane and made his way to customs and immigration. He had been waiting for this moment for a long time — to meet his people, to return to his native land, to use the magical powers of the beloved passport he held in his hand, so that everyone could see who he was, where he was born, and what privileges he had. People around him smiled (because that's what most Canadians do). He found his land. He was one of them.

"May I see your passport, please?" An officer approached him. It was his time to shine. Ashiq gave the woman his papers and his biggest grin. He waited for her to hug him and smell the cologne he had sprayed on himself in the airplane washroom. He wondered if he should kiss her on the cheek, because that's what he saw white people do in British movies. *After all, the Queen is our queen too,* he thought.

"Please come with me," she said, and took him to a secluded room behind the passport control area where he met three other officers. *This is what it feels to be a Canadian: proper VIP service.* He smiled, but they didn't. He looked for the spotlights to come on, but the room got darker. He expected hugs and kisses, but instead he was strip-searched and touched where no one had ever touched him before. The officer threw his gloves in the can and asked Ashiq to get dressed, pack his stuff, and get the hell out of there. "Welcome to Canada," they said.

He walked out with his oversized luggage and his not-so-magical-after-all passport. He spotted his aunt and uncle in the arrival area.

He shook his uncle's hand, but his aunt pulled him closer, embraced him, and kissed him how he had wanted the lady officer to. They got into the car, rolled the windows down, and Ashiq passed out like someone who had returned home after a long time. They took Grant McConachie Way for fifteen minutes, and when they got onto Granville Street, his uncle accelerated, the car jerked, and woke Ashiq up from his sleep.

"You should put your seatbelt on," his uncle stared into the rearview mirror. His aunt held the side of her seat, peeked from behind the passenger seat, and smiled. "We know you're not used to these things, but …"

"What things?" He pulled the seatbelt and wrapped it around his waist. She pointed at the buckle, raising her eyebrows.

"You dozed off as soon as we left the airport. Have you come here to sleep?" His uncle looked into the rearview mirror and pushed his spectacles further up the bridge of his nose. "You know, people pay so much money to come here. It's one of the most beautiful cities in the world, and the drive down to our place from the airport is spectacular."

Ashiq pulled a magazine out of his bag, flipped the pages and skimmed through the feature on lucid dreaming, which he had read at least twice on the plane ride. "Well, I have all the time in the world. It's not like I'm going anywhere anytime soon," he said. The magazine had a picture of a girl walking a white Siberian husky on the beach, listening to music on her brand-new Sony Walkman that reminded him of Alina. She was the girl he met on the plane, who wore an indigo top with spaghetti straps and had long, black shiny hair, same as the girl in the magazine. He had watched her nap during the flight, her head rested on his shoulder, the fresh smell of Wella shampoo. He knew it was Wella because that's what his mom used.

His aunt raised the corner of her lip and turned to her husband, who was tapping his fingers on the steering wheel and taking a deep breath. "You should put that magazine away," she said as they drove by Queen Elizabeth Park. "You're missing out on all the amazing views."

"I'm just thinking about how I'm going to write my next piece."

"The English here is different," his uncle explained. "Very different."

"I used to write in Karachi. I'm a great writer. Jahanara Aunty, why don't you tell him?" he called for her attention. She frowned, and he didn't understand what made her beautiful face wrinkle.

"Ashiq, this is not Karachi," his uncle sounded frustrated. "We speak proper English here. You won't be able to write for Canadian magazines or newspapers. Don't get your hopes high."

"But my English is good."

"You have an accent. You sound like a proper fob," he hissed.

"What's a fob?" Ashiq asked in his disheartened voice, putting the magazine back into his bag. He glanced at the luxury yachts docked at the marina as they passed the False Creek Yacht Club and wondered who they belonged to.

"I rest my case," his uncle said.

"Rakesh!" she protested. "You don't have to be so mean. He's only eighteen."

"Jenny, the kid needs a reality check. Out there in the real world, he won't be able to find his own ass with both his hands. I'm doing him a favor so that he lowers his expectations."

As Rakesh drove the red Audi into the parking garage, the headlights came on. Ashiq's eyes widened in slight awe. He had never seen the lights come on without a manual command. "Is that automatic?" he asked.

"What? The lights?" Rakesh looked at Ashiq in the rearview mirror. "The car has a sensor. When it gets dark, the lights come on." He shrugged. "It's nothing new, but I guess it is for you."

Jenny put her hand on Rakesh's thigh and made him stop mid-sentence. "Are you ready to see our new condo, Ash?" He nodded, smiling. Aunt Jenny always called him Ash, but his mom hated the idea. She wanted everyone to call her son by his proper name, Ashiq. It means "in love" in Arabic. But Jenny had reminded Ashiq's mom that his name could also mean "a lovelorn, someone who is unhappy because of unrequited love." But his mom insisted on using Ashiq and only Ashiq. But to Jenny, the name Ash sounded more Canadian. Less Indian, less Pakistani, and certainly less *fobby*.

Ashiq scanned the parking garage while Rakesh looped the car around to find a spot. He had never seen so many expensive cars in such a small space before. His heart suddenly felt big and prosperous. Full of hopes and dreams.

Rakesh backed the Audi into a tight spot between two identical Range Rovers, sneering, "Fuckin' twits." Jenny slapped his thigh and gave him a look. "Watch the door when you come out," he warned, staring into the rearview mirror.

"Rakesh is very anal about his car," Jenny sighed.

"I just paid a lot of money for this baby."

Ashiq frowned, unsure what exactly his uncle meant by "a lot." *It couldn't possibly be that high*, he thought. In Karachi, cars usually cost 200,000 rupees.

"Sixty thousand, and I paid cash," Rakesh said.

"Wow. That's a lot. How much would that be in rupees? One dollar is thirty rupees give or take," Ashiq calculated.

"That would be one point eight million rupees."

"Whoa. That much! The house my parents and sister and I are living in right now in Karachi is one point four million! You should sell this car and buy our house and you'll still have four hundred thousand left," Ashiq said.

"When we moved here in the sixties, it used to be four rupees to a dollar. The good old days. Now after three decades … wait, it's almost four," Rakesh said, looking to Jenny for confirmation. "Next year will be thirty-eight years?"

"Forty years in the spring of 2000. The millennium will be our forty-year anniversary as Canadians," Jenny smiled.

Ashiq pressed the silver button on the wall. "I guess the lift is not working."

"*Lift*?" Rakesh cracked up like the whistle of a worn-out engine.

"It's called an elevator, Ashiq," Jenny said with composure and shook her head at Rakesh.

"Umm, but Canada is a commonwealth just like Pakistan, so why don't you use British English here. Isn't that proper, instead of the American version?"

"Oh, you have so much to learn, Ashiq," Rakesh said.

Ashiq pressed the elevator button twice. "Why is this not working?"

"You have to clap for the light to come on. It's a new system," Rakesh winked at Jenny. Ashiq put the luggage down and stroked his hands together. He frowned and tried again.

"Oh God, Ricky," Jenny exclaimed. "He's joking, Ashiq."

Rakesh waved the key device in front of the scanner and the panel turned green. Jenny pressed number twenty-two on the inside panel and the elevator doors shut. "Our place has one of the best views of downtown. You're gonna love waking up every day. Vancouver is like a paradise," Jenny smiled.

"Well, every day *only* for the next few weeks. Let's get that straight," Rakesh said.

Ashiq felt like Rakesh had pressed one of the buttons on his key device to cut the oxygen supply in the elevator. His stomach curled up like a snake. *But Jahanara Aunty said I could stay with them for as long as I wanted,* he thought. *What does he mean by only the next few weeks?*

"I need to use the bathroom," he blurted out. Jenny nodded.

The elevator doors rushed into the shafts, as if to help Ashiq get to the bathroom on time. Jenny opened the apartment door, letting Ashiq enter first. "It's on the left." Ricky pulled Jenny and rolled his eyes. She shook her head and said, "Ashiq, don't throw the toilet paper in the bin. Just flush it."

"I know how to use toilet paper, Aunty ji."[1]

"I just thought," she curved her lips. "And you don't have to call me Aunty. You can call me *Khala*,[2] you know."

"But I've always called you Aunty, and *Khala* is an Urdu word."

Rakesh laughed. "Aunty sounds old. And no one will know what *Khala* means. People will think it's her name or something."

"Shut up, Ricky," she snapped before she turned back to Ashiq. "Just call me *Khala* or *Jenny Khala*, okay?"

"Uh-huh."

---

[1] *Ji* is a gender-neutral honorific used as a suffix.
[2] *Khala* means aunt (maternal).

"And spray the air freshener once you're done dropping your kids in the pool. No one wants to smell that Pakistani shit," Rakesh crackled.

Do they seriously think I am stupid? he thought.

"A shit's a shit, Ricky." His voice echoed in the washroom.

"It's Uncle Rakesh, you brat. Show some respect," he said, sounding enraged.

"If Jahanara Aunty is *Jenny Khala*, then shouldn't you be *Ricky Khalu?*"[3]

"Don't be a smart ass."

He flushed twice, washed his hands with liquid soap, and looked at himself in the mirror. *This shit really smells,* he thought. He sprayed the air freshener as if he was clearing up an epidemic. The smell of jasmine reminded him of home.

---

[3] *Khalu* means uncle (husband of your maternal aunt).

CHAPTER TWO

Jenny and Ricky had planned to take Ashiq out to dinner, but the phone rang. It was one of Ricky's old friends from Texas tipping him off on a sizzling new stock. Jenny wasn't happy with the sudden change of plans, but Ricky was. After all, it meant a thicker wallet and a longer erection.

A year ago, Jenny and Ricky moved to Vancouver from Waterloo, where they had lived since the early sixties after migrating from Karachi. They loved the city of Waterloo, despite the lack of the hustle and bustle that they were used to in Karachi. They got used to the quietness, and Pinehurst Lake was only a thirty-minute drive away. It may have been Waterloo that had transformed Jahanara and Rakesh Poonja into Jenny and Ricky, and perhaps had made them feel a bit more Canadian, but the below twenty-degree weather during harsh winters had made them move. It didn't hurt that Jenny had taken an amazing job at one of the elite private schools that attracted children of celebrities, leading politicians, and filthy-rich immigrants. Ricky had quit his computer science teaching job at the University of Waterloo the day Jenny accepted the new position.

"I can work from home," he had said then. "There's so much money to be made in software developing, and we have savings."

But things hadn't gone as planned. Once, Ashiq overheard his grandmother telling the maid that Ricky and Jenny's passion was fading away, and since then Ashiq had imagined that the sheets on their king-size bed were being changed much less often. One night, Ashiq had a dream that Jenny had discovered newer ways of touching herself. *Meanwhile, Ricky counted sheep or dreamt about his Audi stuck in a ditch, or at times morphed into a rusted bicycle with broken pedals. They started to fall apart.*

Ricky wanted to do something about it and began seeing Dr. Mulley (a name Ashiq felt suited such a doctor), who told him on numerous occasions that there was nothing wrong with his pecker and that it was all in his head. Dr. Mulley sent him to see a shrink who explained to Ricky that he probably felt emasculated.

"Men are funny creatures," the shrink told Ricky on the first day. "They want to provide for the family, but when the lady of the house starts bringing in more money, it becomes a matter of pride, and the first signs are always seen in the bedroom."

Since he had overheard Ricky and Jenny's secrets from his grandmother, Ashiq hadn't stopped thinking about them and their lifestyle. Two weeks before Ashiq arrived in Vancouver, he even dreamt about it, in full color:

It must have been the last week of winter when Ricky woke up with sweats and shivers. He had just dreamt that he had died by choking on red Marlboros. In the dream he was naked, and the people from the Silicon Valley were giggling at his exposed penis that looked like a piece of a diminished, dried date. His doctor, Dr. Mulley, called his manhood "a little woody woodpecker" in his eulogy, and proposed marriage to Jenny, who accepted and granted the doctor a fiery fellatio in front of Ricky's open casket.

Sweaty Ricky went straight to his computer to put in a request to sell all his stocks in the company that produced red Marlboros. The following day, he bought shares in a struggling airline because his friend in Texas had told him that one of his cousins in Saudi Arabia had leaked him invaluable information (Ashiq had skimmed through most of Ricky's financial magazines in the bathroom).

And on Friday morning, March 21, 1997, the phone rang, and his broker told him that Philip Morris Companies, the maker of red Marlboros, had plunged the equivalent of about 18.5 Dow points after the news that a rival cigarette maker had struck a deal with state prosecutors who could undermine the industry's defenses against health-liability suits. But that wasn't all. Ricky not only saved a lot of money, but also made a ton. The broker said that the billionaire Saudi Prince Al-Waleed bin Talal had purchased a five percent stake in Trans World Airlines.

On the first day of spring, Ricky's new stocks weren't the only things that had climbed. His pecker had risen from the ashes and kept Jenny up all night. The next day, Jenny replaced the three-week-old bed sheets with the 400-thread-count satin sheets she got as a Christmas gift from one of her students' parents, and Ricky called Dr. Mulley to cancel all his upcoming appointments.

After this vivid night spectacle, Ashiq woke up to the sound of crows outside his bedroom window in Karachi that he shared with his little sister, Fari. Ashiq slid his palms over his bedsheet, hoping he would feel the satin, but when his hand reached a wet spot on his cotton sheets, he realized it was just a dream.

"It's time to make some money," Ricky said, rubbing his palms together and producing his most cheerful grin. Ashiq assumed that it would be a fun night for Ricky and Jenny, and that she would change the sheets in the morning.

"Go get them, tiger," she winked.

Ricky got up from his chair to grab his wife's rump but sat back down when he saw Ashiq appear out of the kitchen holding a lasagna pan.

"What should I do with the *el-you-min-yum* foil?" Ashiq asked.

"Oh, you mean *aluminum* foil," she said, trying hard not to laugh. "Actually, we're going out."

"We are?"

"Yep. Uncle Rakesh will stay home and work on his new software, and then he'll clean up his office so you can sleep there. Just put that back in the fridge."

"Leave it out, Ashiq," Ricky said. "I'll heat that up and have it for dinner later."

"We can bring you something back, hon." Jenny wore her purse across her right shoulder and checked for the keys.

"Where are you guys gonna go?"

"Not sure. I was thinking of taking him to the taco place."

"That's gonna be packed tonight. It's Thursday." Ricky took off his spectacles and puffed on them, wiping them with his t-shirt.

"True. What do you feel like, Ash?"

He shrugged his shoulders.

"He's not gonna know anything," Ricky said in a patronizing voice.

Jenny's eyes narrowed at her husband. "I'll just get you whatever we have," she said as she slammed the apartment door behind her.

Ashiq imagined that back inside the apartment, Ricky was leaning back on his chair and squinting his eyes, getting the message that his wife wanted him to be nice to the son of her older sister. In fact, Ricky was in there thinking *This too shall pass* as he entered the password *fuckPaki$10* on the computer screen.

Jenny took Ashiq for a long walk around the neighborhood. They stopped at a burrito place and got a steak and shrimp to go for Ricky. She showed him the public library and told him he could go there during the day and research about the schools he wanted to apply to for the upcoming semester.

"Which one is the best?" he asked her.

"Well, that depends on the program. The big names are UBC and Simon Fraser, but they're not easy to get into. You need extremely good grades," she said. "What are you interested in?"

"I don't know. I like to write, but I guess I'm not that good," he said, lowering his eyes.

"Don't let Ricky get to you," she counseled him, squeezing his shoulders. "He means well, but it's just that sometimes he doesn't think before he speaks. UBC has a great program in journalism."

"I am not sure, though. Sometimes I think about international development studies because I want to do something for the society."

"You can be a journalist that writes about international development. Wouldn't that be great?" she smiled.

"I don't know. There are so many choices."

"Just focus on what you love."

"I love so many things," he laughed. "And I love the way you say *international.* You sound like a gori[4] madam. I want to learn how to talk like a white person."

"It'll take some time, but you'll adapt, and your accent will change. The trick is to start thinking in English and to pay attention to how people say things, like how you just did with *international.*"

"*Inttur...national?*"

"No," she laughed. "It's *INN-ernational.* The letter T is almost silent."

"But it's not supposed to be silent."

"It's not baba.[5] It sounds like that with our accent. You'll get a grip on it. Don't think too much."

"I guess." He ogled the two girls sitting on the patio of an ice-cream parlor they were passing on their way back to the apartment building.

"You know what?" she asked. Ashiq turned his head to look at his aunt. "I noticed something about you. Well, it's not just you. It's kind of ... I don't know how to put it. It's a desi[6] thing to do ... something pretty much all brown people do when they first come here."

Ashiq looked at her with curiosity. *Does she think I'm like all the other brown people? But I'm different. I'm not like those losers that smell of curry and make loud noises when they sip their tea. I'm Canadian. I was born here. I have a blue passport.*

"You should not stare at people. It makes them uncomfortable," she advised.

"What you mean? I don't stare at people," he raised his shoulders.

"Don't get defensive. There's nothing wrong with checking people out. Everyone does that, but you must be subtle about it. If

---

[4] *Gori* is an informal word for a white or fair-skinned woman.
[5] *Baba* is a familiar word for "father" but has also been adapted to address male children.
[6] *Desi* is a word to describe the people, cultures, and products of the Indian subcontinent.

you're wearing dark sunglasses, it's a different story," she giggled as they turned around the corner toward their apartment building. "The trick is to look once but briefly, and then let them go like you don't care, even if you do."

"Hmm achha[7] achha," he nodded.

"I guess that's enough for today," she smiled, opening the door. "You're gonna sleep well tonight. You must be tired."

"I am," he said, pressing the button for their floor as the elevator doors shut. "Wow. You don't even feel the lift. Sorry … I mean, the elevator."

"Good," she smiled. "You're a fast learner. We live in one of the best buildings in Yaletown, so everything here is top of the line. Tomorrow I'll show you the gym. Do you work out?"

He shook his head.

"That's okay. I'll take you there and show you a few things. We can be new gym partners."

"What about Uncle Rakesh?"

"Oh, he's a lost cause. I tried, but it's not his thing. Well, at least he eats healthy," she sighed.

They entered the apartment and Jenny peeked her head in the kitchen. "Do you smell that?"

"What?"

"The barbecue." She stepped on the foot lever of the garbage can and the lid flipped open. "I can't believe it."

"What happened?"

"He ate the leftovers. I told him that we would bring him something back. Now what the hell do I do with this damn burrito?" She put the burrito bag on the white onyx kitchen counter.

"Maybe he got hungry," Ashiq said, lifting his heels.

"Do you need to use the washroom?" she asked Ashiq, giving him a peculiar look. He shook his head. "Then why do you keep doing

---

[7] *Achha* is a multi-purpose word, which literally means "good." However, it also takes on a number of other meanings, depending on the intonation it's given and where it is positioned in a sentence. It could also mean "okay," "really?" "I understand," "oh," or "I have a question."

that?" She pointed at his lifted heels. "Wanna be a ballerina?" She poked his arm and smirked, "There are some great schools here for that."

"That's not funny."

"You know you can tell me anything. I'm not like your mom." She came closer to him, held his biceps that touched the sides of her breast and whispered into his ears, "We can have secrets."

He felt an intense sensation in his heart that rushed down into his pants. It was a new feeling for him that came with a touch of guilt, like he was peeking into Jenny and Ricky's bedroom, watching them make love.

"Umm, lifting up my heels? Oh. I just do that sometimes," he said.

"Uh-huh." She showed him the spare room. Ricky had packed the mess into a white banker's box that was on the floor next to a pile of files and folders. "You can use the washroom next to the living room for brushing your teeth or if you wake up in the middle of the night. There's only one bathroom in the apartment and it's in our room. Of course, you'll use that when you want to shower. We'll figure out a schedule or whatever. It's no big deal."

"Thank you, Aunty."

"*Khala*," she corrected him.

"Yes, Jenny Khala." He smiled and got into the blue sleeping bag.

"Good night, Ash. Sleep well."

"Good night."

Jenny turned the lights off and closed the office door behind her. She put the burrito bag in the fridge, wiped the counter, and flipped the switch. The light coming through under the door started to dim and Ashiq heard Jenny go into her bedroom.

As the door shut, his imagination got the better of him. He pictured Jenny getting undressed, opening the top drawer to grab her pajamas. *She remembered that Ricky had sent the new version of his software to his clients in the Silicon Valley earlier that evening, which meant multiple orgasms, and decided to go for her Victoria's Secret chiffon slip. She paused to look at Ricky, who was curled up under the covers, and asked him if he preferred the red or the black one. He didn't answer. She picked the black one because it felt better on her skin, but then recalled that Ricky preferred the red one from the time that he had scored big and they went somewhere afterward for a week. Ricky turned to look at her and flipped over the cover for her to get in. "I ate the leftovers."*

"I saw." She got in and cuddled him. "I'm sure you can make up for that."

She put her hands under his boxers and kissed him on his neck. She brought his hands around her and made him feel the chiffon on her waist. But something was different.

"What's wrong?" she asked as she took her hand out of his boxer.

"Nothing."

"This is not normal."

"What, babe?"

"You're not hard at all." She crossed her hands over her chest. "Did they not like your work?"

"I don't wanna talk about it?" He phrased it more as a question than an actual response.

"We have to talk about it. You've been so good, and now suddenly …"

"I said that I don't want to talk about it!" he snapped.

Ashiq's imagination stopped conjuring up this scenario when he heard a bang in Jenny and Ricky's bedroom. It sounded like someone had slammed the bathroom door or the cabinet. *Maybe she threw the chiffon slip back in the drawer.* He heard Jenny raise her voice, but he couldn't tell if Ricky was upset or just murmuring. He wondered if they were arguing about the length of his stay, or maybe Jenny had accidently called out Ashiq's name while Ricky touched her. *Where will I go after a few weeks?* He worried and looked out the window that reflected the lights coming from the downtown core.

He thought about the burritos they had eaten, and the takeout for Ricky that Jenny had left on the onyx counter in the kitchen. He thought about the white V-neck Jenny had worn that evening and his heart beat faster as he remembered how her breast had touched his hand and how she had whispered in his ears. He got a pulsing hard-on; it was one of those erections that rip the seams of most durable pajamas. Little did he know that Ricky would have traded all his Trans World Airlines stocks for a boner like that.

The bedroom door opened, and Ashiq saw the light sneak in under the office door. He grabbed the zipper of the sleeping bag and pulled it toward him. He wondered if Ricky had come out of his room to confront him for thinking about his sweet wife. The thought drew the blood away from his throbbing penis and back to his pulsating heart, and the mighty mushroom tip turned like the Tower of Pisa.

Ricky turned on the tap in the kitchen to fill his glass of water and walked back to the bedroom. Ashiq was imagining Jenny laying in her pomegranate red Victoria's Secret chiffon slip, waiting for sluggish Ricky to start counting sheep and watch his red Audi morph into a rusted bicycle that he once rode in his early teenage years in Karachi, so that she could think about Ashiq and touch herself until her toes curled.

Ashiq pulled up his pajamas, shut his eyes, and forced himself to sleep. He thought about the time difference and wondered what his family in Karachi was doing as he lay on the office floor of Ricky Poonja.

There was a thought, however, that hadn't left him since that afternoon. It was something he could have resolved in his dreams or in the waking hours of the coming days, but he couldn't wait. He opened his eyes wide as the thought rushed back into the dominant groove of his swarming mind.

What the hell is a fob?

CHAPTER THREE

Jenny knocked on the door twice, turned the knob in slow increments, and peeked her head in. "Good morning, sunshine," she whispered.

Ashiq stretched his arms and realized he was inside a sleeping bag. She entered the room and kneeled in front of him. She wore a white bathrobe that kept the sexy chiffon slip hidden underneath, but she lowered herself and, with the robe slightly open, he got a glimpse of the morning sun that not only warmed Ricky's office but toasted Ashiq's insides like a fresh cup of joe. *She smells so good,* he thought. She unzipped his sleeping bag and flipped it open.

"Oh wow," she said, eyes widening. "Someone's been having happy dreams."

"Aunty! You shouldn't have." He flipped the cover back over him and turned his head in embarrassment. His penis was hard and strong, like the voice of a rooster chasing the first rays of sun.

"You don't have to be shy about this, Ash. It's natural, and actually it's a sign of a healthy body."

"Umm, I need a few minutes."

"Of course, take your time." She got up, took a few steps toward the door, and stopped. "I'm assuming you're gonna wait to wank off till you go in the shower?"

"Oh God, Jahanara Aunty."

"*Khala.* Remember?" she chided him. "The reason I said that," she explained as she adjusted her robe, "is because Uncle Rakesh needs the office. He has a lot of work to do and has a meeting later on, so he wants to take care of things before he heads downtown."

He nodded, waited for her to leave, and checked to make sure it was safe to emerge from the sleeping bag. He looked out the window and couldn't believe he had woken up in Vancouver. He wondered how life could be so different in two parts of the world. Two days earlier, he had been walking the dark and dingy streets of Karachi, and then, within the span of twenty-four hours, he was eating a beef burrito in a posh neighborhood of Vancouver. He stretched his arms, rubbed his eyes with the back of his fists, and yawned. He looked at his composed, cool, and collected penis and smiled. He pushed the sleeping bag to the side and walked out of Ricky's office.

Ricky looked at him, sighed, and went back to the news on the television. Ashiq stepped into the kitchen, saw the bread on his plate, and frowned. "Is this flavored bread?"

"No, it's whole wheat. We don't eat white bread like you do in Karachi, because it's bad for you," Jenny nodded with a smile. "Go sit at the table and enjoy your first day. Starting tomorrow, you can begin helping out."

Ashiq didn't understand what she meant by "helping out" until he saw Ricky wipe the breadcrumbs off the table onto his empty plate and take his coffee mug and dirty utensils to the kitchen.

"Thanks, babe," Jenny said.

Ashiq never saw his father do that. Where he grew up, it was given women were supposed to do those things. Men were born to command and to reap the benefits of having a penis. After all, there was a reason why God made women the way he did, with a womb to carry the offspring. Once they slid out the tunnel, he blessed them with mammary glands to feed. "It's their responsibility," his father had said with conviction when Ashiq questioned why his mom did all the housework in addition to running her boutique, Fairies Fashions.

He spread strawberry jam on one slice of brown bread and margarine on the other. He took a bite of the crunchy sandwich. *This tastes weird,* he thought.

Jenny placed a tall glass of two percent milk on the coaster.

"How's the bread? Can you tell the difference?"

"It's good," he said as he struggled to swallow.

"See, I told you. It's healthy and it tastes way better."

The color of the bread made him feel like he was eating leather, and he took a sip of milk to push it down his throat. He wondered why white people in Canada preferred brown bread, and brown people in Pakistan preferred white bread. This didn't seem natural to him. He left the land of his parents to experience all that was white, not to end up in a room with brown people eating brown bread.

"I've got to get ready for work. Finish your breakfast and I'll show you a few things before I leave," Jenny said, and Ashiq nodded, smiling. He followed her with his eyes as she entered the bedroom and shut the door behind her. He picked up the salt and pepper dispensers and examined the feeding slots. He wondered how the black peppercorns came out of such tiny holes. In Karachi, he used simple bottles with holes on the top that sprinkled ground pepper, but the ones in his hand were different, complicated, and foreign. He looked around the living room and compared it to the one he had left behind. He had grown up in open spaces with people around him. And now, for the first time, he felt lonely. He missed his little sister. *This was a bad decision,* he thought, and his eyes watered. He felt like going into Ricky's office, picking up the phone, and dialing home, but he knew better. He didn't feel like finishing the last bits of the sandwich, and he chugged the milk instead.

Jenny came out of her room and showed Ashiq how to load the dishwasher. She asked him to leave his toothbrush in the washroom after he was done and to hang out in the living room until Ricky came out of his office. "I'll try to leave work early so we can go to the gym. Make sure you check out the library today. Ricky will give you a set of keys so you can explore on your own. Do you want anything before I leave?" He shook his head and picked the remote off the coffee table.

"Bye, Ricky," she called out.

"Wait," Ricky said, emerging from his office, "I can drop you off first and then take the car to Dr. Mulley's."

"But your appointment is not until noon."

"I have to run some errands. We need a set of keys for him," Ricky said as he jerked his head toward Ashiq, "and I need a few other things from Safeway."

"I thought you picked the keys up last week." She raised her eyebrows. "We'll talk in the car. Let's go." Ricky put his hand on her back and walked her out the door.

Ashiq entered their bedroom. It was spotless. The bed was made as if it was in an untouched hotel room. The room smelled like Jenny, but he could tell that there was more to it than just a familiar scent. It wasn't until he saw the bottle next to her jewelry box that the neurons shot inside his brain like madmen. It reminded him of his high school classmate who wore *Eternity*, the perfume she got as a gift from her future fiancé. That was when he realized the power of senses, and the sense of smell in particular. It took him back to the day when his high school classmate shut the blinds in their vacant chemistry lab, the day he smelled the fresh citrus around her breasts, the lily-of-the-valley under her armpits, and the pink sandalwood all over her body.

He put the bottle back on the dresser, in the same position. It was something he learned the hard way from his mother. Once, he had gone inside his mother's home-based boutique in the middle of a hot, summer night in search of a magazine for some inspiration to help stimulate his senses. He was thirteen. It was his birthday month when, in his bathroom, he discovered the act of self-pleasuring by accident, which not only blew his mind but also the free-flowing fluid out his wankie, and since then he never stopped. His fault, however, was leaving the magazine and the bottle of moisturizer behind in the shop's washroom. He thought of himself as a clever one, but his mother, Mrs. Amlani, busted him the next morning and gave him a lesson on how she was able to detect the smallest of variations in the placement of items, not only in her shop but all over their home. Since then, he had mastered the technique of being the invisible one.

Ashiq saw a small book on one of the nightstands — a paperback of *Think and Grow Rich* by Napoleon Hill. As he picked it up, he noticed the 1997 semi-annual sale catalog from Victoria's Secret underneath the book. It had Helena Christensen on the cover wearing a seamless miracle bra. He put the book down and picked up the magazine. He imagined Jenny in it, and his heartbeat got faster. He knew that the thought fluttering through his mind was wrong, but he had left the point of no return and the guilt faded like the denim he held in his hands. He put his clothes on the bed and opened the drawer. His eyes widened, teeth shifted, and mouth opened as if he was ready to take a bite from a big bar of milk chocolate. He examined the shape, color, and texture of each one of Jenny's panties, and then his eyes set on something he had imagined earlier: the Victoria's Secret pomegranate red chiffon slip. He pulled it out, felt it between his fingers, and brought it up to his nose.

He picked up his clothes from the bed, walked into the bathroom with the chiffon slip in his hand, and locked the door.

CHAPTER FOUR

Ashiq looked up from the couch as he heard the keys turning in the lock. Ricky entered the apartment, and the applauding audience on the television chanted. *"Je-rry! Je-rry!"* The host of the show, Jerry Springer, introduced a man that was admitting to a long-term emotional and sexual relationship with his horse.

"What the hell are you watching?" Ricky pulled the remote from under Ashiq's legs and turned it off. He gave him his set of keys and encouraged him to explore the area and to check out the library.

Ashiq made his way out of the building and searched around for landmarks to remember. He walked up to the end of the street, but nothing looked familiar. He wondered if it was because when Jenny took him for a night walk, it looked quite different from how it appeared during the day. He turned around and walked to the other end of the street. When he passed by the apartment building, he stopped and looked at the sign to form an image in his head. *"3-1-4-5, 3-1-4-5."* He repeated the sequence until he reached the end of the lane. He looked around and recognized a set of steep stairs with black grills. When he reached the ice cream parlor, it was packed with people, but the cute girls he saw the night before were nowhere to be found. *Maybe they only come at night?* He wondered why the older lady was sucking on her cone and smiling at him. He didn't smile back and sped up. *3-1-4 … what was the last number?* He paused and felt his heart beating. He didn't want to risk forgetting the number. "3-1 … shit." He walked back to the apartment building and gave it another shot in the hopes that this time he would be able to walk a bit longer and not forget the damn number. *3 plus 1 is 4, and the 3 that I added comes right after the 4 and the next number is 5, which normally comes after 4.*

He remembered the day he won 15,000 rupees on a prize bond he shared with his little sister, Fari. Nani, their beloved maternal grandmother, had told Ashiq that the reason they won the money was because the serial number 518545365548 of the prize bond started with the number 5, had five 5s in it, and when they added all the numbers together it came up to 59. The 5 plus the 9 became 14, and when Nani circled the last 5 that came from adding the 1 to the 4 of the number 14, Ashiq's eyes bulged out of their sockets in sheer bewilderment. Fari smiled despite the lack of her comprehension of the logic behind Nani's numerological genius, and they were just happy to have a lot of cash. "You know why?" Nani had asked them as they both looked at their favorite grandmother with curious eyes. *"Punjtan Pak."* She told them that the number five was a magical number because of the Holy Five: the Prophet Muhammad, his successor and son-in-law Ali, the prophet's daughter Fatima who was married to Ali, and their two sons, Hasan and Hussain. Since that day, Ashiq had looked at the number five as pure magic.

That's it. It's perfect, Ashiq thought, and with the end of the sequence he knew that he would never forget where the Poonjas lived. With the numbers 3145 ingrained in the grooves of his mind, he walked proudly to the end of the street and sped up toward the ice cream parlor like a boy who had grown up there in Yaletown.

He pulled the door to the library and came across another door, one that lacked a handle. It was like one of those swinging double doors found in busy restaurants that appear confusing and hazardous to diners but are mastered by the servers who go in and out without crashing into each other, like hundreds of airplanes swarming across the sky. He looked at his watch. He had an hour and a half to explore; the sign indicated that the doors would stop swinging at 6 p.m. due to a private event. He entered the library and looked around for computers, but there were none. He walked up to the last aisle. There were no computers, but an elaborate magazine section and a teenage couple making out. He never saw such a thing in his life, other than in the movies, or when he read the Sweet Valley High novels that painted a similar picture. He couldn't take his eyes off them. He took a step forward. The girl wore a short pink skirt and when the boy put his hands under it, Ashiq got excited and found another reason to stop searching for the computers. The girl slapped his hands out from underneath, and the boy held her by the waist and turned her around toward the magazine rack. Three copies of *National Geographic* fell to the floor. The girl giggled, opened her eyes, and saw Ashiq starring. "Freak," she called out to him. The boy looked at Ashiq and pulled his shoulders back. Ashiq quickly thought of a response to being caught, and then stammered, "Umm, where are the computers? I'm new here."

The boy pointed his index finger to the ceiling and went back to making out with the girl. The magazine rack jerked, and five more copies of *National Geographic* fell to the ground.

Ashiq walked around the aisle in search of stairs or an elevator, but the setup of the library was convoluted and complex. He wondered why two identical couches had been placed in the middle of the racks for people to socialize when there was an obvious sign that read, *PLEASE BE SILENT*. He looked through each aisle to see if there were other couples making out, but the rest of the library was vacant. He noticed an older lady behind the desk, following him with her eyes.

Why is she staring at me? Isn't that supposed to be rude? He turned in her direction, and before he could give her the glare he learned from the girl in the pink skirt, the lady smiled, took her spectacles off, and waved at him.

"Hi. Looking for something?"

"How can I go up?" he asked her, raising his index finger.

"You'll find the stairs on the right," she answered, pointing in the direction of the red exit sign with a smile. "Just go through these doors and you'll see."

He swung the door open, lifted his eyebrows, and took the stairs. When he reached the second floor, he looked through the glass window in the door to see if it was the right room, which it was, but his curiosity made him continue with the next flight of stairs. The third floor was the highest he could get to, but the door had no glass window, no numbers, and no signage, but a crunched up empty pack of cigarettes inserted between the lock and the groove in the wall. He pulled the door open, and the cigarette box fell to the ground. The door led to a secluded roof of the library that oversaw tall buildings with a familiar looking piece of architecture he once saw in one of the old travel books. He took a step forward, and the door slammed shut behind him.

"FUCK," someone yelled.

Ashiq turned to look at the closed door and realized that not only had he locked himself on the roof of a public library but two other boys as well. They shook their heads and looked at each other.

"Sorry, I didn't know," Ashiq said in his apologetic voice, expecting the boys to flip out and give him a piece of their minds. But they burst out in laughter and signaled Ashiq to join them.

"You might as well take a hoot," one of the boys with a shaved head said and passed him a rolled-up paper with a lit end. He was three inches taller than Ashiq, and his hazel eyes reminded him of the cat his mother once rescued and fostered for a year.

"Umm, thanks. I don't smoke cigarettes."

"It's not a cigarette, bro." The other boy, who looked like a surfer, grabbed the rolled-up paper from his friend and pinched his thumb and index finger to the filter tip. He brought it to his mouth and sucked hard. Ashiq admired his shaggy blond hair and blue eyes. He wondered what he himself would look like if he wore blue contact lenses, or at least the Quiksilver t-shirt that the boy wore.

"What is it then?"

"It's grass, bro," the shaved-headed boy said with an astonished look.

"What does it do?"

"It makes you fly." The surfer boy ran around the roof.

"And it gives you the munchies," the shaved-headed boy laughed.

The surfer boy came back and placed his hand on Ashiq's shoulder. "You have a funny accent. Where are you from?"

"Karachi." Ashiq found the boys hilarious and couldn't stop smiling.

"Where's that?"

"Pakistan."

They both gave him a puzzled look.

"It's in Asia," Ashiq said, finding it absurd that he had to explain.

"Like near China, or something," the shaved-headed boy said, passing the joint to Ashiq. "By the way, nice socks, dude."

"Yes, close to China and India." Ashiq shook his head to refuse the joint, looked down, and wondered what was so special about his simple black socks and why the surfer-looking boy had found his friend's statement hysterical. He had never met anyone like these two and wondered if all Canadians had the same sense of humor.

"India," the surfer boy said, suddenly seeming to remember. "That's what I thought, dude. You sound just like Apu."

"Who's Apu?"

"You don't know Apu? *The Simpsons*, man. *The Simpsons*."

When Ashiq gave him a perplexed look, the shaved-headed boy said, "Dude," and pointed at a nearby billboard featuring *The Simpsons*. "Whoa, that's trippy. No Apu up there but this is like *The Twilight Zone*."

The boys looked at each other and started yammering with an Indian accent. "Thankk yu, comme again!" They gave each other high fives and cackled loudly. Ashiq found it amusing.

"We call this a *taali*," he said.

"Call what a *tele*?" the surfer boy asked.

"Not a *tele*. A *taali* ... like *taaa-leee*. When you slap your hands together."

The boys looked at each other, wobbled their heads, and mimicked his accent. "*Taa-leee*."

He tried hard not to reveal what he felt at that moment, but his face felt hot. He realized that being born in Canada wasn't enough. His looks, his accent, and his connection to Pakistan had made him different, foreign, and definitely not Canadian in the eyes of those two boys.

"Enough of this shit, yo. Let's get the fuck outta heya," the shaved-headed boy said. The surfer boy grabbed the plumbing vent at the edge of the roof with one hand and leaned down to look at the street. He yelled at the people below until he got the attention of someone and asked to help them unlock the door.

While he waited, Ashiq looked out over the view of the city. He thought about his family and what he had left behind. He missed his friends who looked like him, spoke like him, and though they were not born Canadians like he was, shared the same heritage as him.

Ashiq saw the boys coming out of the main entrance of the library and jumping on their skateboards. He took a deep breath and looked up at the billboard.

Who the hell is Apu?

CHAPTER FIVE

When Ashiq returned home, Jenny was on the couch with a cup of tea in one hand and a cordless phone in the other. She wore a burnt-orange satin blouse, a knee-length navy blue skirt, and milky-pink matte lipstick. She smiled at him, took a sip, and placed the tea on a coaster. Ashiq assumed she was on the phone with someone he didn't know, otherwise she would have said, "Hey, guess who just walked in?"

The bedroom door was shut, which meant Ricky was in there and Ashiq was free to go into his office and relax. But when Ashiq walked into the office, he found Ricky there. Evidently, closing doors was one of the ways Ricky thought to let Ashiq know that certain areas of the house were not open for business, especially not to guests who were invited for only a two-week stay.

"You're back. I didn't even hear you come in," Ricky said, and Ashiq nodded in response. Ricky put his hands on the side of his waist and asked, "You want something from here?" Ashiq shook his head and forced a smile. "All right, then." Ricky turned his back toward him and went back to the computer.

Ashiq stepped into the dark kitchen and wondered if he should go into the living room and sit next to his Jenny Khala, so she could rest her legs on his thighs and he could massage them. The thought got him hard, and he wondered what Jenny would do if his throbbing penis rubbed her calves. Would she raise her legs and shake her head? Or would she use his penis as a foam roller and self-massage her calves because Ricky was not around. He wanted to be close to her, but he recalled his mother telling him to be considerate of his aunty and uncle and to give them their privacy if he ever saw them on the phone. He stayed in the kitchen, waited for Jenny to finish her call, and hoped that Ricky would not leave the office to refill his water mug.

Jenny jumped off the couch, slid the glass door open, and stepped onto the balcony. "Hold on," she said to whoever was on the line. "I'm gonna see if he's here."

Ashiq snuck his head out from the kitchen. He saw Jenny leaning bent over the balcony, and he galloped toward the metallic railing like a robust magnet. Jenny spotted Ashiq in the living room.

"Can you do me a favor?" she asked. "Can you go downstairs and get something for me? There's a guy with a package."

"Yes," he said, clearing his throat.

"Make sure you take the keys with you in case you lock yourself out."

He nodded, tapped his pockets to ensure he had the keys, and walked out the door. After taking the brown bag from the guy (who winked at him), Ashiq got into the elevator and opened the package as soon as the doors shut. He wondered why Jenny ordered a leather leash with a silver chain when they didn't even have a dog. *Maybe it's a gift for a friend who has a pet,* he thought.

When he returned with the package, Jenny was off the phone. She wore a white tank top and black leggings. He ogled her like she was the girl next door.

"Are you ready?" she asked. "We're going to the gym, the one in our building." She flexed her muscles and blew air into her cheeks.

"Should I change?"

"No, no. You look so cute in these denim shorts, though we have to do something about those socks." She opened the closet next to the washroom and passed him a pair of white ankle socks. "When you wear shorts, it's better to wear these kinds of socks, otherwise it looks funny. Only old people wear long socks with shorts," she smiled. He threw his black calf-high socks into the laundry basket and shot her a genuine smile. He thought about telling Jenny about the boys he met on the roof of the library, how they made him feel about not being authentically Canadian, but he kept quiet. *Maybe later,* he thought, stepping into the elevator.

At the gym, Jenny showed him how to stretch and with every pull he noticed how flexible she was. "How long have you done this for?" he asked, looking over at the overweight girls struggling on the treadmill.

"It's not just about working out. Half of it is food. After all, you are what you eat." She looked over at the girls. "People don't realize that."

Ashiq mimicked Jenny's moves.

"You know what they say: a second on the lips, forever on the hips," she laughed. He gave her a puzzled look. "You're young, so you don't have to worry about that. But it all starts when you turn thirty, so enjoy the next ten years, maybe fifteen." She looked at herself in the side wall mirror. "I need to work on my glutes."

"What's that?"

She moved her hands to her back. Ashiq wanted to look, but he kept his eyes on the floor. "Let me show you the chest press. It's a great workout, even for women." She pressed her fingers under her collarbone. "Here … you can feel it. A lot of women don't know the importance of this."

He was glad that Jenny gave him a valid excuse to keep his eyes around her breasts, but it felt awkward, so he lowered his eyes again.

"You don't have to be shy." She grabbed his hands and brought them forward toward her. "Here, can you feel it?" She pressed them into her chest. He nodded and his eyes darted over to the girls on the treadmill. He hoped they weren't watching him with Jenny. Even though it was the area under the collarbone that he was touching, the base of his palm still rested on her breasts.

The women's changing room door flung open, and a petite old lady walked in. He pulled his hands away from Jenny's breasts and stretched. When they were done, Jenny asked him to shower in the men's changing room before going upstairs because she wanted to get ready in her bedroom and wasn't sure if Ricky would need to use the bathroom as well. She reminded him that it was Friday evening, and they would all be going for prayers.

He entered the men's changing room, took off his fake Ralph Lauren polo t-shirt, placed it on the bench, and unbuckled his belt. A naked man walked into his aisle and threw his towel on the floor.

What's the point of the towel if you're not going to cover yourself? He wrapped the towel around himself and dropped his denim shorts and underwear. He wondered how these guys were so comfortable walking naked.

On his way to the shower, he avoided every possible eye contact with men who had either finished drying themselves or were about to. He worried that one of them might be gay and flirt with him, so he kept his eyes on the ground as he walked into the shower. He was glad he chose the one with its own private curtains because when he turned the hot water on, he thought of Jenny and her chest and her black leggings. In the colorful faculty of his vigorous mind, vivid images formed faster than the speed of light. He wanted to bring his hands to her hips, he wanted to play with her breasts, and he wanted her to put her hands inside his denim shorts, but he didn't have time for unnecessary foreplay. He knew that in doing so he would miss the prayers, so he went on and did what most teenagers did: he pressed fast forward. Within a fraction of a fraction of a second, Jenny lost the white tank top, the black leggings flew away into nothingness, and he sucked on her nipples. He pumped the pink liquid soap into his palms and Jenny Khala bent down to touch her toes. He completed a set of three, curled his toes, and let out a loud, "Oh, Jenny!"

When he walked back to the locker aisle where he had left his clothes, he couldn't believe what was waiting for him. It was Ricky. He had brought Ashiq a set of clothes to change into before they headed to the mosque.

"I didn't know where you were," Ricky smiled. "But I saw *my* green Nalgene water bottle that you took from my office."

"Umm, I was ... umm, in the ..." Ashiq felt like something was stuck in his throat. *Did he hear me? Oh God, did he? He must have!* He panicked.

"We don't have much time, so hurry up. You don't wanna miss the prayers," Ricky said, walking out the men's changing room. *No, I don't,* he thought. He had a lot to pray for, a lot to repent for, and a lot to be grateful for.

*+.

The next morning, the Poonja residence turned into a hectic zone. Ricky walked back and forth from his office to the living room to keep himself abreast of the latest Silicon Valley news on television. Jenny baked brownies in the kitchen. And Ashiq was on the phone with his mother, Mrs. Roshan Amlani.

"Khala," Ashiq called out from Ricky's office. Jenny came to the door with a large bowl and was mixing the paste with a wooden spatula. "Mummy wants to talk to you," Ashiq said, extending the phone in her direction.

"One sec," she said and walked back to the kitchen.

"She is making brownies so we can take them with us. I think she went to wash her hands," he told his mother.

"How is everything otherwise?" she asked him.

"It's okay. A bit different. I miss you guys."

"We miss you too, Ashiq. By the way, how's Uncle Rakesh treating you?"

Ashiq didn't know how to answer that question. He wanted to tell her about the two-week deadline to move out that Ricky had given him despite Jenny's assurance to his mother that he could stay with them for as long as he wanted to. But he figured that it wasn't the time to burden his mother with such unpleasantness. Ricky was in the bedroom with the door open, and Ashiq knew he must have been listening with both his ears.

"Is everything okay, beta?"[8] She could hear the anxiousness in his silence. "Did he say something to you?"

"Jahanara Aunty is here. I'm going to pass her the phone," he said.

"My hands are messy. Put her on speaker," Jenny said.

"Wait a second," his mother interrupted, but Ashiq put her on speaker and stood next to Jenny. He didn't want to miss out on the gossip.

"How are you?" Jenny asked.

---

[8] *Beta* is a term of endearment for someone younger, like kiddo. It literally means "son," but some people also use it for their daughters.

"We're all good here. Shamsu says hi."

"Roshan Didi,[9] I asked how *you* were, and I know Shamsu Bhai[10] is not even there so stop pretending."

Ashiq leaned forward and crossed his arms.

"I miss him," Roshan Amlani said.

"I know Didi, but don't you worry. I'm taking good care of Ash. We'll go to Victoria for a day, and then to Tofino. He's going to love it." Jenny winked at Ashiq.

"You know ..." Mrs. Amlani paused. Ashiq lifted his chin and pursed his lips. "Make sure he gets busy with things," she said.

"I've taken a week off work, so I'll show him around."

"Wow. What does Rakesh think about that?"

"Um ..." Jenny hesitated, "Didi, don't worry about Ricky. Although, I need to talk to you about something, but not now. You know."

"I know, I know. Call me later then," Mrs. Amlani said.

Ashiq imagined his mother pushing the mounds of her hand hard on the rough edges of the coffee table and tiny bubbles of blood popping out, but he knew that his mother wouldn't feel the pain. The agony inside her heart would take over her entire consciousness. Since his childhood, he had seen her do that whenever she was repressed by Ashiq's father. It was something he hated seeing more than anything.

Ashiq turned off the speaker phone and stood next to Jenny.

"Did you tell her?" Ricky shouted from the bedroom.

"Not now, Ricky. Not now." Jenny looked at Ashiq and shook her head.

"When are you going to tell them? On the last day?!"

"Why do I feel like you don't really want to come with us?" Jenny snapped. Ricky walked into his office.

"I have work to do," he said, and shut the door behind him.

"Of course you do." She took a deep breath, composed herself, and spoke in a soft tone. "Listen, it looks like Uncle Rakesh has work

---

[9] *Didi* literally means "an elder woman" in Hindi. Used as a form of respect.

[10] *Bhai* means brother or friend. It's also used as an expression of friendship.

to do." She rolled her eyes, paused, and smiled. "But you and I will go and have an amazing time."

Ashiq smiled and swept his index finger on the edge of the baking tray. Jenny slapped his hand, told him to be patient, and pulled the oven door open. He thought about the girl with the pink skirt at the library, who did the same to her boyfriend. Though Jenny didn't wear a short-short skirt, and Ashiq's hand only touched the baking tray, his mind wandered off to the forbidden zone.

Ricky pretended to work behind the closed door. Ashiq stood on the balcony, and Jenny sat on her bed with the brown bag that Ashiq had fetched earlier on his run downstairs on her lap. The timer echoed in the kitchen. Ashiq stepped into the living room. It smelled like the sweet scent of a gourmet pastry shop, and he savored the moment before he slid the glass door shut. He passed by Jenny and Ricky's bedroom and saw her through the half-open door. She sat on her bed with the brown bag on her lap, clearly contemplating something. He walked to the kitchen to check on the brownies.

"Khala, how do you close this?" Ashiq said, leaning his head out from the kitchen.

"I'm coming," she said. He saw her throw the brown bag into her handbag.

CHAPTER SIX

Ricky helped them load the Audi, and Ashiq knew Ricky was making up for not going out with them earlier to show Ashiq around. When Ashiq was in Karachi, he once overheard the gossip between Jenny and his mother. Jenny had told Mrs. Amlani over the phone that she hated Ricky's inability to express sincere apology, but the passage of time made her partially immune to his failure to apologize, and after realizing that *his ways* would not change, she came to terms with it. In addition, Jenny had shared with her sister that their marriage counselor had advised her that it would be in Jenny's best interest to accept him the way he was, advising her, "Don't try to change him."

Ricky pulled a cell phone out from his front pocket and knocked on the driver's side window. Jenny lowered the glass, took the phone from him, and placed it in the cup holder. "Call me when you guys are on the ferry," he said as he waved them a farewell. He waited for Jenny to say a farewell in the rearview mirror, but she drove away.

"We do this all the time. It's normal in any relationship," she explained to Ashiq. He kept quiet and aimed his head out the window to soak up the sun. He saw two girls in the back of a car that they passed. He smiled, not at the girls, or at the grumpy old driver who gave a sour eye to him for checking out his daughters, but at the thought that came to mind when he saw the yellow convertible.

"I know what you were thinking," Jenny said, sounding excited.

"No, you don't." Ashiq shook his head and chuckled.

"They were too young for you," she said. He thought that her tone was envious, as if she competed for his attention. Then she breezily asked, "Do you know which direction we are heading in? North, south, east, or west?" The girls in the yellow convertible reminded him of his friends, their shenanigans in Karachi, the motorcycle rides, the random trifles, and the uncontrollable laughs. "I don't know," he said.

"What's the matter?" Jenny touched his knee. "Missing home, haan?[11]" she asked. Ashiq nodded and looked out at the ferry docks. "It takes time. I remember when I first came here, everything was so different." She drove up to the entrance of the terminal where it said *VEHICLE DECK ENTRANCE* and pulled out the tickets.

Once Jenny parked the Audi on the lower vehicle deck, they made their way to the upper deck and walked around for a bit, soaking up the morning sun. One of the passengers on the ferry offered to take Jenny and Ashiq's photograph, and he struggled with the shutter button. He scratched his white beard, adamant that the camera was broken.

"Let me take a look," Ashiq said, stepping forward. "You think it's the battery?" Jenny fixed her hair for the fifth time.

The man shook his head. "Told ya it was broken," he said, raising his hands in the air and walking away.

"It's out of film," Ashiq smiled at Jenny. Her eyes twinkled.

"Let me go to the car and get a new one," she said as she took the camera from him and walked away.

"Change the film in the car," he called after her. "You should always replace film in the shade."

Jenny stopped and turned around to look at him, smiling before walking away.

As Ashiq waited for Jenny on the deck, a middle-aged woman, who one might consider to be a cougar, approached him. He smiled at her, and she played with her long, blonde curls multiple times. Three to be exact; Ashiq counted.

"I love taking the ferry," she said as she stepped closer to him and straightened her spine. He admired how the sunlight illuminated her cleavage popping out of her tight turquoise top, the same color of the waters the ferry floated on.

---

[11] Haan means yes. It expresses affirmation or consent.

"Me too," Ashiq said. He wanted to take a step closer to her, but he saw Jenny approaching him, speeding up.

Ashiq rested his elbows on the rails and felt the wind through his hair, but the truth was that wind couldn't go through his thick hair; it was "a crow's nest," his friends used to say. But that didn't stop him from imagining how elegant he looked. He opened his chest wide. The cougar played with her curls.

"Hi there." Jenny came up from behind her, and the cougar's arm jerked away.

"I love your son. He's quite a charmer."

Ashiq noticed that Jenny clenched her fist in response to that remark.

"She's ... she's not my mother." Ashiq smiled.

"Oh, I'm sorry," the cougar said, walking away.

"This is so beautiful," Ashiq said as he scanned the landscape.

"I knew you'd love it." Jenny put her arms around him. "We should be there soon." She grabbed the brownie from his hand and put it into her mouth. He squinted his eyes at her and saw that she felt free, as if wings popped out from her sides.

She never called Ricky, did she? he realized.

The plan was to change the reservation to only one room, get a parking pass, and explore the city on foot. But when they arrived at the Marriott, the receptionist passed a note to Jenny, and as she did, the charm on her bracelet cuffed the counter.

"That's beautiful," Jenny said.

"Thanks," she said as she rotated it around her wrist. "I'm in love with it." Her smile widened into dimples on both sides.

"It tells me it's not just the *Tiffany* you're in love with," Jenny winked. The receptionist nodded.

"Good eye."

Jenny opened the note:

I'M TAKING THE LAST FERRY. CAN'T FIND THE BROWN BAG. HOPE YOU HAVE IT WITH YOU. SEE YOU TONIGHT.

LOVE, RICKY.

"Your husband has asked that we keep both rooms as per your original reservation," the receptionist explained. "The rooms will be ready around 4 p.m. For now, you can just park in the guest area."

"Sure. Thanks, Sherry," Jenny said.

On their way to the car, Ashiq asked Jenny how she knew the receptionist.

"How could you not have noticed her name tag?" Jenny said. "Calling people by their first name helps make faster connections, and it pays to make little people feel like big people."

Jenny kneeled on the back seat and passed the backpack to Ashiq. "People do more for you if you make them feel important," she continued, reaching into the front to grab the cell phone. They both saw that there were three missed calls. Ashiq pictured Ricky's reaction after getting no response to all his calls. *It must be too late to call now,* Ashiq thought. *Plus, Jenny wouldn't want to pay long distance. He'll understand.*

They spent the day on foot. Ashiq loved both the walking tours and lunch on the pier. Jenny wanted to take him to the zoo, but they were both tired and so they headed back to the hotel to relax before heading out to dinner.

They carried the rest of the things from the car and entered the hotel. Ashiq noticed that the girl with the Tiffany bracelet they met earlier was replaced by a guy with rimless glasses. Jenny was thrilled when she found out that they had been upgraded to a honeymoon suite. She asked the guy with rimless glasses to pass on her sincere gratitude to the girl with the Tiffany bracelet.

When Ashiq asked her why he was left with the same regular room while she had been upgraded to a fancy one, she took advantage of the moment and told him that it was due to his moustache. "Pakistan is different, that's for sure. But here, girls don't like boys with moustaches." She waved at him as he walked out of the elevator and onto the second floor. "See you soon," she said, and pressed a button on the elevator panel.

Ashiq imagined Jenny smiling in anticipation of unwinding with the bells and whistles of the honeymoon suite, but also the thrills that came with the unpacking of the bags. He pictured her heart giggling as she threw her bags on the floor, undressed, and jumped in the shower while thinking to herself, *It's gonna be the best night ever.*

After dinner, they sat by the pool, shared an ice cream, and talked about the Bollywood new releases.

"You know, I have never watched an Indian film on a big screen," Ashiq said. "WHAT?" Jenny exclaimed, raising her eyebrows. "Why not? I loved watching Indian films at the cinema when I was in Karachi."

"Because Bollywood films got banned in the theatres after the second India-Pakistan war," Ashiq explained.

"Don't worry. I'll take you to the movies to watch one when we're back in Vancouver." She winked at him.

"That's great! All my friends will be jealous when I tell them."

"There's a new film out right now in the theaters called *Pardes*. It's a story about an Indian girl who comes to the United States after getting engaged to an Indian-American asshole. You'll love it," Jenny said, and got up to throw the ice cream cup in the bin. "Looks like it's time for us to head back to our rooms. I want to get ready for Ricky. He'll be off the ferry soon."

"I think I'll stay here for a bit," Ashiq said.

"Enjoy your evening," she said. "By the way, *if* you watch porn in your room, I'll know because it'll show on the bill." She pointed her index finger at him.

"Of course not, Khala," Ashiq smiled.

After Jenny left him sitting by the pool, Ashiq imagined Jenny going up to her hotel room and opening a bottle of red wine. Shiraz, he envisioned, recalling the bottle he saw at Ricky and Jenny's apartment. Then Jenny would turn on the radio and search for the right frequency until she found Nina Simone on one of the jazz channels. He remembered her mentioning Nina Simone in the car on the way to the ferry terminal. Then he pictured her changing into her pomegranate red chiffon slip and looking at herself in the bathroom mirror and flexing her glutes. As this series of thoughts ran through his mind, he felt the blood drain from his face, and he knew exactly where it was going instead. He imagined Jenny putting the nail file back into her purple pouch and admiring her nails. Jenny had told Ashiq during their ride to the hotel that she wasn't allowed to have long nails because she worked with first graders, but that she loved getting her nails done during her holidays, this week off being one of them. Ashiq saw in his head that she liked how the nail polish complemented the red pomegranate color of her chiffon slip, and how she looked at her feet and realized that they needed a new coat of burgundy red. But then Jenny searched the dresser for the polish, and her eyes went to Shiraz instead.

Ashiq sat where Jenny left him, by the swimming pool. The last couple came out of the pool, wrapped themselves in white towels, and smiled at Ashiq. He wondered if Jenny would have the same smile on her face when she would see Ricky later that night. He got up and walked around the hotel to see if he could find a new spot. The only people hanging out in the exterior courtyard of the Marriott were smokers. He thought about asking one of them for a cigarette to try it out. He took a few steps toward the chain smokers in the hopes that one of them would help him turn into a human chimney for the evening, but when he saw the lady in a yellow summer dress smile at him, he kept his virgin lungs intact. Though he liked her red hair and beautiful freckles, her extreme wrinkles and toothless mouth sent him in the opposite direction.

He walked around for a bit near the pool, but when everyone left, he went upstairs to his hotel room and took a long shower. He scrubbed himself twice and each time he thought about the girls in the pool, and then about Jenny in her black leggings. He came out of the shower, wiped the steam on the mirror, and looked at himself. *Here girls don't like boys with moustaches,* Jenny echoed in his ears.

He covered his moustache with his index finger and wondered if the girls in the pool would have talked to him if he was moustache-less.

"Screw it," he said to himself, and he changed the blade on his razor, applied a layer of Gillette foam on his moustache, and shaved it off. "Holy shit," he said for the first time as he saw his new face emerge in the fogless mirror. It was like an uncovering, an unveiling, a reclaiming of himself, as himself, *for* himself. The physical sensation was new to him, and he could feel individual air currents moving across his skin. He touched his face and slid his index finger over the freshly shaved area. The contrast between the lighter color of his skin where the mustache used to be and the darker color around it was stark and immediate. He wondered how Jenny would react to his new appearance. *I look like a baby,* he thought.

He put on a fresh pair of white briefs, sat on the bed, and turned the TV on. He paused on the pay-per-view option. Jenny's voice spiraled in his mind like a thirsty shark circling a broken boat, and he flipped the channel. He didn't want to be confronted by Jenny the next morning when the charges appeared on the bill or be given a disgusted look by the gorgeous girl with the Tiffany bracelet, so he did what he could. He clicked the tube off, took off his white briefs, and pushed himself toward the headboard of the bed. He dimmed the lights, emptied the hotel moisturizer into his hand and let his imagination run wild. But before the creative juices could flow, the phone rang; it was as if a corkscrew had jammed in the last bottle of champagne on a New Year's Eve. He sighed and answered the phone. It was Ricky, and he had a message for Jenny.

"You must tell her now," Ricky insisted.

"Yes, of course," Ashiq said and hung up the phone.

Ashiq put on a fresh set of clothes and made his way to Jenny's room to give her Ricky's urgent message. In the elevator, he wondered what Jenny and Ricky's upgraded room would look like. *Maybe those fancy rooms don't have clocks so that people can have long sex without having to keep track of time.* He imagined Jenny picking up the phone to call the reception desk to ask the time, but getting no dial tone, and then raising her eyebrows, going through all the possibilities. Jenny tapping the receiver twice on her palm and putting it back down, and then seeing it was unplugged. *Maybe it's better that way*, she must have thought, so that she and Ricky could play in total seclusion. He pictured her drunk in her room, getting up to pee, stumbling, and giggling, *"Where are you, Ricky? Look!"* And then picking up the empty bottle of Shiraz. *"Look, Ricky. I drank the whole freakin' thing. I've been bad. I need to be spanked."* Ashiq had heard those lines on the Jerry Springer show, and it seemed like something she might say. It seemed like something that he *wanted* her to say.

He got out of the elevator and wondered if there was another bottle of Shiraz in the room, and whether she left it sealed so that Ricky could open it. Ashiq knew it was something Ricky loved to do (he had once seen Ricky uncork a bottle in their Yaletown apartment). He imagined Jenny wondering about Ricky's whereabouts, her slurring, *"Where are you, Ricky? Where are you?"* Ashiq stood outside Jenny's room and knocked on the door three times.

"Finally!" Ashiq heard Jenny exclaim from inside the hotel room. He imagined her eyes widening with excitement. "I'm coming, love." Ashiq heard the toilet flush.

Jenny opened the door, froze for a second, and buried her head in her hands. She wore a leather collar with a long silver chain attached to it. Ashiq suddenly remembered the notorious brown bag he collected for Jenny, and from his thorough examination of its contents in the elevator, it was indeed the same leather.

Ashiq stood mesmerized by the mind-boggling marvel in front of him, but he didn't know what to say or how to say it. He wasn't sure if he was supposed to leave without giving her the message or grab the chain and enter the room, so he waited for Jenny to say what an aunt should say before shutting the door and never speaking to him again or invite him in and fuck his brains out. He knew that the latter would never happen, so he just stood there in silence and lowered his eyes.

"What are you doing here?" Jenny hid behind the door, covered the collar with her hand, and peeked her head out from behind.

"Um, Uncle Rakesh called."

"WHAT? When?"

"Like five minutes ago. He said he tried calling you, but the receptionist told him that you weren't answering."

"Wait a second … let me get decent first," she said as she closed the door.

Ashiq couldn't take the vision out of his head, and every time he tried, he failed in his attempt to decode the mystery. He couldn't fathom why she wore such a thing, a choker meant for dogs. *A dog's collar? For God's sake!* He shook his head.

"Come on in," she opened the door, looking away. "Where is he?"

"Home," Ashiq answered.

"What do you mean, he's home?" She pulled her hair back and tied it together with a band.

"He missed the last ferry," Ashiq said. "He called you more than ten times. Is your phone not working?" Ashiq picked up the receiver to check the dial tone.

"It's fine. I kept it unplugged."

"So, we paid for two rooms for nothing?"

Her face flushed, and she dropped her back onto the bed. Ashiq liked how the flawless fall popped her breasts against the gravity and loosened her unsecure robe. The dimmed lights of the honeymoon suite diffused with the red pomegranate color of her slip.

"Can we get our money back if I go downstairs now?" Ashiq placed his forearms on his thighs and hinged forward.

"It's too late." She sat up, fixed her robe, and folded her legs. "What you saw was nothing. I was playing a prank, but …" she rolled her eyes, "… he didn't even bother to show up. He messed up my buzz."

She got up and threw the empty bottle of wine into the black bin and looked at the sealed bottle that was begging to be uncorked. "He's not the nicest person, in case you haven't noticed."

"I don't think Uncle Rakesh likes me," Ashiq blurted out. He could no longer contain the thought that had haunted him since he first landed in Vancouver.

"What? Come on now, of course he does. He's just awkward sometimes. You shouldn't take it personally."

"I know he doesn't want me to stay with you guys," Ashiq said as he lowered his eyes.

"Oh no, come here darling," she said as she walked toward him with open arms. But he stayed in the love seat with his eyes glued to the carpet. She kneeled in front of him and held his hands. "You know that you can stay with us as long as you want."

He kept quiet because she had said the same thing on the phone before he left Karachi, but since then things had changed. Uncle Rakesh — *Ricky* — entered the picture and didn't want him there. He remembered that Jenny had told him the day he arrived that he would be waking up every day to one of the best views of downtown Vancouver, but Ricky smudged that vision with his foul mouth.

"Did he say something to you?" Jenny asked.

"Yes, he said I could only stay with you guys for two weeks. Don't you remember? It was when I first arrived at your apartment building, and we were waiting for the elevator."

"Don't pay any attention to what Ricky says. I'm the one who decides what happens to my sister's son." She pulled his hands and made him get up with her. "And now I've decided that we're gonna have a party. Ricky didn't want to be with us? Fine. Then we're gonna have a lot of fun, and we won't let his bad *juju* get to us."

"*Juju*?" Ashiq smiled.

"Yes, *juju*," she laughed, walking up to the radio to turn the volume up. When she opened the second bottle of wine, Ashiq asked, "Can I have some?"

"Hell no! I don't want to be a bad influence. I wouldn't be able to look at your mom in the eye if the truth ever came out."

"Just one glass," he rubbed his hands together.

"Absolutely not." She shook her head. "I don't want to be the one who introduced you to alcohol and turned you into a bad Muslim. The truth, Ash, the truth always comes out," she said.

After the second glass from the second bottle, everything Jenny said came out slurred. It wasn't mean; it was comical and entertaining. She told Ashiq how much she hated moving to Waterloo from Karachi, that everything had been different and foreign to her but that as time passed, she had gotten used to all that, and now she couldn't even imagine moving back to her homeland.

"What homeland? This is my home now. I love Canada," she said before singing the Canadian national anthem, twice. She asked Ashiq to join her, but he didn't know the words or the rhythm. Jenny smacked her forehead in mock horror. "A Canadian-born citizen who can't sing the Canadian national anthem?"

Ashiq asked her if they would still go to Tofino as planned. She nodded and yelled, "Fuck yeah!" She then took off her robe, jumped in bed in her red pomegranate slip, and proceeded to tell Ashiq about Ricky's software developing project problems and how it affected their passionate life. *So, it wasn't just my imagination,* Ashiq thought.

"Get in here. I'm already falling asleep," she said, flipping the sheets open.

What is she asking me to do? Does she think something is going to happen between us if I get in that bed with her? I might fantasize about her every day, but that's as far as I can go. She's my Khala! He blushed.

"Wait a second … not even in your wildest dreams, you sicko! I'm not THAT drunk," she said. She told him that she loved Ricky more than anything in the world and that it was insane for Ashiq to have thought that. She said she was his *Aunty*, which surprised him because she didn't call herself *Khala*.

"Let's listen to Nina Simone for a bit … until I fall asleep … then you can go back to your room," she slurred.

But Ashiq's imagination took the front seat. In his mind, she grabbed his hands and pleaded for him to stay, saying that she didn't want to be alone. She said it would be *their* secret and that Ricky didn't need to know anything. She said they would stay up and watch movies. He stayed in her bed and hoped she would remember *their* secret the next morning and not blurt it out in front of Uncle Rakesh. It didn't take long for Jenny to pass out and for Ashiq to get excited, but he also felt guilty for his sinful eyes. His heartbeat was fast, his penis stood hard, and he moved closer. He felt the curves of her hips, but she turned over. He panicked and stood up. The bed jerked and twitched Jenny out of her intoxicated sleep. She opened her eyes and saw Ashiq standing in his white briefs, which were stretched by the force of his erection.

"Go to bed." She turned around. "You crazy, horny boy," she slurred.

He got back into her bed, held his hard penis in his hand, and closed his eyes.

CHAPTER SEVEN

That night in Jenny's hotel room, Ashiq Amlani had a long and vivid dream about Ricky Poonja:

Ricky couldn't sleep. He felt bad for missing the ferry. He knew he would have to make up for what he did. And what better way to redeem himself than to surprise his wife. She will love it, *he thought, and checked the morning schedule for the first ferry to Victoria on his computer.*

He planned to leave the house around 6:15 a.m. so that he could catch the 7 a.m. ferry. He hoped there would be room for at least one more passenger. He went into the kitchen and took out the phone directory from the cabinet under the sink. He grabbed Post-it notes from the top of the fridge and wrote down the number for Yellow Cab. Better safe than sorry, *he thought, and then looked at the clock on the oven. Unlike his wife, Jenny Poonja, who would have used her fingers, he calculated the time in his head, which he claimed was faster than a Japanese calculator. He had a few hours.*

He walked back to his office and read Adam Smith's The Wealth of Nations. *When he got to the end of page thirty-seven, his eyelids got heavy. His body was ready to crash. He placed the bookmark in the middle and closed the book. He got under the sheets and placed his head on Jenny's pillow, but her scent aroused him, alerted him, and awoke him. He got up and went back to the kitchen. He made coffee, watched the infomercials, and thought about buying an Abs Cruncher Heat Pack that promised a six-pack in six weeks for only six minutes a day. But the price of $129.95 was only available for the next thirty minutes, which put him off. He would have purchased it if it was half off. He got up to make another cup of coffee, but the voice-over pulled him back, as if the people behind the shopping* *channel heard his request. The girl said that if Ricky called in the next five minutes, he could have it for only $89.99. She would also accept four easy installments of $24.99 each, which he could pay over six months. Ricky dropped his empty cup on the coffee table and went into the bedroom to look for his new American Express card. He called the number on the TV screen, touched his abs, and sucked it all in. The vision of him with a six-pack and walking with Jenny on the nude beach sent him back to his days at Simon Fraser University when he and his friends spent a whole summer pretending to be lifeguards. They wore tiny red trunks and asked topless girls if they needed help. The infomercial girl took his credit card number with a huge smile. Not that Ricky could see it, but he sure heard it. She told him that the package would arrive in four to six weeks.*

"What's the point then? By the time I'll have my six-pack, summer will be over," he said on the phone. The girl wanted to hit him with her punch hole machine to make him realize that by the end of six weeks there would be no abs, and only a new reason for Jenny to give him shit, but she let it go because $9.99 commission looked very attractive to her since her six-hour shift was about to end.

"Would you like expedited shipping on that?" she asked.

"When will I get it then?" Ricky moved his thumb over the raised numbers on his American Express.

"In a few days, sir," she said.

"Sure, let's do it." He smiled. Ricky was a new man. He showered and wore a white golf shirt. He went for a pair of jeans, but then put on his new khakis instead, as he figured that leaving a new piece of clothing in the closet at this point would be a sin. In just a few weeks he would have to go shopping for new clothes to show off his new body.

He called for a Yellow Cab to pick him up at six instead of six fifteen in case there was an unexpected delay and went into the kitchen to make himself a bowl of cereal with skim milk, but then he saw the Tupperware that Jenny had left. He contemplated for a few seconds. "I'm gonna have a six-pack soon, in only six weeks, and it's gonna be hard work." He opened the Tupperware. "I deserve it, I sure do." He poured himself a glass of milk. "At least this is skim." He smiled and took a bite of his first brownie.

The Yellow Cab arrived on the dot. With his weekender bag next to him, he asked the driver to step on the accelerator and head to the docks so he could catch the first ferry leaving for Victoria.

When he got to the Tsawwassen Ferry Terminal, he paid the driver with cash and rushed out to get a ticket. The lady at the counter told Ricky that the first ferry was at its capacity and that he would have to wait for the next one, on which there were two vacant seats left and, with a special coupon from yesterday's Vancouver Sun, he could travel with his significant other on a buy-one-get-one-free deal. Ricky told her that he was alone, and the lady gave him a flirtatious smile and a coupon for his next visit. "One moment, sir." She picked up the walkie-talkie and responded back to the person standing by the ferry entrance. Ricky felt a rush of energy when he overheard the conversation; the glass barrier blurred out the details, but he knew that there was a light at the end of the tunnel and that he might be able to catch Jenny before she left for breakfast, or at least before heading to Tofino.

"I guess you're in luck. Mister …?"

"Ricky, um, Rakesh, Rakesh Poonja," he said as he passed a fifty-dollar bill to her and gave his biggest smile.

The ferry was full, so he made his way to the upper deck and found a vacant seat. He closed his eyes, a wave of exhaustion took over, and off he went into the dream world: a nude beach, a ripped six-pack, and Jenny with a Tupperware full of fudge brownies. But suddenly, Ashiq showed up in their red Audi, and Jenny fed him fudge brownies. Ricky grabbed Jenny by her arm and asked her to look at his six-pack, but she ignored him like he was invisible. When Ashiq came out of the car, he stood tall. Ricky wondered how he got so tall in only six weeks.

"Did you buy a magic pill from the shopping channel?" he asked. Ashiq devoured all the brownies, licked the Tupperware and then Jenny all over. She giggled every time he licked her armpit.

"No Ashiq! No! Get off her!" Ricky shouted. Ashiq pushed him in the water and licked his face.

Ricky opened his eyes and found a Shih Tzu in his lap.

"I'm so sorry," a gorgeous Bahamian girl said, picking up the dog in her hand and putting the leash on. "He never does that," she apologized.

"That's okay," Ricky said with a muddled smile. He was grateful it wasn't Ashiq who licked his face.

The ferry arrived at the Swartz Bay Terminal, and people began to step off. He disembarked the ferry. A cab pulled up, he put the weekender in his lap, and asked the driver to take him to the Marriott hotel.

When Ricky arrived at the hotel, the girl with the Tiffany bracelet greeted him and asked for his driver's license. She found it suspicious that the man didn't know which room he was staying in. She remembered Jenny saying that her husband was arriving later in the evening, not that morning, and that is why she got a separate room for the freak who couldn't take his eyes off her breasts since her bracelet had hit the counter.

"Excuse me!" Ricky felt like his face was being licked by a mean Shih Tzu again. "I just need to enter your driver's license number in the system because you made the reservation and you weren't here when your wife checked in," she said in a diplomatic tone and smiled. "Would you like a spare key card as well?" She brought her hand forward to emphasize that she needed that proof. Ricky took his wallet out and threw the license on the counter. "There you go. I can't believe this."

"I'm so sorry, sir. I didn't mean to offend you. It's just a procedure we follow so you can have a smoother visit next time you come to Victoria." She smiled again.

"And yes, I'll take that key as well. After all, it's me who's paying for this damn room."

"Of course." She activated a new key card, placed it in a cardholder, and passed it to him. He put the card and his license in his wallet and took the elevator to the fourth floor. He came out of the elevator, walked up to the door, and paused. He wondered if he should wait to confront her about her ridiculous decision to throw away their money on a honeymoon suite or give her a piece of his mind when she opened the door. He decided he would wait. After all, he stayed up all night so that he could take the first ferry and surprise the love of his life.

Ashiq awoke from his dream, and Jenny awoke from her intoxicated sleep by the multiple knocks on the hotel door. The lights in the room were on.

"What the hell are you doing in my bed?" Jenny said, jumping back. Ashiq tilted his head and shrugged.

Someone knocked on the door again three times.

"It's probably housekeeping," Jenny said, rubbing her eyes. "Just tell them to come later."

Ashiq got out of bed, walked to the door in his white briefs, and opened it.

His eyes widened. He held his hands together in front of his crotch and said, "Um … hi, Uncle Rakesh."

CHAPTER EIGHT

"What the fuck, dude!" Ricky thrust his shoulders into Ashiq's chest, shoved him aside, and stood in front of Jenny with his hands on his waist.

"Babes, calm down!" Jenny jumped out of bed, walked toward Ricky, and held his hands.

Ricky pulled his hands away and paced back and forth in the room. Jenny asked Ashiq to return to his room to get ready for the next leg of the trip so that she could clarify to Ricky what happened the night before.

Ashiq returned to his hotel room, showered, got dressed, and packed his backpack for Tofino. He wondered what he would tell Ricky if he asked what happened the night before. He knew Ricky would not hit him because, if he really wanted to, he would have done so when he saw him in his white briefs. And it's not like they did anything wrong. It was *their* secret.

Ashiq shook the memory off and went back to the balcony. His stomach growled, and he wondered if he should go for breakfast without Jenny and Ricky. *But what if she comes here while I'm having breakfast?* The thought kept him on the balcony.

After an hour, someone knocked on his door. It was Jenny, her eyes were red, puffy, and sad. She told him it was too late for breakfast and that they would pick something up on the way home.

"Home? What happened to …" Ashiq took his backpack and shut the door behind him.

"Tofino's not gonna happen. We have a bit of a problem. Ricky suspects that something happened between us. I told him that nothing happened, but apparently, he could smell sex in the room," she said, rolling her eyes. "And the bottle of wine didn't help either. Why didn't you go back to your room last night?"

Ashiq stopped walking and gripped onto the railings.

"Let's go," she said. "We can talk about this later."

When they got into the car, she gave him five hundred-dollar bills and asked him to hide them in his wallet because he would need it later. She told him she spoke to her elder brother, the one who was older than Ashiq's mother, who lived in Sugar Land, Texas. Ashiq would get on a Greyhound bus later that day to start his new life in the United States.

How can this be happening? Ashiq's heart started pounding. *But we didn't do anything wrong. I only just got here.* He started sweating. *Why is this happening to me?* "I don't understand. Why do I need to leave? I don't even have a visa for America," Ashiq said.

"Canadians don't need a visa to visit the States," Jenny said. She told him they would get his luggage from home, and then she would drop him off at the Greyhound station. Jenny said he didn't have to worry and that Uncle Moosa in Sugar Land didn't know anything. She said that she told Uncle Moosa that they had an argument and that Ricky didn't want Ashiq to stay there any longer. Uncle Moosa offered to host him with his family. Jenny said that it would be better for Ashiq to be in Sugar Land. Uncle Moosa would get Ashiq a job right away so that he could save money and start school the following year.

"I wanted you to stay with us. I did. I was also ready to pay for your school, you know. But this shit happened and now it's all a mess," Jenny said.

"Why can't I just get a place of my own here in Vancouver? I don't want to go to Sugar Land."

"*Van. Ve, ve, ve. Van*-couver, not *Wan*-couver," she said, correcting his muddled pronunciation.

He looked away. *Who cares?!* But he *did* care.

"It will be good for you, Ash. And you get to see a different country. There's a lot of money in the US, and it's so easy to get a job there."

"Is Uncle Rakesh mad?"

"He's embarrassed. He said he won't be able to look you in the eye after how he treated you this morning. Whatever happened last night is done now. It's history, and let's leave it where it belongs, in the past," she said and pulled in front of Tim Hortons. "Let's get something to eat, shall we?"

The ferry left the Tsawwassen Terminal at noon. Jenny and Ashiq chose a different section of the ferry; it was quieter and more secluded. She told him that she wanted to relax and that he could go hang out on the deck if he pleased. But he stayed, because that's what pleased him. He thought of telling her about all the times she aroused him and how he went to the shower to play. But before he could muster the courage to reveal all his dirty secrets, Jenny stood up, walked over, and sat across from him.

"Are you a virgin?" she asked.

He looked around to see if anyone heard what Jenny said, but there were no passengers, no crew, and not even a lost dragonfly. He knew it was a *yes* or a *no* answer, but he felt he needed to provide an explanation before he could give a response to her unexpected query.

"Well …" he said, smiling. "You know, there was an incident one day at our school. People got hurt, lots of blood everywhere. I was alone in the nurse room, sorting supplies, when this girl walked in. I had a huge crush on her."

"So, what happened?" Jenny placed her hands under her thighs.

"Well, she closed the door and the blinds too, and that is when it all happened."

"So, you guys did it in the nurse room! In your freakin' school?" Her eyes widened, and he noticed her curl her toes, twice, and play with her wedding ring.

"No, we were just kissing and doing other stuff, and then someone knocked on the door. It was the school nurse or someone … I don't remember now. So, we stopped."

"Then what happened?"

"Nothing."

"That's it?" Jenny raised her hands in the air. "So, what's the point of this story?"

"It almost happened!"

"Yes, *almost*. Let me bring you back to Earth. If you didn't do the in and out, in and out, then you're still a virgin. Nothing wrong with that, you know. Actually, I'm glad that you are."

"Why?"

"Because you're gonna have a *real* story the next time I see you. You're still a baby." She smiled, grabbed his hand, and got up. "Let's go to the deck and get some sunshine. You're too white."

He wanted to defend himself, his boyhood, and his special moment. It was as if Jenny had woken him up from the most beautiful dream and revealed to him that his reality was sunless, moonless, and starless, like a lonely and nebulous planet.

He told himself that the only way he could have a *real* story about losing his virginity the next time he saw Jenny would be to *lose* it. The problem was he didn't know how. Maybe Sugar Land was the destination for his salvation.

CHAPTER NINE

He slept for most of the way. He didn't talk to anyone, except an older fella who told him he was nuts for taking the Greyhound all the way to Sugar Land. Every time he woke up, he found new faces in his surroundings and wondered if there was even a single person who was going to Sugar Land.

Jenny had given him a bag of mixed nuts and a small box of granola bars. She advised him to keep hydrated but not to drink too much water because he would not be able to pee until the bus stopped at a station. She also told him to remember the bus number in case he got disoriented at stops. "It is going to be an adventure. I wish I was traveling with you," Jenny had said when Ashiq looked at her with his watery eyes.

"Khala," he said.

She placed her hands on his face, pulled him closer, and hugged him. "Don't you worry, baby. Everything's gonna be alright," she said. "I promise."

Ashiq had called his family from Ricky's office before leaving for the Greyhound station. Jenny had asked him not to mention anything about what happened and to tell his father he was going for a quick visit. He could tell his family that he made the move once he got to Sugar Land.

When Ashiq had called, he expected his mother, but his father answered the phone. When he told him about the quick visit to Sugar Land, his father got suspicious. He asked Ashiq about what made him change his plans. He said it was just a spontaneous decision. When his father passed the phone to Mrs. Amlani, Ashiq broke down.

"Call us when you reach Uncle Moosa's place, okay beta?" she had said, and she told him to remember to recite the holy words throughout the ride.

He looked out the window now, and it had stopped raining, but it was still too dark to see anything. He thought about his new life in Sugar Land and his legs started shaking rapidly. Ashiq didn't know Uncle Moosa well enough, and he wasn't close to any of Moosa's children. He remembered playing with them when they were little, but that was a long time ago and he knew that they would be different now. They would be all American and would not sound like Apu. He wondered if they would accept him or mock him like the boys on the roof of the public library. He closed his eyes and recited the holy words. He took a deep breath and fell asleep once again.

When he opened his eyes, the bus stood at a new station. The weather was gloomy and it was drizzling outside. He didn't want to pee, so he decided to stay in, but the driver came up and asked him to disembark and go through customs because they were at the US–Canada border. Ashiq put on his backpack and followed the rest of the passengers. The driver asked him to take his luggage with him and said that she would meet him and all the passengers on the other side of the building. He grabbed his luggage and entered. He found it absurd that, unlike him, all the passengers carried small handbags. He wished there were wheels on his big suitcases like the old lady's duffle bag. He dragged the luggage forward and smiled at the customs officer.

"Passport," the officer said with a stern face. Ashiq pulled his shirt up, unzipped the travel pouch, and took his blue passport out.

"What's your name?" He didn't understand why the officer asked his name when it was clearly mentioned on the opened page. He thought maybe it could be his moustache-less face that confused the officer, because his passport photo looked different.

"I recently shaved." His voice cracked.

"Where were you born?"

"Edmonton, Alberta, Canada."

"What is the purpose of your visit to the United States, sir?"

"To see my family."

"For how long?"

"Two weeks." He said exactly what Jenny had asked him to say.

"What's in those bags?"

"Clothes."

"Why do you need so many clothes for only two weeks?"

He didn't know how to answer that question. He knew that the officer was right; he didn't need all those clothes only for a two-week visit. But he wasn't going for a visit. He was going to live in the United States to start a new life, and he would need all those clothes, especially his lucky blue t-shirt.

"To visit many places, take photos in different clothes, and share with my cousins," he said with hesitation.

"Why? Don't they have their own clothes? Please place your luggage on the table." The officer waved for the two female officers to come over. They walked forward without taking their eyes off him.

Ashiq placed both the suitcases on the table, took the keys out of his travel pouch, and unlocked them for inspection.

"Please come with me while they check your luggage." The officer took him to another room.

When they entered, there were two other officers. They asked Ashiq why his Canadian passport was issued in Islamabad, Pakistan. He told them that was where the Canadian Embassy was, and he had gone there with his parents to renew it. They asked him why he had lived in Karachi for so long and now wanted to go to the US after spending less than two weeks in Canada.

"Because of my dad's business. Karachi is a port city, so he exported all of his leather products from there," Ashiq said.

Suddenly, a female voice announced on the loudspeaker, "All passengers with US customs clearance are requested to board their Greyhound buses heading to Seattle."

"I'm going to miss my bus," Ashiq said.

"Your bus is already gone," the officer told him.

That surprised him. He pulled out his ticket from his pouch and showed it to the officer to prove that he paid for a full ticket, all the way to Sugar Land, Texas. The officers ignored him and left the room. Ashiq placed his hands under his thighs and recited the holy words.

After fifteen minutes, the officers returned. They took him back to the main door, gave him his passport, and asked him to walk to the building on the other side. "What is that?" Ashiq looked toward another building through the pouring rain outside.

"It's the Canadian Customs and Immigration. They'll help you," the officer said.

Ashiq raised his eyebrows.

"Sir, you're going back to Canada. You cannot enter the United States."

"Why? I am a Canadian citizen. I don't need a visa for America."

"We believe you want to come here to work."

How the hell do they know? "No, no. Sir, I am going only to visit my family then my university will start. I promise you, sir."

"You're on your own now," the officer said and stepped back into the building. He unhooked a key from the loop of his pants and locked the door behind.

Ashiq's heart throbbed in his chest, his body shivered, and he tugged the luggage behind him. The rain drenched him to the bone within seconds, and he thought about his home, his family, and his friends. He summoned the courage from every part of his body to not break down, to stay strong, and to live the adventure. But he felt lost, defeated, and ridiculed. He stood in the middle of a rough patch, a place that was neither Canada nor the United States, and he paused and looked up to the sky for a revelation. But there was no divine intervention, no clear explanation, not even a mere excuse; all he got was pouring rain. He lowered his head and let the rain draw the tears out of him. They dribbled and drizzled into a swirling stream of sadness. It reminded him of Nani, his favorite grandmother, who loved playing with him in the rain, jumping in the puddles, splashing the water, patting his skin dry with her towel, sipping hot milk tea, biting spicy vegetable pakoras, and listening to old Bollywood songs. *"Everything happens for a reason, my love."* Her voice echoed in his ears. Nani taught him never to lose hope, because difficult times always led to better days. He had to trust that, even in the terrible situation he found himself in now, Nani would be proven right.

He didn't know how much time passed, but he knew that he was closer to his destination because he could see people walking around inside the building. A lady with an umbrella came out and made a gesture for him to come forward. He pulled the luggage with all his might and sped up.

"No wheels, eh?" she smiled. He shook his head. "Let me help you."

She took the smaller suitcase and guided him to the building. When they got inside, a guy with the same uniform passed him a towel and asked him to wait in the seating area. The girl returned with a cup of coffee and a writing pad. She asked him if he took a bus or if someone dropped him off at the border. She told him that he could either call his family to come get him, or they could send him back on a Greyhound bus using the same ticket. She told him not to worry because these kinds of occurrences were normal.

"But I have a blue passport," he said.

"What do you mean?" She smiled.

"I was told I didn't need a visa for America, so how could they refuse me entry?"

"They have the right to refuse anyone, just like we do. It's their country and they can decide who comes and goes. There's nothing we can do."

He called Jenny to tell her what happened, but Ricky picked up the phone.

"Hello?"

"Hi, Uncle Ricky. It's Ashiq."

"What is it?"

"They are not letting me go to Sugar Land," he said. "I don't know what to do."

"Ugh, why are you calling me? I don't control the borders."

"Uncle Ricky, I really need help. I'm stuck here," Ashiq pleaded.

After a pause, Ricky sighed. "This doesn't mean I like it, but we'll figure something out."

Ashiq wanted to speak with Jenny, but it was too late to tell Ricky that there were only thirty seconds left on the call and that he needed to put more coins in. The automated operator reminded Ashiq about the time remaining again, but in French that time, which he didn't understand. There were five granola bars and a few almonds left. No loonies or dimes or quarters. The two shiny toonies in his pouch read 1996 on them, but the machine didn't take them; the two-dollar coins were just a year old and too new for the old phone machines. He was trapped in a situation that he could barely imagine, let alone understand. He hung up, went back to the seating area, and waited for the bus.

Jenny was standing on the curb when he got off the bus in Vancouver at the same station where she had dropped him off. All his energy was drained. He wobbled on his feet, and then looked up. Seeing her so soon after he thought he was saying goodbye to her forever made him calm. He gulped, closed his mouth, and fought back the tears that he held back not from embarrassment but from wanting to validate, not decry, his actions.

"You shouldn't have taken your bags with you when you talked to the officials. I don't understand why you did that," Jenny said.

"The driver told me to."

"What does he know?" She looked over her shoulder and rotated her steering wheel to the left. "I should've bought you a plane ticket. The customs at the airport are hassle free. What was I thinking? I thought you'd love the adventure, to be on a bus, and that you'd get to see all the amazing places, but you didn't even appreciate that."

Ashiq didn't understand what there was to appreciate. He had been too tired to see anything when the bus left Vancouver, and when he got up, it was raining and everything was pitch black. He looked out the window and wondered why Jenny was treating him with such impudence. He didn't do anything wrong. It wasn't like he dragged the heavy suitcases to the customs officer on purpose. It wasn't like there was a choice, but Jenny made him feel stupid.

When they got home, Ricky said the same things Jenny did, so Ashiq kept quiet and listened to the wise old birds chirping the wise old wisdom. They called Uncle Moosa in Sugar Land to tell him that Ashiq would be on the next flight, but Uncle Moosa told them that it was not a good idea because Ashiq would be nervous, and the United States customs and border officers would suspect something. He asked them to wait for a week and then send him off.

After Jenny and Ricky went to bed that night, Ashiq picked up the cordless phone, and with careful consideration, slid the balcony glass door open. It was the safest area of the apartment where he could get the maximum privacy. The scratched calling card on Ricky's desk was out of credit. He threw it off the balcony, and dialed Karachi directly on the cordless. He heard a click sound, and the phone rang on the other side of the Pacific Ocean.

"Hello, Bhai," the voice said. "It's you!"

Ashiq's eyes crinkled up. He didn't question how his little sister, Fari, predicted it was him on the phone or why his father or mother hadn't answered the phone, and instead he savored the moment and smiled. An ambulance passed in front of Jenny and Ricky's apartment building, and Ashiq turned to look through the glass window to make sure the loud sirens didn't wake up the Poonjas from their light sleep. He checked the glass door again and felt content that the barrier did a good job of keeping the wise birds in their weathered cages.

He wanted to tell Fari how miserable he was and how he walked in the rain with two heavy suitcases and how he was forced to eat the brown bread that tasted like rubber. He wanted to tell his sister all those things and more, but he took a deep breath instead. Hearing the voice of his little sister made everything better.

"I miss you," Ashiq said.

"I miss you too, Bhaijan! Mummy is here. Let me give the phone to her," Fari said.

When Ashiq reached the first part of the story, where the US customs officials interrogated him, he heard his mother cry, so he skipped the climax and told her that he just went back to Vancouver.

"Give the phone to me," Ashiq heard his father say.

"He's calling direct, so he only has a few minutes. We can talk to him later," Mrs. Amlani said.

Ashiq told his father he couldn't talk for long because it would cost the Poonjas a lot of money and that it wasn't the best choice. He said that he called to let them know that he was all right and he would be going to Sugar Land in a week. But his father asked him to stay on the phone and told him that he shouldn't worry because he didn't have to pay the bill; he would speak with Jahanara Aunty and Uncle Rakesh and take care of it for him. So, Ashiq continued to tell the story, including the part about the rain and the dragging of the luggage, but Mr. Shamsu Amlani didn't cry. Instead, he said that was nothing in comparison to what he had gone through and how he had been arrested twice in Chicago for working under the table and was asked to leave the country. "Forget the US. I want you to stay in Canada," Mr. Amlani said.

"But how? Daddy, they don't want me here." Ashiq bit his tongue for blurting that out. He knew that he shouldn't have said what he said to his father. He knew that it was too late to take it all back because then the balcony door opened and Jenny came out.

She spoke to Mr. Shamsu Amlani for exactly a minute and a half (Ashiq looked at the clock twice) and passed the phone to Ricky. Ricky and Shamsu talked for a long time. There were a few laughs here and there (Ashiq and Jenny could hear on the speaker phone) but mostly serious conversation. They talked for the next thirty minutes. Well, Shamsu talked and Ricky listened. Shamsu told Ricky how important it was to save money and be financially responsible, and Ricky rolled his eyes, clicked the speaker off, and brought the receiver to his ears. "By the way, Shamsu Bhai," he said. "When are you sending me the five thousand dollars you *borrowed* ten years ago?!" Ashiq's father was known for the mismanagement of wealth, just like Ashiq's grandfather who lost their family inheritance after the second world war, in record time.

They talked for another fifteen minutes, then Ricky hung up the phone and looked at Jenny. "Wow, this guy can talk, eh? He must have a direct link to the Pakistan Telecommunication."

Jenny rubbed her eyes.

"I think we spoke for an hour. You know how much that will cost him, but then again," Ricky said, turning to Ashiq, "your dad doesn't really have a clue about the value of money, now does he?"

Ashiq lowered his eyes and wondered how Ricky would react when the truth revealed itself.

"Get some sleep now. You're going to Calgary tomorrow," Ricky said.

"What's in Calgary?" Jenny asked.

"Shamsu's childhood friend lives there. Apparently, he's gonna talk to him and let me know."

"Uncle Farook?" Ashiq asked. The last time Ashiq saw Farook Hookmani was seven years ago, in the summer of 1990, in Karachi, just before the Hookmani family immigrated to Canada. For Ashiq Amlani, it was an unfortunate year — the year he was transferred to an all-boys school in Karachi (because his parents thought he didn't have enough friends that were boys and that he might become too "girly"), the year someone stole his BMX bicycle, and the year he said goodbye to the love of his life, Shefrina Hookmani, because her dad Farook Hookmani moved her and her family to Calgary.

"Yes, you're gonna stay with him. Your dad doesn't want us to send you to the US and we must do what he says. You are our responsibility until you get to Calgary, then it's up to your Uncle Farook and your dad."

"But ..." Jenny interjected.

"Don't look at me," Ricky said, raising his hands. "You know what he said? He had the guts, that Shamsu, *that guy*, had the guts to tell me that *I, that we,* don't know anything about children. Can you freakin' believe that?" Ricky then gave a stern look to Ashiq. "Your dad is something else." He shook his head and turned to Jenny. "He said he knows what's best for his child. You guys can stay up and cry about it, but I'm going back to bed. Good night."

Ricky filled a glass of water from the kitchen tap, walked into the bedroom, and shut the door. Jenny looked at Ashiq and then turned her eyes to the balcony. They stepped out and shut the glass door behind them.

Jenny placed her hands on the balcony railing and gazed into the distance. Ashiq stood by the glass door and looked at her. "I love the Science World lit up at night. I can't believe I never took you there," Jenny said.

"Where?" Ashiq glanced at the landscape.

"You see the giant ball-shaped structure with lights?" Jenny bent over the railings and pointed her index finger toward the geodesic dome. But Ashiq was looking at Jenny's butt cheeks popping out from underneath her mulberry silk night slip.

Jenny turned her head and looked at Ashiq. "Why are you still standing there?" She stared at him for a moment and then reluctantly extended her hand. He grabbed it, walked up to her, and placed his hands on the balcony railing.

"I know how you feel," Jenny said, and put her hand around his neck.

He placed his palm on top of her hand and intertwined his fingers with hers.

"Don't worry. Everything will be fine when you go to Calgary." She tightened her grip.

Ashiq put his other hand around her waist. "I don't want to leave you."

"You know I'll always be there for you. I'm only a phone call away." She smiled, kissing him on his cheek.

He turned his body toward her and looked into her eyes. He loved how much she cared about him. He thought it was the perfect time to get more comfort from her. He slid his hand over her panties and grabbed her butt.

"I love you, Khala," he said in a wobbly voice.

"What are you doing?" Jenny said, taking a step back. "Ricky is in the next room."

He turned around and looked through the balcony glass door. "He's sleeping." Ashiq extended his arm toward her again, but she shook her head. "You need to go to bed." She slid open the glass door, stepped into the apartment, and turned her head to look at him. "Good night," she whispered, "horny boy."

Ashiq followed her with his eyes as she walked to her bedroom. He stepped into the apartment, closed the door behind him, and thought, *I'm not as horny as you are, sexy Jenny.*

CHAPTER TEN

The next day, Jenny took Ashiq to the Great Wall Mongolian BBQ on Denman Street for lunch, then drove him to Pacific Central Station and bought him a Greyhound bus ticket to Calgary. After a fourteen-hour ride, Ashiq arrived in Calgary just before sunset.

He saw a white Crown Victoria station wagon outside the Greyhound station. The passenger door opened and a girl stepped out. She was different from everyone else around him. She was more like him: the color of her skin, the shape of her eyes, and that beautiful smile. He walked closer to the door. *It's her.* His heart skipped a beat.

When Ashiq was young and in Karachi, he had found perfect excuses to visit her house, just to get a glimpse of her. One day, during the summer holidays, he went up to her house to get sugar for his grandmother's tea, and her older brother, Khalid, told him, "Fuck off, you bastard," because he knew Ashiq's grandmother was out of town. Ashiq saw her standing in the window, waving sadly, as he ran off like a little scared rabbit.

"Look. He's here." Ashiq heard as he saw Khalid pop his head out from the driver's seat, pointing at him. Ashiq opened the exit door of the Greyhound station with his leg, held it open with his knees, and pushed the luggage out the door.

"Hi," she said as she opened her arms. Her hair had grown longer, and her shorts had gotten shorter since he last saw her. She smiled and Ashiq saw the glimmer, the same as the one he had seen in little Shefrina's eyes, the fiery sparks that signified her *joie de vivre*.

"You guys can do your hugging when we get home," Khalid said as he helped Ashiq put the luggage in the trunk, shaking hands with him. "Let's get going," he said.

They got into the car, and Ashiq saw her put her seatbelt on and turn her head to look at him. "How was the bus ride?" Shefrina said. "You must be tired."

Ashiq saw Khalid adjust the rearview mirror and look at him while he worked the seatbelt. "Oh, you don't need to worry about that," Khalid said.

"He means it's not mandatory if you're in the back seat, but …" Shefrina paused to give a look to Khalid, "it's better to be safe than sorry. I'm quite impressed that you thought of it, considering you just came from Karachi," she said.

"Just relax, man," Khalid said. "The ride must have been brutal. Can't believe your aunt sent you on a Greyhound."

"It wasn't that bad. At least I got to see some amazing scenery." Ashiq smiled.

"Yeah, I love British Columbia too, but never take a Greyhound past Alberta going east," Shefrina said.

"Yes, never," Khalid agreed.

"It's the most boring landscape ever," Shefrina said.

"True that," Khalid said. Ashiq saw Khalid looking at him through the rearview mirror. "Are you hungry?"

Ashiq shook his head.

"Don't be shy, bro. Here in Canada, we don't ask twice like how people do in Karachi. We ask once and if the person says no then that means no. So, are you hungry?" Khalid asked again.

Ashiq smiled.

"Let's go to Peter's Drive-In," Shefrina said.

"Perfect. Hey, Ashiq, it's the best burger you'll ever eat," Khalid said.

"Well, the best in Calgary, that's for sure." Shefrina pulled her hair up and tied it with a pink hairband. Ashiq felt an uncontrollable desire to kiss the soft bristles in the hollow of her armpit. It was a new feeling that bemused his own curious mind. He couldn't understand why a part of the body that he believed to be a forbidden zone had turned into an erogenous zone at that moment. *She looks hot,* is all he could think during the drive to Peter's Drive-In.

They each ordered a burger with cheese, but Khalid also ordered a chocolate milkshake and recommended that Ashiq get a strawberry one. He said it was the combination of the milkshake and the burger that made it so good. Shefrina agreed but got none; she said she was watching her weight, but Ashiq insisted she get one because she was in great shape. He saw her cheeks turn pink.

"It's going to be a harsh winter for you, bro. You should've come here earlier. You missed the Stampede. It's the best time of the year to be in Calgary," Khalid said as he crunched up the wrapper and slurped the last gulps of the shake.

"The leaves haven't even turned orange yet, and you're scaring him off," Shefrina said.

"I was just talking about the Stampede. You know, when we went this year with Zahid?" Khalid said.

Shefrina kept quiet.

"Zahid? You mean Zahid Hamza?" Ashiq asked.

Zahid Hamza was Khalid's best friend and the first boy in the neighborhood to own a bicycle, which is why Khalid had accepted his friendship and why Shefrina had accepted his heart. Ashiq had not been so quick to accept Zahid, especially not after he had seen Zahid do funny things back in the day with most of the maids in their Karachi neighborhood, though he had never told anyone that.

"Yeah, man. We had so much fun," Khalid continued.

"He also lives here? In Calgary?" Ashiq passed his empties to the front, and Shefrina stepped out of the car to throw the garbage in the bin.

"No, he was here for the engagement." Khalid took out a pack of Marlboro Reds and tapped it on the dashboard.

"He got engaged?" Ashiq asked.

"Yeah, man. Didn't you hear?" Khalid turned around and offered him the cigarette. Ashiq shook his head. "Shefrina and Zahid got engaged. They're getting married this winter," Khalid said, and flicked the lid of the silver Zippo open, slid his thumb sharply downward, and lit his cigarette.

It burned a hole in Ashiq's heart and revealed to him what the winter would look like: the love of his childhood life going to a man who didn't deserve her. It would be harsh, painful, and lonely.

*⁺⁺

Khalid helped Ashiq take the luggage to the basement of their house and showed him his room. There were no windows, one single bed, and pink walls. "This was Zarmeen's room, but don't worry. You won't be spending much time in here. Hope not." Khalid laughed.

"Umm, so, where's Zarmeen sleeping now?" Ashiq asked.

"She's with Shefrina. They love sharing everything," Khalid said. "And I'm in the next room, so if you ever need anything just knock on my door. Everyone else sleeps upstairs. Let's go say hi to them."

The basement stairs connected to the living room. When they got upstairs, the TV was on mute, and no one was around.

"*The Simpsons* is on," Khalid said as he picked up the remote and unmuted the TV. "It's the funniest show ever."

Ashiq sat on the couch and laughed every time Khalid laughed; he figured it would be the best way to learn why everyone thought *The Simpsons* was the funniest show ever.

When Farook Hookmani arrived, he hugged Ashiq for a minute and a half. Ashiq saw Mrs. Hookmani checking the clock twice. Farook Hookmani said he wanted to look at Ashiq "properly," and he said it three times; Ashiq counted. Farook Hookmani even cried while everyone laughed.

"Wow, Dad. You're a bit emotional today," Shefrina said.

"A bit?" Mrs. Hookmani put her head on her husband's shoulder, and he put his hands around her and smiled.

"I haven't seen him, you know, since he was a little boy," Farook Hookmani said. "Uncle, you look exactly the same. No change at all, *wah wah*,"[12] Ashiq said.

"You should be saying that to my mom. She's the one who deserves the compliment," Shefrina said.

Ashiq looked at Mrs. Hookmani and smiled but didn't say anything. He wanted to, but he didn't know how.

"Oh beta, you don't need to say anything. We all know I'm getting old now. Look," she said, and pulled her hair forward. "You can see." Mrs. Hookmani broke the silence.

---

[12] *Wah wah* is a term of appreciation meaning "good," "very good," "wow."

"Mom, you are gorgeous," Shefrina said and inserted her elbow into Ashiq's ribs.

"Yes," Ashiq blurted out, "Yes, yes. You are, Aunty ji."

"No need to butter me up. I'm fine the way I am," Mrs. Hookmani said. "Not everyone can be like your mom, Ashiq," she said as she rolled her eyes.

"Yeah, man. Roshan Aunty is sexy," Khalid said.

"Watch your language," Mr. Hookmani snapped. "Don't forget where you came from. It's disrespectful to talk about your elders like that, *and,* not in front of him. Beta, Maa, a mother is the most sacred person in our culture. You should always respect the way you address someone, even when they are not around," Mr. Hookmani said.

"Here we go. The lecture starts," Khalid said.

"He's right. There's always a proper way to say things. You can say she's elegant or that she's charming," Mrs. Hookmani said.

"No, Mummy. *You* are elegant and charming, but Roshan Aunty, she's just straight sexy." A girl emerged from behind the bathroom door. She had wet hair and wore a violet bathrobe. The house filled with the smell of fresh lilies and daffodils.

"Um, is that Zarmeen?" Ashiq said.

"You got that right," Mr. Hookmani said. "Same little Zarmeen from your painting class."

She's not that little anymore, Ashiq thought, and smiled at her. *Maybe she'll be my girlfriend if her sister can't.*

Zarmeen blushed.

"Why is your face turning red?" Shefrina asked.

"Is it?" Zarmeen ran back to the bathroom. "It's just the heat from the shower."

"Rrrrrright." Shefrina stepped into the bathroom.

Ashiq heard the girls giggle. Mrs. Hookmani looked at Mr. Hookmani, and Khalid signaled Ashiq that it was time to head back to the basement.

✦✦

In the morning, when Ashiq went to the basement washroom, he found a Post-it note on the mirror that Khalid had left for him, and there was a phone number on it. He went upstairs and called the number. Khalid answered the phone and told him he was covering at the Hooks Motel because his dad was at the bank and that later he would go for his hockey practice. He also told Ashiq to fix breakfast by himself, as there was no one around who would serve him. "Everyone's on their own," Khalid said.

"Sure, I can do that," Ashiq said. He also wanted to know if someone had left a set of keys for him so he could go out and explore like how he did in Vancouver, but Khalid just said, "Later, bro," and hung up the phone.

I guess no keys today, Ashiq thought.

He went to the kitchen to get cereal and milk, but he saw white bread on the counter and smiled. *Finally, I'm with brown people that don't eat brown bread.* He made himself two sandwiches with strawberry jam and margarine. He cut the sandwiches in halves, like how his mother did. He found it consoling that every time he dipped the sandwich into the milk and took a bite, the taste made him feel close to home, close to his mother. It was one of those feelings that could not be easily conveyed through paintings or words or convoluted sculptures, though maybe through music, if the composer were not trying too hard.

He finished his breakfast, cleared the crumbs off the table like he had seen Ricky do, but there was no Jenny to say, "Thanks, babe." He missed her. He wondered whether, if he hadn't grabbed her butt during their awkward final encounter on the balcony, Jenny would have let him stay for another week or two.

He walked to the living room, picked up the phone receiver, and dialed Ricky and Jenny's number. The phone rang once, but his eyes traveled to the wooden clock that hung above the TV, and he suddenly remembered that Jenny left for work early in the morning, and the only person around in the apartment at 9:45 a.m. would be Ricky. He slammed the phone down and walked back to the kitchen.

He noticed there wasn't a dishwasher in the kitchen, so he went to the sink and washed everything he found in there. He didn't know what to do with his time, so he turned on the TV and spent the rest of the day watching *The Simpsons*. At first, he didn't understand the hype, but after a few episodes, he started liking Homer (the main protagonist of the show, and a white guy) more than Apu (a recurring character, and a dark brown guy). What boggled his mind was Apu's strong accent. He couldn't understand why people thought he sounded like Apu, when he thought that he didn't. He knew that his accent wasn't Canadian or American. He knew that he didn't sound like white people, but he also knew that he didn't sound like Apu. Just when Ashiq started despising Apu for making his life miserable, he came across one of the latest episodes titled "The Two Mrs. Nahasapeemapetilons," in which, at a bachelor auction, the available bachelors on display were deemed undesirable, and the auction generated no money at all. Marge (Homer's wife) then nominated Apu, who was deemed a success by the women at the auction. He went out on dates with many of the town's women and began to enjoy his bachelor lifestyle.

This gave hope to Ashiq. *If Apu can do it, I can do it too.*

When there were no more episodes left, he turned the TV off, went downstairs to his room, and read for a few hours.

Soon there was a knock on his bedroom door, and he thought that Khalid was back. He threw the magazine he was reading on the bed and jumped up to open the door. "You're already done with hockey?" Ashiq said.

"Hockey?" It was Zarmeen.

"Oh, sorry. I thought it was Khalid." Ashiq smiled.

"I see. Do you play hockey?"

He shook his head.

"I didn't think so. You don't look like a hockey player. You're more like a ..." She slanted her head. "A soccer player."

"I don't play football," he said.

"Definitely not." She put her hands on his shoulders. "You can never be a football player." She took her hands off him and squinted her eyes. "Um, I'm sorry. I didn't mean to."

Ashiq shrugged his shoulders and tilted his head. *Didn't she say I look like a football player ... and now?*

"Ah," she laughed. "You were thinking soccer. Like football soccer." He nodded.

"Well, in North America, football is called soccer."

"Why? Football is football everywhere else in the world," Ashiq said.

"True, but there's another game called football. It's American football, so to make the distinction, we call football *soccer*. Got it?"

"Everything is so different here, so confusing." Ashiq couldn't understand why things were so complicated, why people couldn't just call football *football*, what the hell *soccer* was. A lift is a *lift*, it's not an *elevator*, and Jahanara and Rakesh Poonja are Jahanara and Rakesh Poonja, they are not Jenny and Ricky.

"You'll get the hang of it. Don't worry." She smiled. "Well, I was wondering if you wanted to come with me to pick Shefrina up from work."

"Where does she work?"

"At Fairmont."

"Never heard of it," Ashiq said as he put his socks on.

"It's the best hotel in Calgary. It's a huge name. She's actually doing her internship there, and it's part of the co-op program for her undergrad."

He turned the lights off in the room.

"Oh, I forgot to ask you: how do you like the color in the room?"

"Pink? Seriously?" he said.

"Suits you, doesn't it?" She laughed. "Why don't you wait outside. I'm gonna get the keys."

She came out, walked up to him, and pulled his t-shirt out of his jeans. "There, now it looks much better."

Before they could get in Zarmeen's car, the white Crown Victoria station wagon pulled over and Khalid dropped Farook Hookmani off. "Where are you guys going?" he asked.

"To *fur mount* hotel," Ashiq said.

Ashiq saw Zarmeen and Khalid smirk, but he didn't understand why. "What?" he asked. He gave an indecisive smile because he didn't know what else he could have done in that situation.

"It's *Fairmont*, not *fur mount*," Khalid said.

Ashiq was transported back to the roof of the Yaletown library.

"Anyways, I'm going to my hockey practice. Wanna come?" Khalid said, looking at him.

Ashiq shook his head.

"You should go. It'll be fun," Zarmeen said.

"No, I'll go with you." Ashiq opened the passenger door of Zarmeen's car and got in. Zarmeen shrugged her shoulders and waved a farewell to Khalid.

Ashiq and Zarmeen didn't talk for the first five minutes. The radio was on, and he soaked in the new scenery of whatever he could see in the twilight of the late evening, but when the advertisements came on the radio, she said she knew Khalid shouldn't have corrected him in front of her like that, and that it must have hurt his feelings, but that Khalid meant well. She said that they had all gone through what Ashiq was going through now, and that it would get worse. Ashiq said that his aunt had told him the same thing, and he understood that being corrected was better than getting mocked in front of strangers. It was something he needed to keep learning.

As he saw the upcoming traffic lights turning yellow, he said, "You should slow down." When she instead accelerated through the red light, he said, "Oh shit!" and clutched the sides of his seat tightly. "You're crazy."

"You have no idea." She turned to look at him and winked. "You know what?"

He looked at her and then looked back at the road. She gently touched his earlobe and added, "I'm so glad you're here."

Does she want to fuck me? he thought. *But I can't do that! Shefrina will never talk to me.* Even though he loved the feeling of Zarmeen playing with his earlobe, he didn't want to jeopardize losing the chance of being with Shefrina, so he turned his head toward the passenger window and looked out at the people standing on the curb.

They took a longer route to the hotel. Zarmeen said there was time to kill, so she took him to Crescent Hill for a bit; it was her favorite spot in Calgary, and it was spectacular at night. She said that she wanted to show him around and tell him stories, starting with the first time she went there with the family, the second time with a boy, and the third time when she thought she might be a lesbian, though Lushana Watson's bad breath had kept Zarmeen Hookmani away.

But before she could add the juicy details, Ashiq felt the wind in his bones and asked if they could sit in the car. He saw her rolling her eyes and then unlocking the car for him. "Get in, you wuss," she said, getting into the driver's seat.

"What's a lesbian?" Ashiq asked.

Zarmeen jumped forward in her chair and wrinkled her nose. "Are you serious?" she asked.

He shrugged. "What? How should I know?"

"Oh my God. I can't believe this." She turned to look at him. "Okay, imagine." She held his shoulders and turned them toward her. "Imagine that you're a girl."

"Why? But I'm a boy," Ashiq said.

"I know baba, but just imagine that you're a girl for a second, and that you like me," she said.

He raised his eyebrows again. "You mean like ... *like* like?

"Yes," she winked at him. "Now, what would you do?"

"I don't know. Smile?" Ashiq said.

"Oh God, you're hopeless. Just forget it. You'll figure it out someday. Speaking of which, Ashiq, what do you really want to do with your life?"

"Umm, journalism. I used to write in Karachi."

"Hmm," she said. "The *money* is no good. Writing in general is one of the worst things you could do to yourself. It won't pay the bills. You remember Shirin Appa? She was married to a writer here in Calgary, but they got divorced within six months. And she went back to Karachi."

"Why?"

"Why? Because he couldn't pay the bills, that's why. You should look into computer science. There's so much money in it."

"That doesn't interest me."

"So what? When you have money, everything will look interesting."

"But life is not all about money. What about your passion, your purpose in life?" Ashiq said.

"Oh Lord," she laughed.

The hazard lights from another car blinked in the rearview mirror and distracted them.

"Shit, what time is it? I think we should get going," Zarmeen said and turned the ignition on. "We should come here again. I have so many stories to tell you."

When they arrived at the Fairmont Hotel, Shefrina got into the back seat and told them about what happened at work and how much she would love to get a full-time job there. Zarmeen reminded Shefrina that she was getting married that winter and would have to move to the US because Zahid Hamza would make more money with his job developing software for a multinational corporation and that she would easily find a job there.

Ashiq wanted to tell Shefrina that she shouldn't marry Zahid, because she would regret it later. "Are you happy?" he mumbled.

He was the only one in the car who heard himself ask Shefrina if she would consider staying in Calgary and maybe take him to be her lover, like they did when they were ten, when they played *Ghar Ghar,* the pretentious game in which Ashiq was the *Daddy,* Shefrina the *Mummy* and the rest of the kids were their offspring. They made chicken biryani, baked birthday cakes, drew the curtains to make the room darker (Ashiq's favorite part), and he would ask everyone to close their eyes and go to bed. Only then he pulled Shefrina closer to him and she giggled. He blew air on her face, and she giggled, and everyone wondered if Shefrina would end up with a big stomach the next day.

Ashiq wanted to know if Shefrina was happy, and he wanted to tell her that Shefrina Amlani sounded better than Shefrina Hamza.

"Ashiq," Zarmeen interrupted his thoughts.

"Amlani, Shefrina Amlani," he blurted out.

They all saw the red light. Zarmeen slammed her foot on the brake and turned to Ashiq. "Have you gone nuts? I asked you about the name of her hotel, but …" Zarmeen touched his forehead with the back of her hand. "But you said Shefrina *Amlani.*"

"Yes, and?" He saw everything was normal in the house, in their *Ghar*.

"Ashiq?" Zarmeen said.

"That's what we used to call her back in the day. Don't you remember? We used to play *Ghar Ghar*."

"*Ghar Ghar*. That's funny, but I asked you ..."

Ashiq pointed at the green traffic light.

The next day Ashiq got up early and left the house with Farook Hookmani to spend the day at the Hooks Motel. It was a single-story establishment. The reception desk was in the middle, and each side had eight rooms. They walked around from room to room. Ashiq studied the standard, the superior, and the deluxe, rooms that were vacant but didn't understand why all the rooms had the same small windows, burgundy doors, beige walls, and a distinct scent that smelled like cigarettes and roses. When they reached the last room, his eyes widened. That was the only room that had a black door, red walls, a metallic pole in the center, and chains hanging off the walls "Wow, is this for magic shows?" he said.

"Um, no," Mr. Hookmani cleared his throat. "This is the red room. We sometimes get these fourteen-wheeler truck guys, and they like to do crazy stuff in here. Not a big seller though. Most of the time we store fresh towels and bed sheets in here."

When they returned to the reception desk, Ashiq looked at the price list and converted them to Pakistani rupees. Farook Hookmani revealed to him that they always marked up prices on all the rooms except the standard ones, because Hooks Motel was the only motel in that part of northeast Calgary. Ashiq thought that was unethical, but Mr. Hookmani clarified that there was a reason why a business like his was called a motel and not a hotel. It was the *convenience* that the customers were paying for. He told Ashiq that especially during winter, when the temperatures went anywhere from −5 to −45 with the windchill factor, his customers didn't mind paying an extra twenty dollars on a well-heated room. Mr. Hookmani found it funny that Ashiq couldn't understand why these drivers would stop at the motel and pay for a room rather than keep driving.

There was a convenience store next door, which was owned by a Chinese family. Mr. Hookmani told Ashiq that he could have anything he wanted from the store for lunch, except for McCain's Pizza Pockets because of the pork inside them. Ashiq tried the frozen burrito, which was nowhere close to the burrito he tried with Jenny in Vancouver, but it satisfied him. He finished the Coke and threw the bottle in the garbage. Mr. Hookmani asked him to take it out and throw it in the recycling bin because that is what people did in Canada. When Ashiq asked him what the difference was, he said he didn't know but that it had something to do with the high salary the City of Calgary paid people who came once a week to collect all the stuff that didn't go in regular garbage cans.

After lunch, Farook Hookmani asked Ashiq about his father and his business. Ashiq didn't tell him much, other than that he was doing fine and trying to find new importers from around the world who wanted hand-manufactured leather products. Mr. Hookmani told him that he didn't agree with what his father did. Not so much the line of business, but rather his methods. He said that he always saw Ashiq's father as a great negotiator but not as an entrepreneur, a middleman at best, but not the owner of a proprietorship. "That's not his game," he said.

Ashiq nodded and stayed silent. No one ever described his father the way Farook Hookmani did. He remembered all the times when people came up and asked his father to represent them and talk on their behalf to solve their problems. Not only business problems, but family problems, couple issues, and even recommendations to help with admissions to good kindergartens.

The Hookmanis ran a textile mill in Karachi. It was run by Farook Hookmani and his younger brother, but the day Farook received a letter from Canadian Immigration saying that their permanent residency application had been approved, his younger brother said that he deserved to have full ownership of the textile mill in Karachi. This was because Farook had borrowed money from their business for the lawyer's fee and all the paperwork that went into the five-year-long application process. That day, Farook Hookmani visited Ashiq's father, Shamsu Amlani, and asked him to intervene on his behalf and tell his brother to come back to his senses. Shamsu Amlani went to the Hookmani residence to have a word, and Ashiq remembered that day because he blew air on Shefrina's face, which had made her giggle, and Farook Hookmani's younger brother had shouted at all the children to stop pretending life was good. If they didn't, he would pick a plastic hanger and show them the cruel reality of life, where brothers steal from brothers, and wives pretend they lay next to Bollywood superstars and not their husbands when the blinds shut and the room gets dark at night.

One afternoon when the laundry delivery guy came, Mr. Hookmani asked Ashiq to watch the reception desk while he went to the red room to help the guy unload the fresh laundry. The first customer gave Ashiq a roll of loonies (which has twenty-five Canadian one-dollar coins) for his standard room, but Ashiq remembered Mr. Hookmani's explanation about the seven percent general sales tax rule on all the bookings, so he told the customer that he owed a dollar and seventy-five cents. The customer took out a loonie from his pocket and passed it on to him. When Ashiq picked it up, placed it on his palm and turned his head sideways, the customer flipped over the ashtray that was filled with silver quarters and copper pennies. "There you go, smart ass," he said as he lit a cigarette and took a drag.

"You can't do that," Ashiq said.

"Of course I can. Anyone can. Ask Freddie," he said as he left the reception desk.

Who the hell is Freddie? Ashiq thought.

The second customer gave him two twenty-dollar bills for a superior room. Ashiq passed her the change, but when he picked up the three pennies from the counter, the lady asked him to keep the change. He wondered how two customers were so different: one didn't want to pay the seventy-five cents, and the other overpaid. *White people are weird,* he thought and refilled the ashtray with all the pennies that were dispersed on the glass counter. It was then when he realized that Canada wasn't necessarily as magnificent as it was made out to be in Pakistan. People were people, just like back home. Some with extra pennies to disperse, some penniless, and some were straight up rich, hoarding motherfuckers.

The third customer looked familiar. He had seen her that afternoon in the convenience store next door with her mother buying a few pens and an eraser, and she wore the same school uniform. She gave him a flirtatious smile and walked around the reception area. "I like popsicles," she said. Ashiq wondered what popsicles were and whether he should go to the red room and ask Uncle Farook if they carried any. "And I love the brown ones," she said and placed her hands on the counter, bending over. Ashiq saw she wore a pink bra with blue polka dots.

"You didn't find any on our price list?" he smiled. She shook her head and took a deep breath that raised her breasts, and Ashiq's pants got tighter.

"Shall we go next door and see if you can get me a *popppsssicle*?"

"You know what? Wait here, and let me check first." Ashiq walked to the red room to ask Mr. Hookmani what a popsicle was. He pushed the black door in and came across something mind-boggling. It wasn't the discovery of the popsicle, and it wasn't a wild imagination. It was the laundry delivery guy, and he was shouting at the top of his lungs, "Yeah, Freddie … Give it to me!" Ashiq didn't know what it was that the laundry delivery guy wanted, so he moved closer, and his eyes opened wide when he saw them having sex standing up. After espying the niche behind the metallic table that Uncle Freddie padded, he ran back to the front of the motel.

Ashiq remembered that his father once told him that Farook Hookmani liked boys since he was little, especially Ashiq's dad, Shamsu Amlani. In the early sixties, during a camping trip, Farook put Shamsu's hand on his boner, but Shamsu punched him in the face and pushed him into the lake. They didn't talk for a few months, but one day Farook saved Shamsu's little brother from a bully, and that restored their friendship. Shamsu advised Farook to investigate moving to Canada. "You'd be happy there. Canada is a gay-friendly country," he had said. And that's why Farook Hookmani moved his family from Karachi to Calgary. He told his relatives that the move was for the kids and for their "better future." But Farook knew that he couldn't keep living as *Farook* anymore. He needed to feel more himself. He needed to be *Freddie.*

"You should come later," Ashiq said to the popsicle girl. He wanted to tell her that Mr. Hookmani was the only one who knew what a popsicle was and that he was busy, but he didn't. It felt like a struggle to say Freddie's name. "This is not a good time," he said instead.

The girl lifted her breasts off the counter and went toward the door. She paused to look over her shoulder and smiled at Ashiq, his leering eyes on her short skirt, a sneak preview that he imagined teased every guy in the neighborhood, young and old, raw and stale. But it wasn't her butt cheeks he ogled. Instead, he replayed the scene from the pilot episode of *Freddie Does Larry* — or whatever his name was.

She took the red lollipop out of her mouth and blew him a kiss. That is when he realized it wasn't the popsicle (he still didn't know what a popsicle was) that she wanted. It was *him*, and she wanted him the same way the laundry delivery guy wanted his Uncle Freddie.

Maybe I need a new name too, he thought and adjusted his underwear to make room for his now erect popsicle.

CHAPTER ELEVEN

Farook Hookmani came out to the front of the reception area, lit a Du Maurier Extra Light, and smiled at Ashiq through the glass door as if nothing had happened in the red room. Ashiq couldn't fathom his uncle's cool, calm, and composed demeanor. *He didn't even lock the damn door,* Ashiq thought and wondered if Khalid had ever witnessed his father doing the deed.

Farook Hookmani threw the cigarette butt on the ground, stepped on it, and walked into the reception area. He examined the missing keys on the wall behind the counter and told Ashiq he did a great job. He also said that running a motel was not rocket science and that he only did it because it was better than staying home. But Ashiq knew that Uncle Farook did it because he saw himself as more of a *Freddie Mercury* who liked *Larry the Laundry Man* than Farook Hookmani, married to Farida Hookmani, a determined drifter who gave up on her dreams of becoming a pilot (something he had heard from his father when he was in Karachi) and instead popped out Khalid, Shefrina, and Zarmeen Hookmani.

When Ashiq was thirteen, he overheard his father telling his mother that once, during the summer of 1974, when the Hookmanis ran a textile business in Karachi, Farida Hookmani suspected her husband of doing more than just dyeing the clothes in the back of the mill, because she saw how beautiful the labor girls were. But Farook Hookmani convinced his wife that it was her wild imagination, because the girls went home an hour before sunset and the only reason he came home late every Thursday was because he played poker at the back of the textile mill with his guy friends.

"Uncle," Ashiq said.

"Yes, son?" Farook Hookmani lit a new cigarette.

"What's a popsicle?"

Before Farook could answer, the laundry delivery guy walked into the reception area, and Mr. Hookmani took a long drag of the Du Maurier Extra Light. "This is James Dick," he said as he exhaled the smoke.

Dick? Really? Why would you name your family after a PENIS? These white people … I don't get it, Ashiq thought.

"You can call me Jim," the man said, extending his hand.

James Dick was taller than Farook Hookmani and had an athletic build — a well-developed chest and shoulders that were significantly broader than his waist and hips.

Ashiq noticed the enlarged veins on Jim's forearms. He didn't want to shake the hand that had done more than rearrange the fresh laundry in the red room, but Jim wore a glove, and Ashiq shook it. His face was longer than it was wide, with a narrow chin and a wide forehead, and the most unique set of eyes Ashiq had ever seen: a mix of colors, a combination of gold, brown, and green with a fleck of blue that complemented the Drumheller Dry Cleaners logo on his white t-shirt and his loose faded jeans. Ashiq thought he looked like a work of art.

"This is my nephew, Ashiq," Farook said.

"Nice to meet you *Ars-kick,*" he said.

Really? Ars? I know you like ASS, but my name is …

"It's *Aa-sheek.* I know it's hard to pronounce," Mr. Hookmani said.

Hard to pronounce? How can Ashiq be HARD? Ashiq smiled.

"It's gonna take me a while. You need an English name, bud. Like this guy, *Freddie.*"

"Yeah, we'll get him one," Mr. Hookmani said as he tapped on Ashiq's shoulders.

"See you on Thursday, Freddie." He winked and walked out the door with his wheeled cart.

"So," Farook Hookmani turned to Ashiq. "You were asking about popsicles?" Ashiq nodded. "Let's go," Mr. Hookmani opened the glass door and held it for Ashiq. They walked to the convenience store next door.

"Go to that cooler beside the newspapers," Mr. Hookmani waved as James Dick drove the truck out of the lot. "Yes, that one. You see those long ones? Those are popsicles. Jim likes them." Mr. Hookmani smiled.

I'm sure he does, Ashiq thought as he took one chocolate popsicle out of the cooler.

"The strawberry one is the most popular these days," Mr. Hookmani said. *Now he's gonna tell me about Jim's favorite flavor.* Ashiq wondered if he should exchange his for the strawberry one or wait until he knew what Jim preferred and then make his ultimate decision. "Would you like one, Uncle?"

"No no, beta. I've had my quota of sugar for the day. If I have one and your aunty finds out, she's going to kick my ass." *If she finds out you had a popsicle in your mouth while I watched the motel, I'm sure she'd do more than just kick your ass.* "I won't tell her," Ashiq said.

"Oh. Well, pass me the lemonade one then."

"Is that Jim's favorite too?"

"As a matter of fact, it is. But how did you know that?" Mr. Hookmani ripped the plastic off the popsicle cover with his teeth.

"Just a wild guess," he said and waited for Mr. Hookmani to pay.

He watched groggy customers go in and out of the convenience store with cheery smiles. "I'll walk around for a bit," he told Mr. Hookmani, who opened the glass door of the motel and walked behind the reception desk.

Ashiq saw through the glass door that Farook Hookmani made people laugh. Ashiq remembered Khalid telling him that once his father gave a laughing fit to Mrs. Thompson, the neighborhood's favorite grandma, and later found out that her husband had passed away that same morning. He felt horrible all week, but Farida Hookmani told Farook that he had not done anything wrong and that, if anything, he had brought a few smiles to Mrs. Thompson's sad life.

While Ashiq was pondering this memory, he saw the popsicle-loving girl, accompanied by an older lady, approach the store once more. He threw half of his popsicle in the bin and wiped his hands on the back of his jeans. She wore a shorter skirt, and the tank top left nothing to Ashiq's imagination. She told the older woman to buy her a pack of gummy bears. Ashiq smiled because Uncle Farook had asked him to avoid those because of gelatin, which was made with pig's fat. He did his best not to look at her breasts, even though they wanted to come close to him.

"Where are you from?" She lit her cigarette.

"Oh, I was born here," he said.

"In Calgary?" She blew the smoke out of her nose.

"Actually Edmonton," he said.

"But you have a funny accent."

"I grew up in Karachi."

"I told my mom"—the girl gestured at the woman she had come with—"that you weren't from Mexico and that you have more of an Italian look," she said and blew the smoke to the other side.

"Well, it's in Pakistan," he said.

"You're a Paki? Eww!"

A *Paki*? He didn't like the sound of that. Though the word meant *pure* in Urdu, the revolting way she said it made Ashiq question what she meant. She squashed half of her cigarette under her red flip-flops and went inside the convenience store.

He stood there looking at the half-lit crushed cigarette like it was his identity that she trampled on. He didn't know what to do. He stepped on the cigarette and pondered what it would take for him to be a real Canadian, or at least not a *Paki*. He turned around to look inside the motel's reception area and wondered if Uncle Farook had told James Dick that Freddie was not a *Paki,* but rather a Canadian with an Italian sausage.

For the rest of the week, Ashiq avoided Uncle Farook so that he wouldn't call him Uncle Freddie by mistake. Not that the Hookmanis weren't aware that Farook Hookmani was Freddie Mercury for the rest of the Calgarians, but it was more of the replay of the events in his head that he wanted to avoid.

On the ride home from the Hooks Motel, the day Ashiq watched the pilot episode of *Freddie Hooks James Dick*, Khalid told him that his father wasn't the only person who adopted an English name. Most of them did, and it was imperative for assimilating in that god damn society. Zarmeen was the first one who had taken the plunge. Her problem was bigger because, since day one, the kids at school had called her *Zar-Mean,* and her counselor suggested that she instead be introduced as Zoe. Khalid wanted to be Kyle, but everyone agreed he looked more like Kevin. Farida Hookmani refused to be called Fanny because she didn't see a need for a Pakistani housewife to have an English name. And like her mother, Shefrina kept her name because people thought it was exotic. Plus, she was beautiful, so she could be anything she wanted: Brazilian in summer when she was tanned, and Italian in winter.

Ashiq wanted to tell them how he felt when the popsicle-loving girl had walked away in disgust after he told her he was a *Paki.* But he figured that they wouldn't understand; they didn't have an accent like he did, and they dressed like Canadians, walked like Canadians, they even wiped their backs with toilet paper like Canadians. He wondered if he would ever fit into a society that hated people from Pakistan. *But why?* he thought. He thought about it many times until it dawned on him.

It's the fucking accent.

The following Thursday, Ashiq waited for Uncle Farook to leave the house before coming out of his room because he didn't want to go to the motel and watch the reception area while Freddie and Mr. James played poker in the red room. He walked to the dining room, and everyone turned to look at him.

"Am I right? Or *am I right?*" Zarmeen said to the others.

"What?" Ashiq felt self-conscious because he didn't know why everyone was looking at him.

"You need a haircut, buddy. Look at yourself. That's a huge afro you have going on," Zarmeen said as she spread strawberry jam on her toast.

"Why are you so concerned, *Zoe?*" Ashiq asked.

Everyone laughed except Zarmeen.

"Good one, good one, Ashiq," Mrs. Hookmani said. "More toast, Zoe?" She took a bite and raised her eyebrows at Ashiq. He smiled.

"You look like an *Afro-sheek*," Zarmeen said.

"Don't be so *Zar-Mean*," Ashiq retorted and put two breads in the toaster.

"Whoa, man. You're on fire. What's going on?" Khalid said.

"Never mind," Ashiq said. "All jokes aside, Zarmeen, did you get a chance to pick up the prospectus from U of C for me?"

"Talk to the hand. You're dead to me," Zarmeen said.

"What did I do?"

"What did you do? All I said was that you needed a haircut. It's for your own good. But no, you think you're funny, eh? Well, you can get the prospectus yourself. How's that for funny?"

"I don't see how that is funny at all. Okay, I'll give you two minutes and maybe you can make me laugh. Go, but no peekaboo, okay?" Ashiq laughed.

"Oh, you two." Shefrina got up, put her hands around Zarmeen and Ashiq, and brought them closer. "Go get a room you two. It's becoming obvious what's going on here," she whispered.

"Not even in his dreams," Zarmeen said.

"That means she likes you." Shefrina smiled.

"No, I don't," Zarmeen said. "I'm not into *fobs*."

"Zarmeen! That's just wrong. How dare you?" Shefrina said. "Don't forget where you came from, you brat."

That was the second time someone had called Ashiq a *fob*, but he still didn't know what it meant.

"Sorry about that, Ashiq. Sometimes she doesn't think before she opens her mouth," Shefrina said.

"What's a *fob*?"

"Nothing, Ashiq. Don't worry about it." Shefrina put her hand on his shoulder. "She needs to be disciplined, that's all. Don't worry about it, okay?" He nodded.

Khalid came up the stairs from the basement and walked toward the dining table. "Hey Ash, are you free tomorrow?" Ashiq nodded.

"Did something happen?" Khalid said. "Your face looks like you just got hit by a bus." Ashiq shook his head. "Anyway, not sure if daddy got a chance to tell you, but they are planning a trip to Karachi for a month," Khalid said. "You and I are going to run the motel while they're gone."

As long as I don't have to see the popsicle girl, he thought.

"There are a lot of sluts in the neighborhood that we can shag in the red room," Khalid whispered in his ear.

"Stop putting rubbish in his head," Mrs. Hookmani said.

"Oh shit," Khalid laughed and gave him a high five.

"What's a *fob*?" Ashiq asked again.

"Who said anything about *fobs*, man? You and I are going to be the new Italian cousins. Kevin and Ash are going to take over the world," Khalid said.

What's so different about Italians anyways. Don't they have an accent too? Ashiq thought.

"Does it mean *Paki*?"

"Did someone call you a *Paki*?" Khalid stopped at the door and turned to look at him. Ashiq shook his head. He didn't understand why he was lying to Khalid.

"Never let anyone call you that. *Fob* means *fresh off the boat*. It's just racist, man. These people, these white fuckers. Don't worry about these things, bro. I'll turn you into a stud in no time."

If stud means Italian, then no, I'm not interested. I just want to sound like a proper Canadian. Not an Italian, not with a funny accent, just Canadian. Ashiq waved at Khalid and did the dishes.

Uncle Farook told Ashiq that there was a family issue he needed to sort out in Karachi, and that it could take a month or so. Mr. Hookmani's younger brother had filed a case against him to take over full ownership of the family business. Ashiq pretended he didn't know anything about their family quarrels, even though he remembered his childhood days in Karachi, when everyone in the neighborhood knew the reasons behind those loud noises that came from the veranda of the Hookmani residence.

"You are like my son," Mr. Hookmani said. "And I'm trusting you with my daughters while I'm gone." Ashiq nodded. "You understand what I am saying?" He lit a cigarette. "Not everyone was thrilled when I agreed to have you here with us, especially your aunty." He rested his elbows on the railings of the balcony and blew the smoke. "Don't get me wrong. We all love you, but you know, after all, you're a boy and I have two daughters."

"They are like my sisters," Ashiq swallowed his words.

"I know, I know. That's what I told Farida. But your aunty … you know, she's chary. So typical, very, very suspicious of everything. But I trust you, and I believe you'll do the right thing."

"Of course, Uncle."

"I don't know you that well, but it's the blood in you that I am familiar with. I've known your dad since we wore diapers. Well, since we wore *langot*. We didn't have diapers in our times." He laughed. Ashiq pictured two infants that looked like his father and Uncle Farook with their bums wrapped in white cloths.

"The point is that your blood carries within you the integrity, the values, and the ethics of your grandfather Karamali Amlani and his grandfather, whatever his name was," Mr. Hookmani said, looking at Ashiq.

He shrugged his shoulders. He knew his ancestors were Hindu and had converted to Islam and started following the Aga Khan, but he didn't know their names or what kind of integrity they infused into the blood that glided through his veins.

"As I've said before, this is your house, and you don't have to worry about anything. Just ask Khalid for whatever you need, and I believe Shefrina is helping you out with your school selection and stuff."

"Zarmeen is," Ashiq said, though he wondered if that was still true. After all, she had called him a *fob*, so what help could she really give him?

"Well, I hope you'll have good news for me when I return. I want to see you independent and be like my kids. Like Shefrina, and like

Khalid." Mr. Hookmani threw the cigarette butt out the balcony, and it landed next to his white Crown Victoria station wagon.

Ashiq helped Khalid take the luggage to the car. Unlike Karachi, where the whole family would have gone to the airport to see them off, Shefrina kissed them goodbye at the door because she wanted to stay home. Zarmeen was working on her school assignment at Kirby Zimmerman's house, so she said her goodbyes over the phone. It was only Khalid and Ashiq that got into the car with Mr. and Mrs. Hookmani and headed to the Calgary International Airport.

On the way there, Farida reminded Khalid that she left bite-sized food in the freezer and all they needed was to defrost it in the microwave. There were other items in the spare freezer in the basement that would need to be thawed for a few hours in the kitchen sink before being put in the microwave to achieve the best taste. She told the same things to Zarmeen over the phone and to Shefrina before leaving the house, and by then Ashiq had memorized the temperatures the oven needed to be at and the buttons that needed to be pressed on the microwave. "They'll be fine," Mr. Hookmani said.

"I'm the mother, I worry about these things. What if ..."

"What if *this*, and what if *that*? Nothing bad is going to happen. They are not going to starve to death. There's a McDonald's five minutes from our place, for Pete's sake."

"McDonald's? My kids are not eating that junk while I'm gone. You know how long it took me to prepare all that food? Did I tell you boys about the biryani?"

"Yes, you did," Ashiq said. "We have to thaw it first, otherwise the potatoes are going to stay like rocks."

"Go ahead, make fun of me. You'll thank me when the mouses are running in your stomach."

"*Mice*, mother. It's *mice*, not *mouses*," Khalid said.

"How many times have I told you not to call me *mother*? We are not a white family."

"Mummy, mother ... it's all the same," Mr. Hookmani said.

"No, it's not. He is patronizing me."

"Mummy, you think too much," Khalid said.

"You guys think just because I am a stay-home mom that I don't understand these things."

"Let it go. You want to leave Calgary in this mood? You'll be gone for a month. A month," Khalid said.

"Okay, baba, make sure you guys take care of each other. Ashiq, I feel like you're the only one who has listened to everything I have said. Make sure you guide them through the process."

"Don't worry, Aunty. We'll be fine. Just relax and enjoy your trip."

"What enjoyment? I know what I'll have to do once we get there," she said.

"There you go. Now you have given her something else to talk about," Mr. Hookmani said and tapped Ashiq on the shoulder. Everyone laughed, including Mrs. Hookmani.

On the way home, Khalid reminded Ashiq that they would have to get up early the next morning because they had to reopen the reception desk at 6 a.m. Ashiq asked if he could join him the following week, but Khalid said that he would have to try harder if he was planning to be funny. Waking up at five in the morning was serious business. He promised Ashiq that he would make up for it and that it would be something beyond his imagination.

When they got home from the airport, the girls were asleep, but they had left the stairway lights on so that the boys could go straight to the basement. And they did. Khalid went into his bedroom and shut the door. Ashiq went into the washroom to brush his teeth. It was a habit he had formed during his stay with his Jenny Aunty and since moving to Calgary, he had thought about her every night while brushing his teeth. He wiped his mouth with the hand towel, turned the washroom lights off, and walked into the pink-walled room. There was a prospectus for the University of Calgary on his bed, and on top there was a Post-it note with a smiley face. He needed to give her another chance, and maybe the mean Zarmeen, the mean Zoe Hookmani, would not be mean anymore.

CHAPTER TWELVE

Just after five in the morning, someone knocked on Ashiq's door. He came out of the room and rubbed his squinty eyes. "Do I have time to take a quick shower?" he asked Khalid.

"If by 'quick' you mean five minutes, then yes. But make sure you're quiet because the girls are sleeping," Khalid said.

Ashiq tiptoed to the upstairs bathroom and stood under the hot shower. He squeezed Shefrina's face wash into his palm and massaged it onto his face just like how the back label indicated. He didn't have time for a full body massage, so he rubbed the body wash where it was needed the most and rinsed it off. He came out of the shower and wrapped Zarmeen's purple towel around his waist.

The news on the TV was muted. Khalid looked at Ashiq, and he looked at the towel. "I'm gonna have a smoke outside," he said.

Ashiq got dressed and looked at the prospectus on the nightstand. He took it, closed the bedroom door, and went upstairs. He reached the front door, and his eyes darted back to the Post-it note. He wondered what Khalid would think of that. He didn't want to give him any wrong ideas. Not that there was anything going on between him and Zarmeen, but at the back of his mind he knew that there could be *something* in the future. But he had promised Uncle Farook he would remember the values ingrained in the red blood cells that ran throughout his body. He picked up a pen from the coffee table, wrote "Thank You" under the smiley face, and stuck the note on her door. He paused, uncapped the pen, and added an exclamation mark. He smiled and went outside.

"You're like a girl," Khalid said.

"What?"

"Why did it take you so long to get ready?"

"It's not even five thirty," Ashiq said.

"I got ready in ten minutes, and that includes taking a big dump."

"That's nasty."

"I rest my case," Khalid said.

"What do you mean?"

"That's okay. You look good, and there's gonna be a lot of girls coming in around seven-thirty on their way to school."

"To our motel?"

"No, dumbass," Khalid slapped the back of Ashiq's head, "to the convenience store next door."

"Oh, I forgot to tell you something," Ashiq said.

"What?"

"The other day when I was at the motel with Uncle Farook, this girl came in and said to me that she wanted a popsicle. You know, a *popsicle*." Ashiq winked.

"Oh, yeah? What did daddy say?"

"He was busy ..." He cleared his throat as he thought about the red room.

"Did you get her number?"

Ashiq shook his head. He had seen the crushed cigarette and her disgusted face. "I think she only likes white guys."

"Why do you say that? Wasn't she flirting with you?"

"I don't know."

"Don't worry, man. There are tons that are color blind. Yes, there are many haters out there, but there are always those that are looking for guys who are *different*," Khalid smiled. "Once, there was this girl ... she was big, but she fucked like crazy. I've never met anyone like that before, and guess where it happened?"

Ashiq shrugged his shoulders.

"In the red room. I'll show you the spot when we get there. You'll need it soon." Khalid smiled.

Hell, no. I'm never doing anything with anyone in that room. I'm never even gonna touch anything that's in that room, Ashiq thought.

"Welcome to Cowtown, where all it takes is a cowboy hat for brown guys to transform into white cowboys, even the ones with desi accents. Dun matter if it's made with fur-based felt or just cheap straw." Khalid slapped his thigh. "As my friend Tony says, 'When the drinks flow freely and the sun shines surely, no one cares if they have a dime, because everyone is having a good time.'"

"That sounds like a poem," Ashiq said.

"He makes up the best shit ever, but only when he's drinking." Khalid laughed. "Do you?"

"Do I what?"

"Drink?"

Ashiq shook his head.

"That's okay, but you're not against it, are you?" Khalid said.

Ashiq shook his head again. "And I don't mind trying, though," he said.

"All in good time, all in good time. Now let's go and get this place ready for business." Khalid unlocked the front glass door and entered the code into the security alarm, and the fluorescent lights of the sign outside came on: *HOOKS MOTEL. Vacancy.*

They walked to the convenience store next door. Ashiq grabbed a 200 ml bottle of chocolate milk and tore the plastic off a strawberry Danish pack. Khalid told him to wait for the fresh ones that were expected to arrive in half an hour, but Ashiq couldn't wait because he was starving. Khalid filled a tall mug with coffee, paid with cash, and walked out.

They stood outside the motel, and Khalid smoked two Marlboro Reds in a row.

"How many do you smoke a day?"

"I don't know. Half a pack … sometimes more if I'm out with friends drinking," Khalid said.

"Is that a lot?"

"What are you? My fuckin' therapist? Trying reverse psychology and shit on me? If you want to have one, then just take one." Khalid took out his soft pack of cigarettes from his shirt pocket.

"Um, I was just asking." Ashiq lowered his head. *Maybe I should start smoking. Everyone else around here seems to do it.*

"You know what you can do?"

Ashiq looked up.

"Bring those piles of newspapers from inside and replace them on the rack next to the door. The guy's gonna come later to pick up the ones from yesterday. That's old news, literally. You see what I did there?" Khalid put a pair of scissors on the counter, and said, "Take this, you'll need it to cut the cords to unbundle them."

Ashiq smiled, picked up the scissors, and walked out the door. He picked up the two piles of newspapers, brought them inside, and dropped them in front of the rack adjacent to the entrance. The first pile, which was smaller, was the *Calgary Herald*. The second one, bigger and more colorful, was the *Calgary Sun*. He divided them equally on two racks and stood with twenty extra copies of the *Calgary Sun* in his hands.

"Bring me one of those," Khalid said, "and leave the rest by the door."

"Do they always bring more of the *Calgary Sun*?"

"Yes, the clientele of this motel is the *Sun* type. Did you notice there were no copies left from yesterday?" Khalid said.

"What's the difference?"

"It's all about the Sunshine Girl, man," Khalid said, flipping the pages and finding a blonde in a polka-dot bikini. "You like that?" Khalid winked at him. He explained to Ashiq that the *Calgary Sun* was somewhat like the British tabloids, and their signature feature was a daily glamour shot of a female model called the Sunshine Girl, originally situated on page three, to emulate the UK tabloids (which also featured such photos on their third pages), but then the feature was recently relocated to the sports section in the last few pages of the newspaper.

These girls must hate Pakis too. Ashiq thought about the popsicle girl and her pink bra with blue polka dots.

"If you want real news, good writing, and ethical journalism, then you can't go wrong with the *Herald*, but most of the people here don't give a rat's ass about all that. They want to see a new girl every day in a bikini, even if it's forty below outside," Khalid said.

Ashiq thought about the articles he had written back in Karachi, but Ricky Poonja's voice echoed in his head: "We speak proper English here, not what you're used to. You won't be able to write here, so don't get your hopes high."

"Here," Khalid said, passing him the *Sun*. "Go spank your monkey to Paula. You can call her Parveen or Parvati if that rocks your boat." He laughed.

"No man," Ashiq said. "I was thinking about ..." He contemplated whether to reveal his journalistic aspirations to Khalid (and for Khalid to mock him just as Ricky had done) but there was something about Khalid that said he could be trusted. Even though he was more candid than Ricky Poonja, he gave out a vibe that Ashiq connected to, and that made him feel like he was talking to a friend. Khalid reminded him of his best friend in Karachi. He couldn't put his finger on what that was, but it could have been anything, like his love for cigarettes, the chewing tobacco, or the way he drove.

Ashiq looked up. "Writing," he said.

"What?"

"I was thinking about writing an article." Ashiq hesitated. "I used to write back home."

"Get out of here," Khalid said.

When Ashiq gave him a puzzled look, Khalid smiled. "*Get out of here* is an expression. So, you want to write, eh?"

Ashiq nodded.

"Well ..." Khalid walked around the counter and picked up a copy of the *Calgary Herald*. "You should start by looking at this and see which section speaks to you most."

"But why would they publish my article?"

"Why not?" Khalid unwrapped the newspaper. "There's the front page, then there's the business section, then you've got the sports section." He spread the newspaper around the counter. "I'm sure it's the same as the ones you get in Karachi."

"No, I mean, isn't the English different here? My uncle said that I wouldn't be able to write for newspapers or magazine in Canada."

"Fuck that shit, man. Some people are just full of negative energy. They don't do shit themselves and then when someone else tries, they don't like it." Khalid flicked his Zippo and lit a smoke. "I tell you what: why don't you write one and I'll take a look. If it needs small changes, I'll help you out. How's that?"

"Great! Thank you, Khalid." Ashiq smiled.

"Call me Kevin when we are outside," he said and winked.

A guy who looked like he was in his late fifties limped into the motel.

"Howdy," Khalid said and walked behind the reception desk.

"Man, I need to sleep, drove all night long," the guy said. "Give me your cheapest room."

Khalid pushed the newspaper aside and looked at Ashiq. "Now take this shit off the counter so we can make some money."

"Yeah, get that shit away from me," the dopey guy said as he placed his cup of coffee on the counter and counted his change.

"How about this Sunshine Girl to go with that cup of coffee?" Ashiq said.

"You want all my money, don't ya?" The customer smiled.

"Just look at her." Ashiq winked. "And it's on the house."

"A'right … give me one of those bitches."

Ashiq picked a fresh copy from the pile in front of the glass door and passed it to the customer. "Have a great sleep, man."

"You're a fast learner," Khalid said.

"Well, now I know what you mean by the *Calgary Sun* type." Ashiq laughed.

"You got that right."

They spent the rest of the day talking about their childhood and about when Ashiq visited the Hookmani residence to play with the girls. Khalid pushed Ashiq to reveal what he did with his sisters during the *Ghar Ghar* game, but Ashiq said there was nothing more than making tea and biryani in imaginary pots and pans.

They ordered a pizza for lunch. Ashiq wanted beef and pineapple, but Khalid told him that real Italians never ate that, and because they were pretending to be Italian cousins that day, they ordered just plain cheese with extra marinara sauce.

Khalid let Ashiq take the reception desk every time a pretty girl came to the counter, and he gave him pointers on what he could have done better. He learned how to touch a girl's hand while giving the change back, how to lightly touch her on the arm if she smiled at his jokes, and especially how to go for that kiss if she was one of the "easy ones." Unlike the chain hotels, the Hookmani family's Hooks Motel had a very small and narrow reception area, which made it easy for Khalid to lean across the counter and make his move. Ashiq saw Khalid make out with two blondes and one brunette, but he couldn't understand why none of these girls came closer to him when he went in for a kiss, too. He knew it wasn't anything to do with how he smelled, because he showered in the morning and Khalid didn't. On top of that, Khalid reeked of cigarettes. Despite all that, the "easy ones" locked lips with him and avoided Ashiq. Ashiq even attempted to write an article for the *Calgary Sun* titled "How to Pick Up Women at a Motel's Reception Desk," but then he thought about Shefrina reading it and finding out about his shenanigans at the motel, so he discarded the idea.

"What am I doing wrong?" Ashiq asked.

"You try too hard," Khalid said with a laugh.

"How?" Ashiq frowned.

"Just like how dogs can sense fear in people, girls can sense desperation. If there's anything that you need to learn to master your game, it's this."

"But I don't know how."

"It takes time, but you'll get it. Just imagine that it's *them* who want you, and not the other way around."

"Man, I don't know how to do that. They are all so hot. I just lose control."

Khalid laughed and passed him the *Calgary Sun*. "Go. Take this to the washroom at the back and take care of business."

"Shut up. I'm not *that* desperate," Ashiq said.

The glass door opened, the fluorescent lights on the ceiling flickered twice, and a small, somewhat fragile-looking girl walked in. Ashiq thought she must be in her early twenties.

"Move. I'm gonna get this one," Ashiq told Khalid, and he stood behind the reception desk. She had long blonde hair and a pierced eyebrow, and when she walked to the reception desk, Ashiq saw a tattoo of a horseshoe on her neck. She wore a black tank top, black jeans, and black Caterpillar boots.

"Love your hair," Ashiq said.

"Oh, thanks. Haven't washed it in two weeks." She held her hair up, grabbed her black hair tie from her wrist, and tied her hair in a ponytail.

"That's a nice tattoo," he said.

"Yeah, I love it. Got it last year during the Stampede." She touched her tattoo with her left hand.

"Did it hurt?" Ashiq extended his hand toward the tattoo. She shook her head and arched her neck. He touched the horseshoe with his index and middle fingers. "Do you like how this feels?" he asked.

She raised her eyebrows. "Easy, tiger," she said and took a step back. "Where's Freddie?" She looked around.

"He went to Italy to see my parents," Ashiq lied.

The front door opened, and a tall white guy entered the store holding a six-pack of Bow Valley beer. "Howdy, motherfuckers," he said and walked straight to the *Calgary Sun* pile. Ashiq followed him with his eyes, then looked at Khalid to see if he was aware of this guy, but Khalid was reading a magazine, so Ashiq continued watching him. He wore a red plaid flannel shirt, blue jeans, and cowboy boots. His hair was brown and dusty. He took off his sunglasses and put them on top of his head.

"I've never seen you before," the blonde said to Ashiq, putting her arms on the counter and leaning in.

"I'm not that easy," Ashiq said. It was one of Khalid's lines.

"What?" She smiled.

"It's obvious that you want me, but you gotta do better than that," Ashiq said.

"Nice try," she said. "Give me your cheapest room." She pointed at the key panel on the wall behind Ashiq. "I only need it for a few hours."

"Only if you give me your phone number," he said.

"Freddie always gives me a deal. *Please.*" She pulled out the hair tie and her long blonde hair fell and covered her horseshoe tattoo.

The tall guy walked up to them, slammed the six-pack on the counter, and said, "Chop-chop bud." He pulled a can of beer from the six-pack, cracked it open, and took a long swig.

Ashiq ignored the guy, put a pen in front of the girl, and winked. "Your digits, *please.*"

"What the fuck's wrong with you?" the tall guy shouted, shoving the pen off the counter. "Give her the room."

"*Pata mangna,*" Khalid said to Ashiq in Urdu. *Ask for his driver's license.*

"What the fuck did you say, yo? Speak English! None of that Indian shit!" The guy looked at Khalid.

"He's Italian, not Indian," the blonde said.

"In his fuckin' dreams." The guy looked at the girl, then turned his attention back to Ashiq. "Yo, keys! Didn't you hear me? Let's get goin'. I don't got the whole day."

"Can I please see your driver's license?" Ashiq said.

"Are you fuckin' kiddin' me, yo? I always come here. Where's Freddie?"

"He's in Italy," the blonde said, smiling at Ashiq.

"Yo," he said to Khalid. "Tell your cousin I'm a regular here."

"Don't look at me. I'm not at the counter. He's just following the rules. Show your driver's license and get it over with."

"I don't have it on me. It's at home, I swear."

"I trust you, but he can't give you a room without looking at it. He doesn't know you," Khalid said.

"C'mon, bro."

"Oh, now I'm your bro, eh?" Khalid said. "You're holding up the line. No ID, no rooms. Simple as that."

"Fuck this shit." The guy threw the opened can of beer onto the floor. "Y'all fuckin' Pakis are all the same. Fuck you." He pointed his middle finger at Ashiq and turned to Khalid. "And fuck you, *Paki.*"

"What did you say, you cunt?" Khalid ran around the counter.

The guy pushed two customers behind him and rushed out the door.

"Watch the motel!" Khalid shouted at Ashiq and ran after the guy.

Why did he call me a Paki? All I did was ask for his ID, Ashiq thought.

Khalid came back, furious. He told Ashiq that the guy got away, but he would get him the next time he came around. "I'm gonna crack the motherfucker's skull open when I see him again," he said.

"Why did he call me a *Paki*?" Ashiq put his hands on his waist.

"We will never be accepted as equals by white people in this country," Khalid said. "Regardless of what the world thinks of Canada and of its multiculturalism, it is indeed racist."

"So then why do you call this place home if all these people make you feel like an outsider? You weren't even born here."

"There isn't a country on this planet that doesn't have immigrants." Khalid lit a cigarette. "Home isn't where you are born, it's where you feel alive." He took a long drag and exhaled the smoke from his nose. "And I feel alive here. This is my home, this is where I belong."

On their way home, Ashiq didn't say a word as he absorbed, analyzed, and assimilated everything Khalid had said earlier. *Where is* my *home?* he wondered.

Khalid smoked his red Marlboros one after another and Ashiq kept his head out the window. Ashiq remembered Khalid mentioning that he had dealt with such situations many times before and had even gotten a few customers banned from the store, but for Ashiq, that was a new feeling. Those words stabbed him and penetrated his soul. Those words made him feel dirty, like murky water. They made him question his identity, his color, and his heritage.

Fuck Pakistan, Ashiq thought. *What has it done for me anyway? I might as well change and be someone else. Someone who doesn't have to keep proving his worth, someone who can belong to this wacky world of white wranglers and crazy cowboys. It's time to be Ash.*

CHAPTER THIRTEEN

The next few weeks were business as usual at the Hooks Motel. Khalid told Ashiq to be extra vigilant in the late evenings because that was when most of the prostitutes made their appearances.

James Dick arrived both Thursdays and managed to load the laundry trolley, unload in the red room, stack the pile of towels, and refill the trolley twice, all in less than half the time he normally took when Farook Hookmani was there.

There wasn't a morning when Ashiq missed the racks. First, he sorted the newspapers, then he flipped the back pages of the *Calgary Sun* and envied the staff photographer. He wondered if the Sunshine Girls changed into their bikinis in the photographer's office or if they always had them on. Just like the girls that came to Hooks Motel to ask for standard, superior, and deluxe rooms, Ashiq saw the Sunshine Girls in the same way. Some had perfect breasts, but not so perfect lips; some had the best set of legs he had ever seen, but then their behinds were as flat as cricket bats. To Ashiq, the only girl who ever came close to perfection was Shefrina, but she was engaged, and he knew he would never get her. So, every morning, he hoped that it would be the day he would discover the perfect Sunshine Girl, but that day never came either.

Then, on one Monday morning, a tall brunette walked into the motel and went straight to the counter. Ashiq thought Khalid must have sprayed air freshener that turned Hooks Motel into a spring orchard. She had qualities of the Sunshine Girls that he had seen in the paper; her eyes reminded Ashiq of Paula from his first day at the motel with Khalid, her hair was exactly like Tracey's from the previous Sunday, her legs belonged to Samantha who liked being called Sam, her breasts looked like they were transferred directly from Stacy's chest, and her rump (Ashiq's favorite part) was as round as Rachel's. She was the perfect Sunshine Girl.

"You can be the Sunshine Girl," Ashiq said before he could stop himself.

She smiled and tapped her long nails on the glass counter.

"Is there anything I can help you with?" Ashiq knew that he had no chance with her, but he wanted to try. At least he would end up with a perfect picture for his spank bank.

She stepped closer to Ashiq and whispered into his ear. "Can you help me find a pack of condoms? Make sure no one sees you. You know these creeps," she said, winking.

Ashiq didn't know that getting an instant boner was even possible. In his experience, there was always that time lag from when the blood leaves a man's head and rushes downtown, but this moment defied nature. He nodded, adjusted his pants, walked slowly around the counter, and opened the door for her. She walked out, he followed, his eyes glued to her round rump.

When they entered the convenience store, Ashiq looked at the owner and nodded. He picked a box of condoms, saw his reflection in the glass door of the cooler, and smiled at himself. He saw the Sunshine Girl walk around a few aisles, but she didn't select anything.

"Here you go. Hope this is the right one. They have more, but I didn't know what you wanted." Ashiq passed her a pack of Trojans.

"That's okay, sweetie. I forgot I'm on the pill, but thanks. You're awesome." She lightly pushed on his shoulders, and a few things fell off the pharmaceutical shelf.

"That's okay, no problem. No problem at all." Ashiq picked up the things from the floor and she helped him stack them back on the shelves.

"Are you single?" she whispered in his ear.

Ashiq wondered why a gorgeous girl like her was asking him if he was single. Even Farook Hookmani would have told him that she was out of his league. *So why then?* Ashiq nodded and smiled at her. *This is too good to be true.* The bell echoed throughout the store, the front door swung open, and two police officers walked in.

"Howdy officer," the store owner said.

Ashiq saw her looking at the officers, and her eyes widened. "I gotta go. See you soon," she said and walked away.

He saw the store owner, the two officers, three construction workers, a high school–aged kid, and a grandpa all ogle at the two sublime, round haunches that walked away toward the door like it was a divine choreographed dance she had perfected just for that scene. At that moment, it all made sense to him: she was a prostitute.

"Ma'am," Ashiq called. But she didn't respond. "Hey you!" he shouted. She placed her hand on her hip and turned her head as if taking the last step on her catwalk. "Are you going to pay for that?" Ashiq asked.

She shrugged her shoulders.

"That," he said, and pointed to her back pocket, where she had inserted a pack of condoms. She pushed the door with all her strength and rushed out, but her heels got stuck to the base of the door railings and she fell on her face, and her short dress rode up around her waist. Ashiq saw that her panties matched her shoes. *What is going on with these damn polka dots? Seriously,* he thought.

The officers had their first assignment for the morning, and the store owner offered them two complimentary coffees while they wrote her up. The grandpa walked up to the girl and gave her the folded copy of the *Calgary Sun* and a felt marker.

"Can I get your autograph, please? Make it to Allan Dick. Allan with two Ls," he said.

What's up with all these Dicks in this town? Ashiq sighed, picked up a copy of the *Sun*, and examined the photo of Nikki, the Sunshine Girl of the day. She did resemble the prostitute a fair bit. He looked at the grandpa, shook his head, and put the newspaper back on the rack.

I wonder if there's even a perfect Sunshine Girl out there, he thought and then saw Shefrina in his mind, her long hair blowing in the wind. *Even if there is, no one can compete with her.*

CHAPTER FOURTEEN

Over the next few weeks, Ashiq memorized the Basic Driver's License Handbook for the Alberta Road Tests. Zarmeen asked him if he wanted to go out for a picnic after he finished the learner's permit test. "It's my treat," she told him and said that it was her way of apologizing for calling him a *fob*. He told her that even though he forgave her now, her insult had bothered him for a long time. He didn't understand why a friend would ever do that to him. "It was really mean, *Zar-MEAN*," he said.

"I know, I'm sorry. I really am," she said.

They decided that once they left the test center, they would pick up burgers on their way to the park. Ashiq wanted to go back to Crescent Hill, but Zarmeen suggested that they go to Nose Hill Park instead because it was closer to the university, as she had booked him an appointment with a counselor. Summer was coming to an end, and she told him she wasn't sure if he would get admitted to the fall semester, but that she was hoping he would so that they could go to school together.

After the picnic, they made their way to the university and walked toward the library building where the counselor offices were located. Ashiq protested that the meeting was pointless because he didn't even know what he wanted to take at school, and she insisted that this was exactly why he needed to see the counselor.

Susan Surani, the counselor, asked Ashiq a series of questions that he thought bore no significance to how he should pick his major, let alone get admitted. She asked him what his parents did for a living, what he would do if he had a million dollars and didn't have to work, and what kinds of things he did in his spare time. They spent forty-five minutes in a small cubicle. He stared at her cleavage every time she looked away at the evaluation forms. She suggested he take introductory anthropology, a prerequisite for the advanced journalism course, a general studies elective, and a couple of other easy ones, but Ashiq didn't like the sound of that. He thought that would be a lot of work for nothing. What was the point of *trying out* a few things to figure out what he really wanted? Susan told him that a lot of students didn't know what they wanted to do with their lives in their first year, second year, or, in her own case, ever. She told him that she got engaged in her last year at the University of Alberta and that on one of their ski trips, her fiancé was on a black-diamond run when he hit a tree and died on the spot. Since then, she had spent most of her days with psychologists and career counselors. One of them, a tall man twice her age, got her drunk one evening and took her dancing. There was an epiphany the next morning in bed, and he told her that she would make a great student counselor. The next morning, he got her an internship with the Counseling Services department of the University of Calgary. Ashiq wondered if Susan Surani shared such intimate details with all the potential students, or if she was interested in him.

Ashiq came out of his session with a few pamphlets and magazines in his hand that he wanted to throw away, but he saw Zarmeen waiting for him with an iced tea. "How did it go?" She smiled.

"I can't even start school until the winter semester," he said, frowning.

"Did you get the forms for the winter semester?"

He shook his head.

"I know it can all be overwhelming, but trust me. It will all work out."

She took him to a showcase in the middle of the courtyard. There were several documents in various glass slots. They picked the right form, and she also gave him the financial aid forms, explaining to him that he could borrow money from the government to study. At that, he perked up a little. Maybe he could be a student here after all.

Zarmeen took him around the campus and showed him everything from the campus bar to the soccer field to the university theater. He wanted to stay longer and watch the pretty girls do ballet, but she grabbed his hand and dragged him to the university food court where they shared an ice cream.

"You're gonna love it here, Ash. Trust me. It's a bit scary at first, but then you'll get into the flow of things." She scooped the vanilla ice cream with her tiny pink plastic spoon.

"Well, can we go home now," he said and threw the empty cup into the bin like he was shooting a three-pointer in a basketball game.

"You're boring," she said.

"But you still like me," he said, grabbing her hand.

"Shut up. In your dreams, you *fob*." She laughed.

"It doesn't bother me anymore," he said.

"And why is that?" Zarmeen asked.

"I'm not that *fresh* anymore. You know … *fresh off the* …"

"Yes, yes. You can be quite witty, you know, and I like that about you."

"So you like me, *haan*." He winked.

"Oh God." She grabbed his hand. "Let's go home."

Ashiq was surprised when he and Zarmeen came home to find Khalid on the couch, watching a hockey game between the Calgary Flames and the Vancouver Canucks and eating ice cream straight from the two-liter bucket. It was too early for him to be home. They both wondered if he came home to check on them, but he told them that there was a gas leak at the convenience store, and, as a precaution, he had evacuated all the guests and had closed the motel for the day. He also told them that his parents were coming home early, that the family case was taking too long, and that they speculated it could go on for a year, so there was no need to be in Karachi.

Khalid asked Ashiq and Zarmeen if Shefrina could take the bus home from work, because he wanted to take Ashiq downtown to party. But Ashiq didn't want to miss the opportunity to see Shefrina, so he suggested they go for a drive. They all got into the white station wagon and headed downtown.

When Shefrina entered the car, she told everyone she scored a $200 gift certificate from Earls restaurant and that they could all go for dinner. Zarmeen told her about the boys' plan and said that it would be perfect for them to go to Earls before they went to the movies and let the boys be boys.

"But Ashiq has never been to Earls before," Shefrina said. "I was thinking …"

"It's not like Earls will be closed anytime soon. Plus, Ash would rather go with Khalid and his friends." Zarmeen looked at Ashiq.

"Well, then we can go next weekend when I'm not working. One last night out before mom and dad are back." Shefrina put the gift card back into her purse.

"Actually, they're coming back the day after tomorrow," Ashiq said.

"Oh." Ashiq saw Shefrina looking at Khalid in the rearview mirror. After hearing the news, Shefrina seemed surprised and annoyed at the same time. Khalid nodded. "Well, then we go tonight," Shefrina said.

"If we're gonna drink, then I'm not driving," Khalid said and pulled the car in front of their house.

"I can drive," Ashiq said and pulled out his wallet, showing them his new learner's permit.

"Well, then it's settled. We're going to Earls and I'm getting tanked," Khalid announced, getting out of the car and slamming the door shut.

The Hookmani residence turned into a fish market when Farook and Farida Hookmani returned home from their trip. Four large suitcases were opened and scattered around the house. Farook threw the smaller bags and bundles within the suitcases to Farida, who then threw them to their right beneficiaries. Ashiq imagined that the smaller bags were like sheepshead fish leaping out of water and falling into the mouths of brown pelicans. He took his stuff and went straight to his room to open the package Farida had brought back for him from Karachi.

The folds on the sides were perfectly aligned, and he knew it was carefully wrapped by none other than Mrs. Amlani. The way his mother swathed and bundled packages was a skill that could only be mastered through ages of trial and error, and Mrs. Amlani certainly put in her ten thousand hours. He didn't bother to remove the tapes and tore the covers to see what was inside. He wondered what his mother would have said had she seen him tear the gift wrap with such ruthlessness. Mrs. Amlani taught him to open his gifts with careful consideration so that the wrap could be reused and the gift giver honored. She told him she never understood why people tore apart and threw the gift wrappers away. It was such unnecessary waste.

There was one CD and one cassette, among other things. He didn't understand why his mother sent a cassette when he asked her for CDs, until he found a letter in the package written by his mother that said she couldn't find a CD of his favorite qawwali singer, Nusrat Fateh Ali Khan. The store only carried cassettes. It was a master recording, and she paid twice the price, not because it was a higher quality tape, but because the legendary qawwali singer had died the week before. He put the cassette in the tape recorder, pushed the play button, and examined what else was in the package, while Nusrat Fateh Ali Khan sang *Afreen Afreen*.

Ashiq picked up his mother's letter. It said, "Love you mera bacha" (which meant "love you my child"). He then read the last line in the letter: "P.S. Say hi to everyone, especially Shefrina."

Ashiq had always suspected that his mother knew about his crush on Shefrina, but after re-reading the last line in the letter (three times), he knew that she always *knew*. He examined how his mother wrote the letter *S* in Shefrina, and he felt nostalgic. It was a strong wave of emotion that had nothing to do with Shefrina, but the letter *S* itself, the cursive *S*. He reminisced about his childhood days when he copied his mother's cursive *S* hundreds of times on the advertisement pages of the fashion magazines that Mrs. Amlani kept in her boutique. He wondered why he loved the letter *S* so much. He picked up a blue ballpoint pen from the top of the nightstand and wrote "S" at the back of the envelope that carried his mother's letter. He realized it was the motion of writing the letter *S* that he loved so much.

Nusrat Fateh Ali Khan continued singing, and Ashiq hummed along as he wrote the letter *S* again. When the tip of the pen came to the end of the letter *S*, he didn't lift his hand. Instead, he added the letter *h* next to the *S*. And then an *e* and then an *f*, but he stopped when he heard the voice of Farook Hookmani calling Shefrina. *Who am I kidding? I will never get her,* he thought and went back to examine the package his mother sent him.

He found copies of his old articles that he had published in youth magazines and in the children's section of *The Dawn* and *The News*, the leading Pakistani newspapers. He had asked his mother to send photocopies of whatever she could find because the counselor at the University of Calgary mentioned that including them with his application would increase his chances of getting an early admission for the winter semester. He sorted the ones he thought would make a difference. He picked the one he wrote in the summer of 1994 about his vacation but saw a few typos and left it aside. *These are all so bad,* he thought. *I can never be a writer in Canada. Ricky was right.* His mother mentioned in the letter that he should include his latest article, titled *The Privileged PPP,* the one he wrote about the dark side of the politics in Pakistan, which exposed a few big names and got him in some trouble. The letter also mentioned that his favorite high school teacher, Sir Omar, arranged for the transcripts and the letters of reference to be delivered directly to the University of Calgary. Ashiq thought about him and wondered how he was doing. *Susan Surani will like that,* he thought and placed the article on top of the pile he wanted to submit with his university application.

※+.

Ashiq heard a knock on his door. He got up and opened it to find Zarmeen standing before him.

"Hey," she said, smiling. "I was wondering if you wanted to go to a party with me tonight."

Like a date? His eyes widened and he nodded. "Sounds like fun."

"Well, I planned it a while ago, but now that Mom and Dad are back unexpectedly, they won't let me go unless you come with me," she said.

So it's not a date? He wondered why Zarmeen was bringing up her parents and why she was making up this fake excuse, because he saw the spark in her eyes when he opened the door. *I'm thinking too much,* he thought and said, "For sure. I would love to."

She took a step forward and put her hand in his hair. "You might wanna do something about this Afro, though." He examined his hair, and his hand touched hers, but she didn't pull it away, and he liked that.

"Wear something nice tonight," she said, just before she walked out of his room and shut the door behind her.

Ashiq unzipped his backpack, reached for the white envelope that Jenny Poonja had given him before he left for Calgary, and counted what was left in it. He found two hundred-dollar bills, one fifty, and a twenty. He had used his first hundred-dollar bill at the University of Calgary for the application fee, $48.95 for a pair of jeans and a t-shirt from the Gap, and he'd paid for the tickets and popcorn when he had gone to the movies with Zarmeen and Shefrina. But he couldn't figure out where he spent the other thirty dollars. *Where else did I go?*

Suddenly, he remembered where the money had gone. The week before, Khalid had stopped the car in a back alley and sent Ashiq toward a redheaded prostitute. She told him he could call her Candy because she was "Candilicious." Ashiq looked back twice to make sure Khalid wasn't watching, and then he called her Candy before she went down on him. But afterward, she ran after him. Khalid kept the car running and they fled, leaving the redhead with a mouthful and thirty dollars in her hand. Ashiq felt guilty but Khalid told him that she ripped him and his friends off the week before. "It's a win-win for everyone," Khalid had said.

He took out a twenty-dollar bill and put the envelope back into the backpack, then walked up the stairs to where Khalid was waiting.

"Good luck taming that Afro," Zarmeen said at the door, waving at Ashiq.

When they got to the salon, Khalid introduced him to Fatima, a Lebanese hair stylist who immigrated to Canada in the early nineties. She gave him a quick shampoo and examined his hair and his face. She told him he reminded her of her first boyfriend who was half Persian and half Spanish. Ashiq said people have told him that he looked like anything and everything from Italian, Mexican, Arab, and kinda Indian (although not the Native Indian but the Indian from India). He even got Afghan at one point, but never a mixture of Persian and Spanish before.

"And he came from Pakistan. Who would've known that, eh?" Khalid said to Fatima.

"I'm not from Pakistan," Ashiq blurted out and surprised himself that he said that.

"Of course you are. Where else are you from then?"

"I was born here."

"In Calgary?" Fatima said.

"Edmonton. Same thing."

"It's not the same thing, young man." Fatima turned off the electric trimmer and put her hands on her waist.

"Don't get her started on that. Her ex was from *Deadmonton*," Khalid said.

"You got that right. It sure is dead as hell." She turned the trimmer back on. "Sorry to hear that you were born there," she laughed.

"You asked for it, man." Khalid got up and raised his hands up in the air.

"Let me give you a piece of advice." She held his chin in her hands and turned it to the side to check how much more she needed to take off. "Never, never tell anyone that you were born in Edmonton."

"Especially if you're in Calgary," Khalid said.

"That's right. There's a big rivalry," she said.

"What am I supposed to say then?"

"Just say Alberta. Or even better, you can say the Rocky Mountains. Your mom was skiing, and you came out right there," she said and burst out laughing.

"But I was born in July." Ashiq raised his eyebrows.

"Oh, he's taking this seriously." Ashiq saw Fatima wink at Khalid. She picked a pair of thinning scissors and trimmed around the top and the front. She shampooed and conditioned his hair and gave him a head massage. She put some product in his hair, styled it with her fingers, and gave a satisfied look to Khalid.

The till showed $15.50. Ashiq thanked her, passed her a twenty, and told her to keep the change, as Khalid had suggested. He waved at Fatima and headed out the door.

"This would've covered a whole year of haircuts in Karachi. Seriously," Ashiq said.

"You need to stop converting dollars into rupees. You're now in Canada, not in Pakistan anymore."

"I know I know, it's just that …"

"I understand. I used to do this too when I first came," Khalid smiled.

When they got home, Ashiq showered, put on his new jeans and the t-shirt he bought at the Gap, and sprayed the new cologne Jenny Poonja had hid in his bag with a note saying that he should use it on his first date.

"That's a great haircut," Zarmeen said as she felt the back of his head. "And you smell amazing." She came closer. "I love it. Let's go." She grabbed his hand and reached for the door.

"Zarmeen …" He wanted to know what tonight really meant.

But she wouldn't let him finish. She simply smiled and said, "You can call me *Zoe*, now that we're going to a different world."

"Can I drive?"

She passed the keys to him, opened the passenger door, and got in.

He reversed the car out of the driveway, drove to the end of the street, and turned left onto the main street. Zarmeen turned on the radio in the car. Backstreet Boys sang *Quit Playing Games (With My Heart)*.

"Hell no," she said and changed the radio station. Aqua sang *Barbie Girl.*

"I love this song," Ashiq said.

"What are you? A twelve-year-old girl?" Zarmeen changed the station again. Puff Daddy sang *I'll Be Missing You.* "This is it. Don't change the channel," she said. *If you ever stop changing it yourself,* Ashiq thought.

Zarmeen then told him that she loved this song. It had been recorded in memory of her favorite singer Christopher "Notorious B.I.HI." Wallace, who died earlier that year.

"You see the house up ahead with the lit-up tree?" Zarmeen said. He nodded. "Park right behind the Range Rover." She pointed toward the house.

The front door was open, and they could hear the loud music playing inside. "*Chumbawamba,*" Zarmeen said.

"What?" Ashiq looked at her and raised his eyebrows.

"The song." she jumped up. "I'm so stoked!"

"I don't know this song," he said.

"Not surprised."

When they entered the house party, Ashiq looked around. He had never seen so many young white people together at the same time.

"Are these all your friends, Zarmeen?"

"*Zoe!*" She rolled her eyes.

"Oh yeah. Sorry." He laughed.

"Enjoy yourself." She pulled herself away from him and waved at a tall blond and muscular guy who was standing across the room.

"Should we ..." Ashiq wanted to ask her if they should hold hands, but Zoe sped past the kitchen island counter, which was full of beer bottles, and ran toward the tall guy who kissed her on the lips and embraced her with all his might.

Ashiq felt like a hapless groom left alone at the altar. He realized that the little Zarmeen Hookmani he once knew was now the new Zoe Hooks, and he had no chance with her, not even with his slick haircut, or new clothes, or the blue bottle of Polo Sport. Zoe belonged to the tall blond Kirby Zimmerman, that was the truth. And it was all because of the redheaded hooker who had cursed him.

"I curse you, motherfucking Paki!" Candilicious Candy's howling echoed in his mind.

CHAPTER FIFTEEN

One day, when *That '70s Show* was on television, Ashiq overheard Zarmeen tell her friends that "my cousin kinda sounds like Fez," and they all laughed. Ashiq stuck his head out from behind the staircase to see who the hell Fez was, but the credits rolled, and he returned to the basement to stay hidden inside his room, surrounded by pink walls. It explained why Zarmeen had been avoiding him all this time.

Since the house party where Ashiq saw Kirby Zimmerman kissed Zoe Hooks on the lips, Ashiq and Zarmeen didn't talk much, other than random nods now and then whenever they passed each other in the living room, or during family dinners, or outside the house when Ashiq went to throw the trash in the large green bins and Zarmeen happened to arrive home at the same time. He didn't know how to talk to her anymore. He felt betrayed, confused, and isolated. He was hurt. Not in the sense that his heart was broken; only Shefrina could do that, but that would never happen. He was hurt because he thought Zarmeen could have been his good friend, and all that time he thought that she liked him. He still didn't know whether Zarmeen's flirting had been real or if she had just been using him and having fun with it.

After the party, Zarmeen had talked nonstop about Kirby, about how hot he was, how perfect he was, how tall he was. *Everything I am not,* Ashiq thought. "He even goes down on me," Zarmeen said. *Eww, so dirty and smelly,* Ashiq thought and stayed quiet.

In the next few months, Zarmeen Hookmani moved to Zurich for her geography exchange courses. Ashiq heard Zarmeen promise Shefrina that she would be back in time for her wedding in December. Before Zarmeen gave Ashiq a goodbye hug, she told him that she would probably be his date during Shefrina's wedding banquet, because her parents would never allow Kirby Zimmerman to attend the wedding in a million years. *You wish,* Ashiq thought and tried his best to produce a smile.

No one at the Hookmani residence saw Khalid for days. Farook Hookmani suspected that he was smoking weed, but Mrs. Farida Hookmani told him that Khalid was enrolled in six courses that semester and was finding it hard. Shefrina told Ashiq that she would never take more than four courses at a time so that she could have a social life. She also told him stories about people who took five or six courses to finish their degrees sooner than everybody else, but therefore school was all they did, and there were no friends around.

Shefrina was busy preparing for her big day and took on more hours at work to pay for the wedding. Ashiq heard Shefrina tell Zarmeen over the phone that her fiancé, Zahid Hamza, was looking for a job, but word went around in Karachi that he would soon be married to her and immigrate to Canada, so no one wanted to hire him. He thought about moving to Dubai for a few months to work for his uncle, but Shefrina's lawyer suggested he stay in Karachi, or the immigration process would take longer. So Shefrina chose to work more hours, including weekends and statutory holidays. But Ashiq was suspicious, so one day he called his best friend in Karachi to find out what Zahid Hamza was up to.

"He's a lucky bastard as always," his friend said on the phone. "No job, just smokes hash all day and fucks his maid on the roof of his house."

"How do you know?" Ashiq asked.

"Everyone knows! The other day I went to Yasin's roof to fly kites. You remember Yasin, right?"

"Yeah."

"We heard some pots and pans clanging really loud, then Yasin pointed at Zahid's roof. Zahid was kissing the maid's neck, and she was pushing him away. Then he turned her around, shoved her against the wall, pulled her shalwar[13] down, and went for it."

---

[13] *Shalwar* are loose pajama-like trousers worn by people from the Indian subcontinent, especially women. The legs are wide at the top, and narrow at the ankle.

"What the fuck? You mean, against her will?"

"Who knows, bro. This is very common," Ashiq's best friend said. "I think you should tell Shefrina."

"I don't know how to do that. She will never believe me," Ashiq said.

After the phone call, Ashiq contemplated how Shefrina would react if he told her the truth, not about Zahid Hamza's deception, but about his feelings for her. *But I hardly see her these days,* he thought.

Ashiq went for long walks around the neighborhood because Zarmeen wasn't around to drive him to the parks, nor Khalid to take him to hockey games or to Peter's Drive-In for burgers and milkshakes. He didn't see Uncle Farook for months. All he could do was walk, think, and regret his decision to leave Karachi. *What's the point? No one is around, no one wants to be around, no one even cares.* He walked past a dry patch of grass, a sort of small open field where the neighbors brought their dogs to pee in the morning. *This is my life,* he thought. *If I was still back home, life would be so much better. What am I even doing here?* He walked for what seemed like forever. There was nothing else to do, but to think about how bad his life was, how boring and unlucky.

He ran into Shefrina once, late at night after she returned from work. Ashiq came out of the shower, smiled at him, and went straight to her room, and that was all that happened. Only Farida Hookmani spoke to him and asked him occasionally how he was doing and if he needed anything. He wondered what was so great about Canada and why people wanted to come here. The white envelope with money that Jenny Poonja gave him when he was leaving Vancouver for Calgary was almost empty, and he didn't know what he would do once he used up the last fifty-dollar bill.

One day when he came back from his long walk, Farida Hookmani gave him a letter from the University of Calgary. He tore the side of the envelope and pulled the letter out. It said that his application was incomplete and that they couldn't process it in time for him to start school in January. When he called the registrar's office, they put him through to a counselor. He asked for Susan

Surani, but they said that she was no longer there, that she moved to Africa to build houses for underprivileged kids. It was a program offered by the local church group, and it was good for her soul. Instead, a lady named Tamara Jeggels explained to Ashiq that they never received his transcripts, nor the letters of reference from Karachi, and that he would have to reapply. He could ask to be enrolled in the spring and summer semesters, but he would have to pay the hundred-dollar application fee again because the last one was non-refundable. He told Tamara Jeggels that there were only fifty dollars left in his white envelope and there was no way for him to get the other fifty dollars to apply. He asked her if he could get the phone number for Susan Surani because she believed in him, but Tamara Jeggels told him that it was her job now to believe in him, and that is what the university paid her for.

When he got off the phone, Farida Hookmani told him to get ready because she had packed lunch for them both, and she wanted to take him to her favorite place.

They walked for twenty minutes; it was a path he had never taken before, because he thought it led to nowhere, but Farida Hookmani proved him wrong. She said that her mother taught her to always explore patches that no one else touched before because it led to amazing experiences. And she was right, because they ended up in a small cul-de-sac surrounded by wild plants that had turned orange from the fall. They sat down and ate peanut butter and jam sandwiches. She told him that it was her favorite food in the entire world, and he found it shocking that a lady who cherished making Indian cuisine loved a simple sandwich that could be made in minutes by anyone and anywhere. They spent the rest of the day walking around and talking about life. She pulled a wildflower from its root and passed it to Ashiq. She asked him to look at the flower carefully, to observe its wilderness, its vulnerability. She told him that he was like a wildflower that was pulled out from its root and needed to survive. He needed to get serious about life.

She told Ashiq that she had known his parents for a long time and liked the way they brought him up, except that they didn't teach him the value of money — they had always just given him what he wanted. And Ashiq's father, Mr. Shamsu Amlani, told him that he would not have to worry about anything once he got to Calgary and that his best friend, Farook Hookmani, would take care of everything, including his schooling, but that wasn't true. She told him that he would have to come out of his comfort zone and get a job, any job, and start saving so that he could start school in spring. She told him that nothing was free in this world, and he needed to confront the fact that his father won't be paying for his expenses for the rest of his life.

Shamsu Amlani was famous for making grand promises and not keeping them. He had told Ashiq that he would not have to work the way he had in his youth because he wanted his son, his prince, to have a better life than his, but the truth was that Mr. Shamsu Amlani stole money from his wife's business. He said it was a family business and that it was her duty to support her husband. He was an international businessman, and he couldn't look bad in front of his clients. He insisted that he keep a fancy showroom even though he couldn't pay for it.

Farida Hookmani told Ashiq how she made each of her kids work since they were sixteen. It was not easy for them, but there was no choice. That was why all Hookmani children were independent.

No one ever talked to Ashiq the way Farida Hookmani did that day. In the future, every time he would see those wildflowers, he would think of this very moment, the moment of insight, the moment of wisdom, the moment that pushed him out of his comfort zone.

When they got home, he told Khalid that he was planning to go out the following day to look for work. Khalid gave him a copy of his resume and told him to use it as a guide to format one for himself. Ashiq was worried that he didn't have any previous experience, but Khalid told him that he should include his experience of writing for magazines and newspapers in Karachi, and his volunteer work with the boy scouts and other non-profit organizations.

He sat on the computer for three hours and wrote a four-page resume. When Khalid came downstairs to proofread, he laughed and told him that no one would read four pages and helped him condense it to two. Khalid also suggested he shorten his name from Ashiq

Shamsu Amlani to just Ash Amlani, and to get rid of the word *Pakistan*. He told him that if anyone asked, he could just say that it was in Karachi because most of the people couldn't make the connection. And no one would ask where that was because no one would want to appear ignorant.

Khalid said that he would drop Ashiq off downtown before going to school the next morning, and that he could walk around and circulate his resume to different places. He gave him a few pointers on how to introduce himself and inquire if they were looking for help.

"Always call yourself Ash. That is who you are now. Ashiq is history. He doesn't live here. He is back home grinding wheat. You are Ash Amlani, who can look like whoever he wants," Khalid said.

I already decided that I'm Ash. Ashiq felt hopeful and content for being one step ahead of Khalid. *But why would I grind wheat?* he thought. *Never mind.*

The next morning, Farida Hookmani packed him sandwiches and put two juice boxes in his backpack. Shefrina lent him a file folder for his resumes and asked him to go see her at the Fairmont so that she could introduce him to her bosses to see if there were any opportunities for him. Khalid dropped him off downtown and reminded him to keep the map handy in case he got lost. He also showed him which bus to take if he wanted to get back home and marked the bus stops on the map. Ashiq loved how the Hookmanis helped him, supported him, and gave him hope. *But it's a bit too much. I'm not a child,* he thought.

After Khalid left, Ashiq looked up at all the tall buildings and wondered which one looked the best so that he could go in there and hand out his resume. He followed the crowd that wore suits and carried fancy briefcases and handbags. He went in and out of eight tall buildings, and every single receptionist told him that they didn't hire high school graduates; they all required a minimum of an undergrad degree, and they emphasized that he should take oil and gas courses if he was interested in working for them. But Ashiq didn't like oil or gas, so he walked out.

He looked at the map and made his way to the Fairmont, but the bellboy stopped him at the door and told him that he would have to go around the building, where he would find the human resources office. When Ashiq found the back door that led him to the right department and asked for Shefrina, the lady at reception laughed at him and told him that there were hundreds of people that worked at the Fairmont, and she didn't know anyone by that name. She told him that she didn't even know the names of all the people that worked in her own department. She gave him a fresh application and asked him to look at the postings on the notice board and apply accordingly, but he found the process daunting. He left the application on the table and walked out of there. He wondered where the hundreds of jobs were that Khalid had told him about.

He decided to check out the restaurants because he remembered his father had told him stories about how he got shifts as a server at multiple restaurants when he was a student in Edmonton. But when Ashiq walked into the restaurants with his resume, they all told him that he didn't have any previous experience. He told them that he just needed a chance to prove himself and that his father had been a server in Edmonton, but they told him that he was not his father and that he should come back after he got some experience. He wondered how in the hell he would get any experience if no one would give him a chance in the first place.

After walking around downtown for four hours, he took a break and ate. He devoured the sandwiches Mrs. Farida Hookmani made for him. He drank one of the fruit juices, flipped open the sides of the box, blew it up with air, and placed it onto the ground. Him and his friends did that at school every time they got *Frooto* juice boxes. He lifted his foot and smashed the box with all his might. The box burst open with a bang, which attracted multiple looks from people in suits and fancy handbags. He realized that his friends weren't with him and that no one found it funny, so he picked up the smashed box and threw it in the next recycling bin he passed.

He looked at the file folder Shefrina lent him and saw the twenty copies that Khalid printed for him. He was told to leave a copy with every potential place he visited, but no one wanted to keep his resume. He knew that Khalid would never believe him, so he went back to the recycling bin and dropped ten copies in it, and then two more. *I can work with eight,* he thought. He walked for another three hours and after getting the same answers from what felt like the entire city of Calgary, he hopped on the bus and went home.

He told Shefrina what happened at the Fairmont. She said that she spoke to her boss and passed off his resume to them and that they would get back to her if they saw a fit. But Ashiq knew nothing was going to fit.

"Not a single place?" Khalid asked. "That's not possible."

Farida Hookmani came to the living room.

"So, you think I'm lying," Ashiq said.

"Restaurants would hire you in a second. They wouldn't even ask for a resume," she said.

"But I went to all the restaurants," Ashiq said.

"Come on, man. So you're saying *all* the fast-food restaurants said no to you," Khalid said.

"Fast-food restaurants? You mean McDonalds and …"

They nodded.

"Oh, I didn't go to those. I went to the proper restaurants," he said.

"Why not?" Khalid stood up.

"I don't want to work at those places. They're so nasty." He turned his head down.

"You gotta start somewhere, Ashiq. We all did that kind of work. Do you know how many front desk jobs Shefrina had before she landed that internship at Fairmont?"

The next day, Khalid dropped him off in front of a glass building on 9th Avenue. He said that there was a food court on the top floor, and the crowd that went there was fancy. If he was going to work at a fast-food place, then that would be the best possible location in Calgary.

Ashiq saw Tim Hortons, which was the first window he noticed from the escalators. He walked up to the counter, and they said they weren't looking for anyone, but he dropped off his resume anyway. The second one was a burrito place, and he insisted they keep his resume. He was on a mission and left a copy at every window, except when he saw that the owner of the Greek fast-food place threw it in the garbage. He asked for it back and took it to Wendy's.

"Why should I hire you?" the manager at Wendy's said, emerging from behind the counter.

"Because this is the last copy of my resume and I don't want to go back home," he said.

The manager found his honesty amusing. "You'll be a perfect fit for us." He laughed. "Can you start now?" Ashiq nodded. "Let's get you started, and we can do the paperwork after lunch."

"So do I stand here?" Ashiq walked up to the spare till.

"No, you're gonna start over there," the manager said and pointed toward the back where two guys were scrubbing pots and pans.

"I'll be better at customer service," he said.

"Do you want the job or not?" Ashiq nodded and walked to the back to introduce himself to the two boys working there, who invited him to go to the strip clubs with them after work and offered him cheap booze that they hid in soda cups, but Ash Amlani shook his head and smiled.

Jayton Anderson, the manager at Wendy's told Ash that he would make five dollars an hour, the minimum wage in the province of Alberta. There would be no guaranteed hours, but after a three-month probationary period, they would do an evaluation and if he did the job right, they would give him a permanent part-time position, which would guarantee four hours per day, five days a week. The first day was a test day. Ash wanted to ask if he would get paid for the test day, but he thought that might jeopardize his hours for the rest of the week, so he stayed quiet, smiled, and wondered how long it would take them to figure out if they liked him or not. He himself wasn't sure about them yet, other than the boys who did the dishes and blew bubbles. Ash thought they looked like fun.

Then there were two girls making fries and they both had braces. Ash couldn't figure out if they were Chinese or Thai or from one of those other East Asian countries. To him, they all looked the same.

Then he remembered the movie *Rush Hour* that he had watched in the theater the other day with Shefrina and Zarmeen. There had been a fighting scene where Chris Tucker accidently hits his partner Jackie Chan and says, "I'm sorry! All y'all look alike." Ashiq had laughed during that scene, but when he turned to look at Shefrina, he saw her shaking her head and rolling her eyes, and he didn't understand why. After the credits rolled, and they threw the empty bags of popcorn and fountain drink containers in the trash bin, Ashiq asked Shefrina if she loved the movie as much as he did.

"It was fun, but I feel like I have a knot in my stomach," she said.

"Why?" Ashiq didn't understand what bothered Shefrina during that fighting scene. "It was funny. All the East Asian people do look alike." Ashiq laughed. But Shefrina and Zarmeen didn't.

"Are you freaking serious?" Shefrina said. "Think about it, Ashiq." And he did. That day, he realized that many of the major Hollywood movies that appealed to young people presented these stereotypes very subtly disguised in humor. Most Asians might not even know it, but the damage was there just underneath the surface.

Ashiq couldn't believe that he was being a racist himself. He looked at the two girls again who were making fries. He looked at them carefully and saw their different features. He noticed that one of the girls had a single eye lid and shallow eye sockets, but the other one had double eyelids and deep eye sockets. But they also looked like they were twelve and had been eating at Wendy's since they were born, so he tried his best to avoid the overweight, underage, braced-up Asian twins.

There was also a blonde. Two blondes to be exact, but only one of them mattered to him. The problem was she didn't like being approached by new employees. Every time Ash tried, she said, "Can you stay in your area?"

Mr. Anderson told Ash that he could have anything he wanted from the menu for lunch; it was their way of saying thank you for being a part of the team. He then introduced him to the other blonde, the one that didn't matter.

"Why don't you observe Melissa and see how she flips those bad boys." Ash nodded and followed him to the grill.

"This is no rocket science. You see, these bad boys are kinda pre-cooked," she told him. He wondered why Melissa and Jayton called the beef patties "bad boys," but he kept quiet.

"No one knows this about the patties being pre-cooked but, after all, this is fast food. People are always in a hurry to get back to their jobs and make moola." She laughed.

Melissa turned to look at the blonde that mattered. "I should be on the till, but you see, Tiffany is prettier than me." She came closer to him and whispered, "and everyone knows that Jayton is a sucker for pretty girls."

"Less talking, more working guys. We're getting close to the lunch hour. What's your name again?" Jayton asked.

"Ash."

"Yes, of course. Melissa, let's show him how it's done. Come on everyone, step up. Tiffany can't do all the work here." He went behind the blonde that mattered and said something in her ear. Ash saw that she blushed and that she liked Jayton Anderson touching her butt. It wasn't the accidental touch; it was the actual hands going down and sliding across the rear end.

"Did you see that?" Ash said.

"What?" Melissa looked toward the counter.

"Never mind." Ash wondered how Melissa would react if he accidentally touched her butt while she scrubbed the grease off the grill.

When Melissa went back to flipping the burgers, Ash stepped back and compared Tiffany's back to Melissa's and concluded that Tiffany ate less Wendy's than Melissa.

"Hey! When I said 'eyes on the patties.' I meant *these* ones." Melissa slammed the spatula on the grill.

"Um, I was just …"

"Yes, yes. I know what you were checkin' out, freak. You know, that's sexual harassment," she said. He lowered his head and thought about what he would say to Jayton Anderson after Melissa ratted him out.

She laughed. "I'm just kidding, dude. Take it easy."

"Oh, you scared me," Ash said.

"Well, then we're even." She smiled. "So when are you going home?"

"After lunch, I think. Are you working tomorrow?"

"Yep, every day. Ten to two."

"Wow, that's good money," he said.

"You're joking, right?"

"Well, that's $100 a week."

"I'm assuming this is your first job, right?"

"Yes, why?"

"There are taxes and other shit that comes off the paycheck, so what's left at the end is nothing spectacular."

"Oh."

"That's right. Sorry to disappoint you, but it's better you find this out before it's too late. Hope you're not planning to buy a ring for the girl of your dreams with this money."

He thought about Shefrina and shook his head. But he realized that it would take him longer than he expected to put together the $100 for his new application to the University of Calgary for the spring and summer semester.

Melissa told him to try the Frosty when he ordered his lunch and that it was the best dessert she had ever tasted in her life. But when he asked for the number one combo on the menu and a large Frosty, Tiffany turned to Jayton. He could only have one item from the menu, except for the combo meals.

"I'll just have a Frosty then," he said.

"What size?" Tiffany gave him a bothered look.

"A small, definitely a small," Jayton Anderson said.

"I'll get that." Melissa left the spatula on the grill, filled a large cup with Frosty, licked the extra layer she topped up, and walked to the till.

"Here's your *small* Frosty, Ash," she winked.

CHAPTER SIXTEEN

Winter had officially started. Khalid gave his winter jacket to Ash, because he got a new Helly Hansen for his birthday. The brown Columbia jacket was heavy and a size bigger for him, but Melissa said it made Ash look bigger and stronger, and he liked that. He liked a lot of things Melissa said, but he worked odd hours and rarely got the same shifts she did. He believed it was Jayton Anderson, the manager at Wendy's, who didn't want him to have the same shifts as hers, but she told him that it was all in his head and that Jayton wasn't even responsible for making the schedule; it was Tiffany who was recently promoted to be the new assistant manager.

Nevertheless, Melissa and Ash became good friends. She had worked at Wendy's as a permanent part-time staff member for the last two years and Ash found it bizarre that Tiffany, who had been with that branch for less than a year, was promoted over her and given full-time hours, but Melissa didn't think too much of it. She was happy. But Ash wasn't; he wanted more, and he wanted his life to get better. He saw how the Hookmani children went out into the world to get the things they wanted in life. He wanted to do the same.

On one particular day, a couple of months after Ash started working at Wendy's, he went to the washroom at the end of the food court and changed into his favorite clothes after his shift. The blue shirt was an imitation of Ralph Lauren polo that his mother had bought for him from Zainab Market in Karachi and had picked the color herself. The owner of the shop guaranteed that no one would be able to tell that it was a fake, and he was right because every time Ash wore that shirt, he got compliments. "This color suits you," or "Is that a new shirt?" or "Lookin' sharp, Ash," they said.

He took the file folder out of the plastic bag and put his Wendy's uniform in it. He removed a sheet of paper from his pocket and scratched off the first restaurant on it. The night before, Shefrina had helped him make a list of all the restaurants in the downtown core, and he had spent an hour looking up the addresses in the yellow pages and writing them down next to the names.

As he made his way to the next restaurant, he thought about how he had walked the same streets with a map in his hand a few months ago, and he realized that now he knew those streets like he had spent all his life there. He even knew which alleys to take for shortcuts and which ones to avoid. The two dishwashers at Wendy's turned him into an expert at navigating downtown Calgary in the shortest time possible.

He printed twenty resumes based on his list, but Shefrina asked him to print five more, "just in case" he came across a few that were not on his list. He was glad he did, because he found one Greek and one Italian restaurant before he completed half of his list.

He noticed that he was more confident than the last time he went looking for work and that people were more courteous and welcoming to him than they were before. He wasn't sure if it was the fake Ralph Lauren shirt he was sporting or something about how he carried himself, but he didn't waste much time thinking about the reasons and just focused on circulating his new resume, which now included his first job in Canada.

He expected that they would all fight over him and would offer him a job on the spot, but their responses were the same as before. He couldn't understand why he needed more experience in order to apply. His resume showed the experience they asked for, the three-month probationary period was over, and Jayton Anderson and Tiffany Mason were ready to offer him a full-time position at the best food court in downtown Calgary any day now. *That must count for something*, he thought. But the rest of them didn't see what he saw.

After walking out of the last place on the list, there was still a copy left but he was too tired and disappointed to find another restaurant. He left the resume in the file folder and sat down on the bench beside the bus stop.

He got off the bus and walked home at the slowest possible speed. If there had been a tortoise next to him, it would have reached the house, taken a long bath, made spaghetti with marinara sauce, cleared off the plate, done the dishes, watched a few episodes of *The Simpsons*, brushed its teeth and gone to bed before Ash had even reached the front door. That's how tired he felt.

When he reached the house, all he wanted to do was sit next to Shefrina, put his head in her lap, and tell her about how he was disregarded at every place she had recommended the night before. But Shefrina put her head in Mrs. Farida Hookmani's lap, and she cried.

The wedding was off. Mrs. Hookmani told Ashiq that Zahid Hamza did something naughty with the house maid, who now carried his child, or rather, children — triplets, to be exact. No one would have found out, but it was Zahid Hamza who shouted on the phone to one of his friends, "I have a magical penis," and the maid's older sister brought her hands up to her mouth, let out a loud "Ya Allah!" and went straight to Mrs. Hamza.

Later that evening, Farook Hookmani knocked on Ashiq's door to tell him that "due to unexpected circumstances," Shefrina wouldn't be moving out of the Hookmani residence anytime soon and that Zarmeen's exchange studies were coming to an end, and therefore, she would be returning to Calgary. It was time that he looked for a new place to sleep. After Mr. Hookmani went upstairs, Ash went into his backpack, checked the white envelope and his bank statement, and realized that he would need to make a phone call to Tamara Jeggels, the university counselor, to see if she could help him solve this issue. He didn't know how much it would cost him to find a new place.

He woke up in the middle of the night from a dream, in which Shefrina stood at the altar. Zahid Hamza begged her to take him back, because Ashiq Amlani stood in front of her, wearing a garland, a big gold ring on his third finger, and the biggest grin he ever produced.

He looked at the alarm clock and saw that he had two hours and twenty more minutes before he would have to get up, get ready, and get the hell out to flip burgers, scrub dishes, and clean the Frosty machine. He closed his eyes and went back to the altar in his dream. This time, he dreamt that Jayton Anderson and Tiffany Mason exchanged rings and thanked him for cleaning the Frosty machine. He looked around but there was no Zahid Hamza or Shefrina Hookmani. Someone pulled the fire alarm in the church and things went haywire.

He woke up, turned the alarm off, and rubbed his eyes. He pulled the towel from the back of the door and tiptoed his way upstairs to the bathroom. When he got closer, the door opened and Shefrina came out, wrapped in a purple towel. He remembered that she was working the morning shift at Fairmont. She looked into his eyes. He saw she had been crying, and he put his hand on her shoulder. She stepped closer and put her head on his chest.

Should I tell her about the dream? he thought.

"I'm sorry," she said, taking a step back.

"I love you," he said, then immediately thought, *what the fuck!*

"What did you say?" she asked, her tears suddenly gone.

"Um, I'm sorry, I meant to say …"

"Oh, forget it," she said and pushed him into the bathroom. "Go shower, you weirdo." But as she turned away, he caught the hint of a smile on her lips. He smiled too, did a fist pump, and closed the bathroom door.

CHAPTER SEVENTEEN

The local meteorologist, Sunny Mayani (aka Uncle Sunny), predicted that the weather would take a turn and that it would be a bad one, so everyone listened to him and stayed home, except for Ash Amlani, who arrived at work with a clean shave and a double spray of Polo Sport. The food court had been empty since the early afternoon. There were a few people who lined up in the morning at Tim Hortons to get their morning fix, but afterward it looked like a dead zone.

Jayton Anderson picked up the phone and canceled most of the shifts for the day, except Tiffany Mason's. But when he put the phone down and went to the front of the store, it rang. He asked Ash to pick it up. It was Tiffany, and Ash put her on speaker. She said she wouldn't be able to make it. Jayton offered to pick her up, but she said she was nursing a cold and didn't want others to catch it.

Ash offered to stay longer and cover for her. Ash knew that Jayton was aware that Ash couldn't do what Tiffany could for him, but Jayton agreed and said, "Sure, why not? I don't want to be alone in this horrible weather."

At around four o'clock, Jayton said he was going home because the roads looked slippery, and he didn't want to risk it. His winter tires weren't that good. He locked up the cash and all valuables in his office and showed Ash what to do and how to lock up after he left. He told him that he wouldn't need any keys because once the shelter was down, it would lock in place.

An hour and a half after Jayton Anderson left, Ash made a double patty burger for himself and Denzel, the janitor who had arrived to start his night shift. He threw half a bag of fries into the oil, let it sit for a few minutes, and sprinkled salt on it. Instead of boxing it, he poured the fries straight onto the tray and Denzel said they were perfect, even better than the ones his wife made at home with real potatoes and not those chemical-induced bites they called French fries. They spent the next forty minutes eating burgers, fries, and nearly expired chili. Denzel told him that he was from Malta and immigrated to Canada with a dream to revolutionize the medical system, but his degree was not valid, and so he decided to take the job of a janitor so that his wife could continue to cut potatoes and make fries for their two sons and daughter. Ash told him that French fries weren't invented in France even though people thought they were. Denzel didn't believe him and told Ash that he didn't know what he was talking about.

Ash cleaned up everything, signed out *6 p.m.* on the time sheet, and pulled the shutters down right at 5:30 p.m. He put on his toque, his gloves, a fleece, and then the Columbia jacket that Khalid had given him. He told Denzel to enjoy the night and walked out the door into freezing rain.

There were hardly any cars on the road, and not a single bus in sight, but he waited inside the bus shelter. According to the timetable on the pole, the next bus was scheduled to arrive in five minutes, but it didn't. He thought he must have just missed it and waited for the next one, which was supposed to come in fifteen minutes, but that one didn't show up either. He felt uneasy because he had already pulled down the shutters at Wendy's, and Jayton Anderson didn't leave the keys with him in case he needed to go back in.

He wondered if the bus drivers at the Calgary Transit were told by their bosses (who must have listened to local meteorologist Uncle Sunny) to call it a day, even though buses usually ran no matter how bad the weather got. He put the hood over his toque and walked back to the building.

Denzel took Ash over to the wall phone, which was hidden in one of the closets. Ash called home to see if Khalid could pick him up, but no one answered. He called Hooks Motel, but Farook Hookmani was gone for the day. He called home a few more times, but it kept ringing. He wondered where everyone was in this harsh weather. Denzel mentioned that the next day's flights might be canceled, and Ash remembered that Zarmeen Hookmani was scheduled to arrive that evening from Zurich.

"They must have gone to the airport," he said to Denzel.

"In this weather?"

"Yes, my cousin is coming back from Europe today." Ash put the receiver back on the wall and walked out into the food court.

Canadians knew all about snowstorms, but this one was particularly bad. The freezing precipitation kept Denzel and Ash inside the building overnight. They pulled anything and everything through the shelters, whatever was left on the counter: a few muffins, packs of condiments, and croutons for salads. They drank stale coffee left by the morning customers, and Ash was glad that Denzel hadn't done his job of cleaning up because otherwise they would have gone on a forced hunger strike.

When Ash finally made it home, Shefrina hugged him for thirty seconds. Ash thought she would confess her love to him, but she didn't. Mrs. Farida Hookmani made him a large bowl of soup when he came out of the shower, and Mr. Hookmani told him that the storm had resulted in many downed trees, causing power outages and traffic accidents all around the city.

Ash thought a lot about something Denzel had said on their night of hibernation in the food court. He told Ashiq that he could get him a part-time gig with the night shift staff and that Ashiq could sleep in one of the storage rooms for the rest of the night. Though it was an obvious joke, there was some truth to it; he did need a new place. The Hookmanis gave him a date to move out. It wasn't a deadline that was written in stone, but everyone knew that it was time he moved on.

"To better things, better places," Farook Hookmani said.

"To new adventures waiting for you with arms wide open," Farida Hookmani added.

He wanted to wait another week to see what other options were out there, but Zarmeen was back from Zurich and was getting tired of listening to Shefrina cry in the middle of the night. They all needed their privacy, and they needed it fast. He picked up the phone and called Denzel to see if his offer had been genuine. It would be a perfect arrangement. The only thing that made him think twice was the shower situation. Ashiq Amlani grew up showering every day. It was the first thing he did after waking up and the last thing on days he did something vigorous or sporty during summer, which was most of the time in Karachi.

"You can freshen up in the sink," Denzel laughed. Ash wondered what he could have said to make him realize that, to him, personal hygiene was as important as having a new bicycle is to a kid on the first day of summer vacation.

"That's the only deal breaker," Ash said.

Denzel took him to a corridor attached to the next-door building, which people used during harsh winters to access the food court. Denzel used a pressure hose to wash the floors every day to keep them spotless for the businesspeople. Denzel joked that Ash could shower with the hose in the corridor before the floor got washed and that it would be a perfect setup.

"I'm not getting naked in front of everyone," he said, and that was the end of the conversation.

When Denzel Albani picked up the phone, Ash knew that he couldn't start the conversation from where they left off during their storm lockdown, because it was necessary to point out that the matter was urgent. He needed an immediate answer.

"The night shift, the hose in the corridor," Ash said.

"Oh, you're serious?"

"Well, yes. You know, here ..."

"Don't say another word. Why don't you come see me tomorrow night and we'll take it from there."

"Cool. Thank you so much, Denzel."

Ash hung up and walked into the dining room, where everyone was having the leftover lasagna that Zarmeen had made from scratch, except Farook Hookmani who was still at the motel. Ash wondered if Freddie was making his rounds outside the occupied rooms or loading and unloading with James Dick, who was now the district manager and came only on weekends.

When Ash blurted out, "I think I found a new place to live," everyone turned to look at him, but no one said anything except Mrs. Farida Hookmani, who asked, "Did you try Zarmeen's lasagna?"

"No, but it looks delicious. Zoe is an expert cook now."

"Why don't you have some?" Shefrina said to Ashiq.

"Maybe later. So I'll find out the details tomorrow, but I just wanted to let you guys know."

"There's no rush, beta," Farida Hookmani said.

"You can have your room back," Ash said to Zarmeen and placed his hand on her shoulder.

"You know I don't mind." She touched his hand. "*We* don't mind," she said, looking around at everyone. The Hookmanis nodded in sync.

"Actually, I'm kinda tired of the pink walls," Ash said, and everyone laughed. He pulled up a chair next to Zarmeen. "Why don't you heat up some of your gourmet lasagna for me?" When Zarmeen ignored him, he went on to say, "Okay. Well then, I think I'll stay here a bit longer. Those *lovely* pink walls have started to grow on me."

"Fine, fine. I'll get you your damn lasagna." Zarmeen pushed him and got up from her chair.

He saw that Shefrina was watching him, and he wondered if she was reminiscing about the other day when she fell into his arms and how he had declared his love for her. Ashiq thought that he was the perfect rebound; he probably reminded her of Zahid Hamza, the same color of skin, the same sex appeal. He wondered if she would want him to stay a little bit longer. He looked at her and blinked. She smiled and lowered her eyes.

CHAPTER EIGHTEEN

Shefrina Hookmani came up with the perfect plan. An annual free ski trip, courtesy of the Fairmont hotel, part of her year-end bonus that had arrived late. Ash didn't know how to ski, so she promised to get him lessons from a pro when they got to Lake Louise, which would include boots, skis, and everything he would need to go down the slopes. All he needed were warm clothes.

Shefrina reminded everyone in the car that the room was booked under the corporate account and allowed one additional guest, Zarmeen. Khalid and Ash were supposed to pretend they were visiting a friend, just in case someone asked where they were staying. In addition, they weren't allowed to go to the guest services desk, even in the case of an emergency.

The girls claimed the king size bed next to a glass wall overlooking the majestic mountains. Ash wondered if the boys would sleep on the floor, but Khalid called him from the other side of the bathroom, an ensuite spa station with a Jacuzzi and a fireplace. Khalid offered the couch to Ash, which was against the glass window, and he took the love seat, which reclined all the way down.

The bathroom doors could be accessed from either side of the room, and Shefrina demonstrated the locking and unlocking of the doors so that the girls could have their privacy. Khalid asked them to make sure they remembered to unlock their side of the bathroom door after they were done with their business, or the boys would be stuck on the other side and would have to resort to peeing in the Jacuzzi. The girls assured them that the doors would always be kept wide open so that the boys didn't get a chance to be boys.

Shefrina told Ash that he would find a lady named "Louisa Something-Something" at one of the booths on top of the mountain. She was one of the best instructors in Lake Louise and came highly recommended. The lessons would take half a day, after which he could come back to the hotel room where they would all meet and go for lunch at one of the resort restaurants.

The girls changed into their ski pants, opened the bathroom door, and told the boys that they would see them around 1 p.m. Khalid kept the spare key card because Ash's lessons would take longer than Khalid's runs. Khalid told Ash that since he started smoking, he had lost his stamina and could no longer do the multiple black-diamond runs without taking breaks. Ash wanted to know if there were black diamonds that could be collected on that trail. Khalid fell to the ground, curled up, and laughed for fifteen seconds, then apologized and told him it was just a name for a more advanced route that he would not have to worry about. They left the hotel and went straight to the slopes. Khalid helped him locate the station for the first-time skiers. "Virgins" he called them. Then he wished him luck and disappeared into the crowd.

Ash learned that "Louisa Something-Something" was Louisa Brampton and, according to a fellow first timer, a foxy cougar. The foxy cougar gave the newbies a formal overview of how much fun skiing was and that it was okay to be nervous. Ash wanted to ask her if she was named after Lake Louise, but he kept quiet and waited for her to come to him and help him put his feet into the skis.

As soon as Ash made his first attempt to ski, he fell down and stayed there. He looked at the passerby skiers and their color-coordinated apparel. With every fall, he felt more self-conscious about what he wore and wondered if he should pack up and return to the hotel, but Khalid had the spare key card, so he stayed seated in the snow.

Louisa Brampton came over and helped him get up. She told him that he was doing great and gave him additional pointers. That time he didn't fall and did a fist pump. He did a few more runs without any breaks and, after the seventh run, he waited for Louisa so he could tell her how much fun he was having. He asked her if he could try something different, like a black-diamond run, but she laughed and told him to continue exploring the same area. She said she admired his enthusiasm but that maybe when he returned to Lake Louise the next season he could go on that trail. He declared that he would come every season and take lessons from her, but she told him he already mastered the basics, and his next move was to gather more courage. He realized he was capable of such a feat and was glad that Shefrina had invited him on that trip. He returned the gear to the registration window and admired the mountains for a while.

When he got back to the hotel and knocked on the door, Shefrina opened it and looked at him from top to bottom. He could see her thoughts lingering around the room, telling others to turn their heads to watch the spectacle being brought to them from the hilarious gods and goddesses of the unkind universe. He felt anxious, and their scorching eyes poked holes in his one-of-a-kind apparel.

"What?" He looked past Shefrina and saw that Zarmeen was also in the room.

"You look like a …" She got up from the couch, put her hands on her waist, and looked at him from top to bottom. "Like a Pakistani snowman."

The girls burst out laughing, and he saw that they couldn't keep it inside any longer.

Ash Amlani, with his head down, walked through the shared bathroom and sat in the empty Jacuzzi. He wore baggy jeans, an oversized green fleece over two sweaters, and Zarmeen's pink toque he had found in the room with pink walls. *How am I going to make it through if I don't even know how to dress like Canadians?* he thought. *This sucks.*

He told Khalid he wasn't hungry and that they should go without him, but after finding out that Zarmeen called Ash a Pakistani snowman, Khalid went back to the boys' enclave and dragged him out of the Jacuzzi. She came over, apologized, told him to get rid of the sweaters, and gave him her spare snow pants. He refused to wear them because he thought she was trying to fool him, but she attested that they were unisex and that no one would be able to tell. He lowered his guard and put them on. Zarmeen wanted to say something else, but he saw Shefrina stopping her. They made their way to the restaurant like one big happy family.

They were starved to the point where they couldn't decide what to order. After asking the server for a few minutes to think, twice, Ash suggested they all get burgers and fries. Zarmeen concurred by saying that it would be perfect because they had burned more than enough calories skiing. Khalid ordered a beer, a Coors Light. Shefrina and Zarmeen each ordered a Molson Canadian. The waitress asked Ash if he would like a beer as well, and he shook his head. Zarmeen laughed and asked her to bring a baby glass of milk for him, but Ash said he detested the word milk. The waitress raised her eyebrows and left.

Ash explained why he would never be able to look at milk the same way again. He told them about the day a week earlier when he had visited his friend Denzel, who wanted Ash to meet his family and to discuss the possibility of him moving in with them, given that his family liked him, and he liked them.

Ash told them that when he had met Denzel's family that day, everything was great in the beginning. They went for a walk in the neighborhood, Ash touched the snow-covered bushes, flicked the snow off them, and the wildflowers popped out and invited him to feel their foliage. He told the Hookmani clan that the wildflowers reminded him of the walk he once took with their mom, Farida Hookmani, who helped him dream bigger. He realized how much he had changed since then, and how much he saw himself in that foliage. He was one of those wildflowers; he was now courageous, audacious, vigorous enough to survive the harshness of life, the uncertainty it brought with it, and the unexpected twists it presented.

Khalid snored, "Booooring. Get to the fucking point."

"Okay, okay, baba," he continued. He relayed to them that when he told Denzel's wife that he loved everything about winter, the snowfall, the white trees, and even the shoveling, because it made him sweat in thirty-below weather, something he would have never imagined before, she laughed non-stop. And he didn't understand why.

Everything was great until Denzel went out to get beer. He left his wife and Ash in front of the TV. When the twin boys came to the living room, Ash thought Denzel's wife might take them to their room and tuck them in but, to his surprise, she pulled her breasts out and the twins went for it. Ash tried to leave, but she insisted he stay and watch the news with her.

"Hell, yeah," the Hookmani clan said.

"Go on," Shefrina said, raising her eyebrows.

Denzel's wife took her shirt off and wasn't wearing a bra. "She was topless," Ash said. She told him that the twin boys didn't like anything touching their face and that they were very particular about that. What scared Ash the most was that Denzel wasn't around. What if he walked in and found them together on the couch? What would Denzel Albani think? Before Ash could make another attempt to leave, she laughed and told him that she couldn't stop thinking about his first experience of sweating in the cold. She raised her arm and asked him to sniff; she wanted him to know that she wasn't lying when she said that she never sweats, regardless of winter or summer. He refused, but she shoved his head into her armpit and raised her eyebrows at him.

"No way," Shefrina said.

"No fucking way," echoed Zarmeen. Only Khalid shrugged and seemed to think it wasn't a big deal.

The waitress came back with a tray bearing drinks in her left hand and a shot glass filled with milk with her right hand. She placed it in front of Ash and said she overheard his story and that if he took the shot, she promised he wouldn't look at milk the same way again, and that his portion of the meal would be on the house. Ash didn't want to look at the shot glass, but the Hookmanis and the guests on either side of their booth cheered him on. He didn't want to come off as a poor sport, so he took the shot and slammed the glass on the table. Everyone clapped, and Ash looked at the waitress and asked her what was in the shot glass, because it tasted good. She told him it was a gift sent directly from Denzel's wife, and the crowd cheered again. Ash said he would like one more and the waitress obliged and filled up a $6.50 shot glass with fancy liquor.

Khalid told him he might as well get a beer now that he broke the vow of not drinking alcohol, so Ash took a sip of Coors Light and made a face, saying that he would be happy with just a Coke.

After the third Coke, Ash Amlani spilled the beans. When the Hookmanis found out that the twins were not infants, but three-year-olds who spoke clear sentences, they asked him not to go there again because that was not normal. Shefrina said that once a baby could say the word "booby," the mother should stop breastfeeding, regardless of how much the kid cried. The waitress said she did the same with her kids; if children knew what was good for them, they would eat ice cream for every meal. They ordered more drinks and Ash enjoyed how the world got blurrier and blurrier. The last thing he remembered from the restaurant was saying, "I've never had Coke that tastes like that," and Shefrina laughing and saying, "That's because I told the waitress to spike it with rum, dummy."

In the evening, he took two Tylenols and went to bed. When he woke up, he found himself sandwiched between Shefrina and Zarmeen. He sat up and realized that the foot resting on his face belonged to Zarmeen. It reminded him of the childhood days when they played *Ghar Ghar* at the Hookmani residence, minus the monstrous headache.

"You should drink raw eggs. It'll help you with your hangover," Khalid said, sticking his head out from behind the bathroom. It was as if Khalid's words made his headache worse. He rushed out of bed, pushed him out of the bathroom, and hurled for the next ten minutes.

When he came out of the shower, Shefrina passed him a glass of freshly squeezed orange and apple juice with ginger that she had especially ordered for him with two caffeinated migraine pills, and she promised that he would feel better after that. He drank the magic potion, picked up his backpack, and went down to the lobby with the Hookmani clan to check out of the hotel.

CHAPTER NINETEEN

The next morning, the bus dropped him at the Brentwood Station where he took the C-Train and got off at the University Station. When he got to the Olympic Oval building, he came across a sign that said *Rundle Hall*. A girl came out from the front door with a journal in hand, and he thought of asking her for directions, but she was too pretty. *She won't talk to me*, he thought. The parking spots in front of the building were occupied by various SUVs, and the rest of the driving path was layered with fresh snow, so the pretty girl took the sidewalk and passed Ash.

"Are you looking for something?" she said.

He nodded with a hesitant smile and said, "Residence Services."

"Oh, you should walk around the building. There's a door next to the Dining Center, and their office is at the end of the hall."

He wanted to tell her that soon he would be her neighbor, that he would be one of the *Rundle Hallers*, and that he would be available to hang out. He wanted to tell her, but she smiled and walked away, so he did the same.

His high school teacher, Sir Omar, had mailed his high school transcripts and the letters of reference, and Tamara Jeggels at Counseling Services had pushed his file to the Admissions Office and recommended him for an early admission.

He got to the Residence Services office and asked about what options were available for new students. The receptionist brought him to the waiting area. His eyes noticed an internal memo, and he got up and looked closer. The Residence Services was looking for part-time front desk staff. It was a new position funded by the Student Services, and it required that they hire a full-time student. The most appealing thing about the posting was that it paid eight dollars an hour.

Eight dollars! Ash marveled. *That's three dollars more than what I make at Wendy's!*

He walked out of the waiting area to ask the receptionist about the position, but a lady in her mid-forties appeared in front of him. Her dirty-blond hair was short, and she wore a blue suit. "Hi, I'm Adrianna Saul." She smiled.

"I'm Ashiq. Ash," he said and shook her hand. "I'd like to apply for this job." He pointed at the internal memo posted on the wall.

"Why don't you step into my office. I'll be right back, and in the meantime, why don't you give your resume to Molly McKenna at the front desk so she can make a copy for me."

He opened his backpack and took out the file folder Shefrina gave him. It had one last copy of his resume. "Could you please make a copy for Adrianna?" he asked as he passed his resume to Molly McKenna.

"Sure." She smiled.

He wanted to tell her that he liked her smile and would love to work with her, but instead he waited and looked around the office.

"Here you go," Molly said and handed him two sheets of his resume. "Thank you so much," he said and walked into Adrianna Saul's office.

Adrianna went through his resume and asked him a series of questions that appeared to be a complete waste of time to him, because none of them were related to anything mentioned on the posting. He wondered if he should excuse himself from further affliction and leave the office, but she stood up from her chair, left his resume on the desk, and asked him why she should hire him for that position. He thought about telling her what he told Jayton Anderson at Wendy's, that it was the last copy of his resume and that he didn't feel like going back home to get more, but he realized that Adrianna Saul wanted to hear something better in order to pay him three dollars more than what he currently made.

"I used to help out my dad with his business. He exports leather products around the world, so I'm familiar with creating documents, and drafting, and filing, and all sorts of office work," he said. "And my recent work at Wendy's has prepared me to provide customer service." He thought that it was the perfect answer and that she would open her arms and invite him into the Residence Services family. But she kept quiet. So, he continued. "And I believe that everything happens for a reason."

"What?" She looked up at him.

"I mean, I could've kept going on with this and lied, but the truth is I came here to ask what services were available for new students, and then I saw the notice."

She smiled. "I like that. I'll tell you what: why don't you bring me a copy of your confirmation of enrollment from the Registrar's Office, and I'll ask Molly to process you in."

He nodded with a smile, thanked her, and walked to the Registrar's Office. The lady there told him that in order for him to get a confirmation of enrollment, he needed to enroll in the courses first. He was accepted into the program, but he hadn't registered in any of the courses or paid the fees.

He sat down with a spring and summer course catalog and picked ANTH 201, the introductory course in Anthropology, GNST 200, the basic general studies course for the spring semester, and two photography courses for the summer. When the lady at the counter enrolled him in the courses and told him that he needed to pay just under two thousand dollars, he froze and stared at the lady with eyes wide open and raised eyebrows. When she saw the look on his face, she pointed him to the financial aid office next door. The University Planning Services positioned the two departments next to each other on purpose, because they knew that students like Ash Amlani would want to visit these departments one after another.

That day, he realized that being born in Canada had its own privileges, like getting interest-free federal and provincial student loans. He started to feel different about this country, about all the racist people here, and about moving across multiple houses. All of that faded away to reveal new possibilities, new adventures, and new horizons. He took the required documents and promised to bring them back the following week.

With a newfound purpose and a sense of accomplishment, he walked out of the building and smiled at everyone who looked in his direction. He wanted to scream out loud to show the world that he was ready for all the good things that were waiting for him, but he realized that in doing so, people would look at him funny.

So instead, he did a fist pump and quietly said to himself, "Yes!"

CHAPTER TWENTY

June 1998

A few months had passed since Ash Amlani moved into the student housing and started his new life as a student at the University of Calgary, as an employee of the Residence Services, and as a boy, who, according to many girls, now carried an *interesting accent*. He learned ways to not come off as a *typical Paki,* a *fob,* or a person with a *thick accent.* He believed that now he looked more Canadian; he got a better haircut, and he corrected himself every time he mispronounced a word. Plus, he had quit his job at Wendy's, so now he no longer smelled like fast food all the time.

The only thing that kept him awake at night was the thought that he was still a virgin. Some days he justified that he didn't have a car and that's what kept him a virgin, and other days he blamed it on his living conditions, but when he realized that everyone else on his floor also didn't have their own pad, yet *they* were busy "doing it," not just on the weekends, but also during the daylight hours, he got sad. He knew that soon the day would arrive when he would no longer have to keep track of all those moments when he *almost* did the in and out, in and out, and that it would be an interesting story, like how his Jenny Aunty said.

The professors for his ANTH 201 and GNST 200 announced a four-day long weekend; it was not a public holiday, but a mini reading week before the spring semester's midterm exams. Ash looked at the long weekend as the perfect opportunity to lose his virginity. He didn't have his eye on a girl because he didn't care whom he did it with. He just wanted to get it over with so that he could brag to his friends and feel better about himself.

One day, he stopped by the mailboxes in front of the Residence Services window and opened the 637 slot, which was his and his roommate's mailbox. There was one brown envelope inside with the wrong name on it, so he took it to the window and told Molly McKenna that someone must have made a mistake, because his roommate's name was Benjamin Holston and all his mail read *Ben Holston*. She looked up the name on her computer, scratched a line across the envelope and wrote, *RETURN TO SENDER* in red.

Ash Amlani admired Molly McKenna's unbuttoned red blouse that afternoon. He wondered if she was the one he would sleep with. He raised his eyes from her cleavage to her face, her lips pursed in silence. He disapproved. He looked at her lips for a few seconds and concluded that they were too thin and that he preferred fuller ones like his own, so he shook his head and started to walk away.

"Hey, Ash!" she called out.

He brought his backpack down from his right shoulder and looked at her. He noticed that her breasts looked better from far away than up close, and he had second thoughts about asking her if she would like to go out for a drink at the university bar.

"Any plans this weekend?" She smiled.

"Umm ..."

"My boyfriend is having a barbecue this weekend at his parents' cottage."

"I see." He pulled the backpack off the ground and slung it over his left shoulder.

"I was wondering," she touched her lips with her index finger wrapped in a black wooden ring, "do you want to take my weekend shifts?"

He figured now that he was not going to get laid, he might as well make some money. He walked back to the window to look at the schedule, erased her name, and replaced it with his. He calculated the hours in his head and saw $100 more in his bank account. She told him the shifts were easy because the Residence Services window would be closed during the weekend, there were a few security guards on call for emergencies, and all he needed to do was go through the boxes of mail, look up the names on the computer to see if they were still there, and if not, to do exactly what she did with the letter he had brought to her earlier — write *RETURN TO SENDER* with a red pen and leave it for the mailman who would return on Wednesday morning to pick up the mail. She thanked him for saving her fun weekend, and he showed his gratitude for the opportunity to make some extra cash.

On his way to room 637, he imagined Molly McKenna at the barbecue party. She took her red blouse off and went down on her boyfriend, who was six feet tall and hairless. He saw them on the patio, surrounded by green grass and white daisies. Her boyfriend took a bite from his massive double patty burger, wiped the ketchup with his bare hands, and kissed Molly McKenna on her thin, thin lips.

On Saturday morning, day one of his four-day long weekend, he opened his eyes and the first thing that came to his mind was nothing related to finding a girl who would sleep with him or how much money he would make that weekend. He was thinking about a big, fat chocolate chip muffin and a tall glass of two percent milk. He got out of bed, brushed his teeth, and took a quick shower in the communal bathroom. When he got to the Dining Center for breakfast, they were out of the big, fat chocolate chip muffins. He frowned and picked a blueberry muffin instead, poured himself a glass of chocolate milk, and sat by the window alone. The girl behind the till told him that an all-girls rugby team was here from out of town, and that they liked their carbs before the game. Ash Amlani asked the girl if the chocolate chip muffins carried more carbs than the blueberry ones, and she told him that he made her day and that she needed the laugh because she was having a bad week. He thought about asking her if she wanted to go out for a drink later, but he saw her goopy eyes and agreed with his gut feeling that it was too early to be thinking about beers, loud music, or dark spaces.

He put the tray away and took the stairs down to the Residence Services office. It was the first time he saw the space without people, without noise, and without any supervision. He kept the shutters down, as Molly had suggested, and turned the main computer on.

He brought the first basket up to the counter and wondered how long it would take to finish all the four of them. Molly had told him that the weekend shift would not be paid by the hour because there would be no one to verify the hours he worked, so Adrianna Saul decided to pay for two full days' worth of work. He could come in and go as he pleased in those four days when the office was officially closed for business, as long as he finished the work before Wednesday morning. Molly had said that it could take him anywhere from four hours to two whole days depending on how he managed his time and how fast he processed the mail. She told him that they would randomly check the names in the database to make sure he didn't just scratch off the names because no one was looking and that he would be accountable for the four baskets of mail. If they were not in the *RETURN TO SENDER* boxes, then they were to be in the right mailboxes. It was a big job and Ash's future hours depended on how he did that weekend.

The first letter was addressed to Danella Wong who lived in room 435 of the Kananaskis Hall. It was an offer for a credit card from the Royal Bank of Canada, but she had moved to Winnipeg for the summer, so Ash put a line across her name and put the $500 credit offer in an empty box he placed on the floor for the mailman to collect on Wednesday morning. The second one was a package, a large bubble wrap envelope addressed to Liam Lenard of 221 Rundle Hall. According to the database, he had left for Europe to attend a music camp.

Molly McKenna had asked him to read the additional note at the bottom of the page because some students requested that the Residence Services held their mail. Those students paid extra for the service, and others left pre-paid envelopes with them to forward important documents that didn't arrive before the end of the semester. Ash wondered who paid for Liam Lenard to fly all the way to Europe and whether he was a pianist, a drummer, or just a rich kid who liked playing flutes by the fountains with big marble sculptures.

The third one was a brown packet. It was heavier than the others and was sent by Columbia House Records for Zahra Dossani, who lived on the all-female floor of the Kananaskis Hall. He took the package to the mailboxes across the office and put it in the slot for 716. That was the first brown person's name he came across in the database, and he wondered if he would ever see her during that summer. Since moving to the student housing, Ash had felt less and less attracted to his own color. There was something in him that woke up; a desire to explore, a hunger to touch and feel all that he never did before, the unseen, the foreign, the mysterious.

After going through half of the first basket, he looked up at the clock and saw it was time for lunch. He went through a lot of mail that belonged to students he didn't see, didn't meet, and would never know in real life, but he found it thrilling to go through the database to see what they were up to, where they lived, what they were taking in school, and when they were born. Even though he knew that there were many students he would never cross paths with, he felt a connection to them. He felt that he knew them. He realized that sorting mail was not a hard job and that he could finish it in no time, but he liked taking the time to go through each of them with care, to guess what was inside them, to wonder how the students would have reacted had they been there to collect, to open, and to savor what was inside of them. He came across birthday cards, wedding invitations, offers for magazine subscriptions, bank statements, credit card bills, and even prospectuses from American universities. He took out one of the magazines from the *RETURN TO SENDER* pile and went back to the Dining Center for lunch.

He looked at the burger and fries, and they reminded him of Wendy's. One of the guys behind the counter brought a fresh batch of chili, but Ash didn't feel like it was a chili kind of a day, so he walked to the spaghetti and lasagna section, but it looked stale. He thought about going to Market Mall food court, but then a girl walked past him, and the smell of her chicken fingers did it for him. He passed his empty plate to one of the servers and sighed. He thanked the lady and wondered how many hours she would have to work in order to make the $100 he would make that weekend. He remembered seeing a posting on the stairs one day from the Food Services that they were looking for servers, cooks, and cashiers. The big *$5.25/hour* sign underneath made Ash wonder why all the food related jobs paid so little when the work was so hard and disgusting, and he was making three dollars more per hour than what he'd made at Wendy's working in an office at Residence Services, where everyone smelled great, and his tasks were a piece of cake.

He savored every bite of the chicken fingers and read the magazine he brought with him from the Residence Services. When the plate was clean, he wiped his mouth with the brown paper napkin, crumpled it into a ball, and tossed it into the farthest trash bin like it was a basketball ring. He slid the food remnants on his tray into the bin and placed the empty tray on the top, then went outside to get some fresh air and see if he could find a girl who would sleep with him. He walked in different directions, took breaks near the pond, sat outside the closed university bar where people smoked, but there was no luck. So he made his way back to the Residence Services and got back to work.

He threw the magazine back into the *RETURN TO SENDER* box and took out a small tube from the basket. There were plastic lids on each end. He pulled open one of them. There was a black and white print rolled up inside, and it was a portrait of a girl. *She's pretty,* he thought, *but not as pretty as Shefrina.* Ash speculated that she must be a blonde with hazel eyes. He wondered how Shefrina was doing. He thought about their ski trip and their time together, and then he thought about her beautiful face. He missed her. He imagined taking a portrait of her and what she would look like in a black and white photograph. *Definitely better than this girl,* he thought and put the photograph into the tube, put the lid back on, and verified that Oisin Bolton was staying in 625 of Rundle Hall.

Maybe Oisin Bolton and I will become friends. Maybe I'll even get to meet this girl. And maybe we'll have double dates, he smiled. He imagined asking Shefrina out on a date, a double date with Oisin Bolton and the girl in the black and white photograph, even though he knew that would never happen. The thought made him miss her more.

He wondered why he had a such a messed-up luck. People spend their life looking for the one. He didn't have to, because he already knew that Shefrina was the one for him. *Forget it Ash,* he thought. *You will never get her.* He tried to put the tube with the black and white photograph in the mail slot, but it was too big to fit, so he opened the drawer under the counter, took out a plastic-coated card, wrote *Parcel For Pickup*, and left that instead for Oisin Bolton.

By the end of the day, he had managed to go through two of the four baskets. He went faster with the data searches and spent less time on pages that belonged to boys or the ordinary-looking girls. There weren't many good-looking girls that received mail in that time period, though he found a few who stayed on the seventh floor of the Kananaskis Hall. He wondered if he would see them on campus or on the grass patch between the two residence buildings, sun tanning in their bikinis or listening to music in their short shorts and tight tank tops.

He placed the completed box in one of the corners for the mailman to collect on Wednesday. He thought that Molly McKenna would be proud of him for doing such an amazing job. He looked at one of the letters on the top of the pile and noticed that his handwriting had suffered over the course of the workday. He dug into the pile and pulled out an envelope from the bottom. That one read *RETURN TO SENDER* in perfect cursive script. He knew that the appearance of his handwriting on the returned mail didn't matter to anyone, but it bothered him.

He recalled the first time he bought a greeting card for a girl in grade six that everyone wanted to date. Ashiq Amlani had spent a few hours practicing writing her name on the newspaper, but when the time came for him to put his pen on the card, the ballpoint leaked the blue ink at the end of the *R* in *DINAR,* so he went back to the shop and bought two more cards and then three more. When he was satisfied with how the message looked, he tore the defected cards into small pieces, took them to the roof of his house, and burned them to ashes so that no one would ever find out that his writing was anything other than perfect.

He looked at the brown package and realized that it could be pushed further into the slot so that it would be easier for Zahra Dossani to access it from the other side. He inspected it again and wondered what was in it. He saw a few other brown packages that he had put in the *RETURN TO SENDER* pile, to be sent back to Columbia House Records.

He went back to the box and found two packages. One was for Megan Hopkins and another for Julie Simmons. He wondered if they carried feminine products because all the packages were addressed to girls. He shook them one more time, but nothing moved inside. The package was relatively heavy, but he couldn't figure out what was inside, and he was dying to know, so he took both packages back to his room. He turned the lights off in the mailroom, locked the Residence Services office for the night, and went to his dorm room.

CHAPTER TWENTY-ONE

Ash Amlani came out of the elevator and ran into Sally Jacobson, who looked taller than the last time he saw her a few weeks ago when he first moved into his dorm room in Rundle Hall.

She was the first fellow dorm resident he had met on the sixth floor, while he carried his belongings to his room, and she had held the door to the corridor entrance open for him. He thought she looked cute in her pink bunny slippers and wondered if there was a pair available in blue and if he should get one.

He noticed her black stiletto heels. "Nice boots," he said.

"Thanks. Whaddaya up to tonight?" she said and flipped her hair to the front.

"Nothing much. Just finished voo … work." He squeezed the top of the paper bag he held in his hand.

"We're goin' to the Tequila Nightclub tonight. You should come," she said. She then got into the elevator and waved at him.

"Cool," he said to her as the elevator doors shut. *Holy shit! Did she just ask me out?* he thought. *I love this place.*

He went to his room and was glad that Ben Holston wasn't in. He liked being alone. Ben had told him on the first day that he would be busy with work most of the time and would hardly be around, other than at nights when he would come in to sleep. For the last few weeks, Ben came into the room after midnight; he was a considerate roommate and always snuck in as if he was a cat burglar. Ash was a light sleeper and regardless of how careful and quiet Ben tried to be, he always woke him up, but Ash didn't mind because Ben never turned the lights on and he went straight to bed, and that helped Ash fall back to sleep.

He didn't want to take any risks, so he put the brown bag under the pillow and grabbed his blue towel from behind the door. He didn't understand why someone placed a mirror on the back of the door, because the towels and other pieces of clothing always covered it up, but Ben Holston speculated that a girl must have stayed in that room last semester, and it was a clever use of space. He told Ash about how people lived in Tokyo. Ben had been there for an internship the previous year and lived in a 45-square foot space.

Ash went to the communal shower, but all the stalls were taken. There was a guy with a goatee, big arms, and broad shoulders. He looked like someone who had played football (not soccer) since birth. He talked to another guy with big shoulders who introduced himself as Oisin. Ash wondered if he was the same Oisin Bolton who received the tube with the black and white photograph of the gorgeous girl. *Well, not as gorgeous as Shefrina.* He thought about asking him, but he felt awkward talking to boys who were comfortable walking topless in towels, especially in communal bathrooms.

Ash could never do that. He was self-conscious of his hairy chest and legs. He had never worked out in his life, and it wasn't something that boys did back in Karachi. Their high school didn't have a gym, and he had never seen his father doing anything sporty. The only thing he saw his elders do was play cards, which only required holding hands up in the air for long periods of time and moving eyes around the circle. Whatever energy they burned in their game of rummy was overcompensated by the intake of calories from the traditional sweets of *gulab jaman* (a milk-solid-based sweet), *rasgoola* (ball-shaped dumplings of Indian cottage cheese and semolina dough, cooked in a light syrup made of sugar), *chum chum* (similar to *rasgoola*, but with a unique taste of its own by stuffing mawa or khoya in between and typically coated with dedicated coconut powder), and the good old golden *jalebi* (spiral-shaped, crispy, and juicy sweet).

After the shower, he returned to his room and found a yellow note posted on the outside of the door. It was from Sally Jacobson who had, apparently, visited him while he was in the shower. She left her phone number for him to call. He knew it was something to do with the night out, but he didn't have a phone in his room. Ben Holston said he didn't want to share the cost of a phone line because he would not be around to use it, and Ash didn't want to pay the whole bill because he knew that Ben would use it once it was installed. He decided to use the phone at the Residence Services whenever there was a need. He liked that his family in Karachi couldn't call him when they wanted to, and therefore he was the master of his time. He was free to roam the nights, with no worries of having to answer to his father, or listen to his mother, or let his conscience guide him.

But when he looked at the note again, he realized he needed a phone.

He hooked the towel behind the door and walked to the window to admire the sunset. He looked down toward the semi-circular driveway, empty as a ghost town, except for a shirtless guy who sat on the curb and smoked a cigarette. Ash knew that in a few hours the driveway would get busy with yellow cabs taking the kids out for a night of drinking, dancing, and debauchery.

Sally told Ash that Tequila Nightclub would always remain in her heart as the first real club she ever went to. It looked like the same pumping lights and writhing bodies she saw in the movies. He thought about the money he was going to make that weekend and that gave him the justification he needed to put on his favorite outfit and get ready for the night.

He heard the key twist and saw the knob turn. Ben Holston entered the room and smiled, "Hey."

"You're too early. What happened? Did you get fired?" Ash said.

"Funny. I'm gonna spend the weekend with my girlfriend. Just came to get a few things."

A girlfriend! Already?

Ash Amlani wanted to feel happy for Ben Holston, but he couldn't understand how a boy from out of town could find a girl who not only wanted to be his girlfriend but who also wanted them to spend the weekend together, at her place, so they could do the in and out, in and out. While Ash Amlani lived in the same town for eight months and still waited for his damned virginity to fade, melt, and dissolve into nothingness.

Ash told Ben that it was great he was going to be away for the rest of the weekend because he planned to bring girls over who were dying to sleep with him. Ben told him to enjoy his time and smiled at him like how an older brother smiles at his sibling, and Ash wondered if Ben knew that there wasn't a single girl out there who wanted to touch his hairy, cursed, virgin body.

After Ben left the room, Ash locked the door and put the brown packages on his bed. He wanted to see what Columbia House Records sent to Julie Simmons and Megan Hopkins. When he opened the first package with careful consideration so that it wouldn't look opened later, it surprised him. He expected an album with a collection of girly photographs, a *record* of Megan Hopkins's memories. Or a journal, a *record* of her daily diaries that she wrote during her Girl Scout years. Or even a box with secret documents, her *records* sent by Columbia House Records. But they were simple music records in the form of CDs. They were individually wrapped in airtight plastic and there were twelve of them.

He didn't recognize the names except *Thriller* by Michael Jackson, which he put aside, the soundtrack of *Titanic,* which had sold over nine million copies that year, and *Spice* by the Spice Girls that had topped the sales the year before, but he left those with the rest of the collection. He picked up the box addressed to Julie Simmons and, unlike with Megan Hopkins's package, he tore that apart like an untrained dog. The CDs went flying all over the bed. He thought that Julie was his kind of a girl; she had also ordered *Thriller*, which he put on top of the one he placed on his desk. He picked up the Backstreet Boys, which included his favorite song at the time, *Quit Playing Games (With My Heart),* and *Evita*, which he didn't know anything about, but he liked Madonna. He heard from Khalid that U2 was a great band and that he wanted to get their album *Pop*, so he put that aside for him. He saw another one from Madonna, *Ray of Light,* and he thought that she looked better in that cover. He also picked Jay-Z *Hard Knock Life* because he'd heard good things about him from Melissa. He examined the Celine Dion disc for a minute but couldn't decide if she was worth keeping.

Someone knocked on the door. He pulled his bed sheet over the CDs and went to the door. It was Sally and she had brought a friend, Jonny. Ash couldn't figure out if Jonny was white or Asian, but he looked interesting to him with his thin face and sharp features, especially his pointed nose and chin. His skin was reddish, like he was sunburned, and he had beady little eyes.

"I see you got my note." She pulled the Post-it off the desk and raised her eyebrows.

"I don't have a phone," Ash said.

"That. Makes. Sense." She smiled. "I thought you dissed me."

Ash didn't know what that meant, but he figured it was something along the lines of not being a good friend. Sally looked over at his collection of CDs.

"Been there, done that," Jonny said. "Remember I was telling you when I bought *Be Here Now?*" He looked at Sally.

"By Oasis." She nodded.

"I hate when that happens," Jonny said.

"Do you have this one?" Ash passed one of the *Thriller* CDs to Jonny. He shook his head. "Have it." Ash smiled. "I insist."

"Wow, just like that?" Jonny looked at Sally.

Ash noticed that one of the Columbia House Records' brown boxes was visible from under the sheet, but he couldn't do anything because they were right there in his face. When Jonny flipped the CD and walked toward Sally for them to go through the list of the songs at the back, Ash pulled the torn cardboards out, and threw them in his laundry bag. He knew that it was better than the garbage can, because no one would ever go in the laundry bag. Sally got up and sat on the other side of the bed and something cracked under the bedsheet. "Shit, I'm so sorry," she said. As she drew back the sheet, she revealed a whole pile of CDs under the covers.

"Oh my God! I love Lauryn Hill, and you have Shania Twain too," she said.

"Man, you have Radiohead. We're gonna be good friends," Jonny said, thumbing through the collection. "And Foo Fighters."

"Wow, OutKast, and Massive Attack. Where the hell did you get all this amazing music?" Sally looked up at him.

Ash felt like the coolest kid alive even though he never heard those names before. "My mom sent it," he said. He didn't know who else could have sent these CDs to him and he didn't want to jeopardize his job either, so he happily lied.

"Where does your mom live?" Sally asked.

Why did she have to go there? Ash didn't feel like opening his mouth. Why, he wondered, when everything was going so well, when he appeared so hip in front of his new friends, why was he being asked to reveal his true identity? He didn't want to tell Sally that he didn't know who OutKast was, or to tell Jonny that he didn't know who the Foo Fighters were fighting.

"Um, Vancouver," Ash said.

"Cool. Your mom is awesome."

Ash couldn't believe how easy that was. He tried remembering the names of all the streets he had come across during his stay with Jenny Aunty and Uncle Ricky, but neither Jonny nor Sally asked anything else about where his parents lived or where he grew up.

"You know what?" Ash thought of something that would not only make him cooler than he already was in the eyes of his new friends, but also take care of the mistake he made, for once and for all. "Why don't you have them?"

"Are you serious?" Sally said.

He nodded. "It's not like I have a CD player, so they're useless to me."

"Why don't you just buy one?" Jonny looked puzzled.

"Oh, I will. I'm just waiting for a new model. So, help yourself. My mom gets great deals so she can send me new ones."

Sally picked five and Jonny took eight, excluding the *Thriller* he initially got from Ash.

They asked him to come to room 657, Jonny's room, for pre-drinks. Sally said they always got drunk before going out because the drinks at the nightclubs were expensive, and it was the best way to save money.

In the evening, Ash went to the common area, opened the door to the right of the elevator where all the single and co-ed rooms were, and heard the music coming out from the end of the corridor. He saw Jonny mixing a drink, two blondes talking about how much they loved *OK Computer* and how that was one of the landmark records of the nineties. Jonny agreed and told them it was in fact the best album that came out the previous year and no one would be able to match it before the upcoming millennium.

"ASH!" Sally yelled from across the room, sort of stumbling toward him in her stiletto boots with a red face, and then she gave him a big, drunken hug.

I just saw you an hour ago, Ash thought as she let him go. But he just smiled at her. Jonny passed him a drink and introduced him to everyone as the music god, the one who had brought Radiohead to them for the evening. The blondes told him that Jonny mentioned the other five CDs on Ash's bed, and they were interested in buying them. Ash couldn't believe how fast he was getting rid of the stolen goods, and there was no more reason for him to feel guilty or be careful, especially because he had broken down the boxes into smaller pieces and flushed them down the toilet.

When he returned to Jonny's room with the five CDs, the girls each gave him a hug and he wished he had more CDs to give away. "Here you go," Jonny said and gave him two fifties and two twenty-dollar bills. "I had taken nine, and the rest was for the girls, so we figured five dollars apiece," he said and shrugged his shoulders.

"No man." Ash took a step back.

"I insist," Jonny said.

"We insist," the blondes said in sync.

"And here's mine for the five I took." Sally gave him a twenty and a ten.

Ash did the math in his head and told her that he didn't have the five dollars in change, and she said he would buy her a drink when they headed to the Tequila Nightclub.

When it hit him that he had made more money by giving away the CDs he stole than he would make by working that weekend at the Residence Services, something lit up inside of him. He excused himself, took his backpack from his room, and went downstairs to the

Residence Services office. He went through the two baskets he hadn't touched and found six other packages from Columbia House Records. He looked up the names in the system and found two living in Kananaskis Hall. He left those in the basket and walked away with the other four.

Four … that's twelve each, so forty-eight. Five bucks apiece. That's …

He knelt down in the elevator, took out a pen from the front pocket of his bag, and calculated *forty-eight times five* on one of the brown boxes. *Two hundred and forty dollars!*

The elevator doors opened, and he quickly zipped up and walked out with the bag slung over his shoulder, as if he was carrying a jacket that he had brought along, but the weather had turned too warm.

"Where did you go?" Sally giggled.

"Why are you laughing?"

"Because I'm happy!" She hugged him.

"She's already drunk," Jonny said and walked out of the corridor with everyone. "You're ready? We're leaving."

Ash nodded with a smile. "I just need a minute. By the way, my mom's sending more CDs next week." He looked at everyone and ran to his room.

CHAPTER TWENTY-TWO

As a young boy living in Karachi, Ashiq Amlani had made a list of things he wanted, but since joining the Toronto School of Academic Excellence (TSOAE) at the age of seven, his list became longer. TSOAE was a Canadian school, located in one of the most luxurious towns of Karachi. His father wanted him to attend a normal English medium school, but Mrs. Roshan Amlani wanted only the best for her favorite child. She promised to design more dresses in her boutique, the *Fairies Fashions*, more fashion shows, more exclusive saris, more lingerie, and more laces, and she even announced a spectacular deal for exclusive prints despite being advised by her doctor to avoid chemical-based products. TSOAE was expensive, so she stood on her feet for hours, getting everything done. She wanted her boy to be inspired by the best, but all Ashiq learned was how to talk posh, how to develop a bigger ego, and the need to have more things.

He wanted the model race cars his friend Fazal Rizvi played with, figurines of *He-Man and the Masters of the Universe* found in Latif Kabir's collections of toys, and a t-shirt with *Teenage Mutant Ninja Turtles* on it like the one Kiran Kazani wore on Fun Fridays. Every month, Ashiq Amlani wanted something new, something more fun, something all his friends had, and Mrs. Amlani continued to shower him with what he asked for, sometimes in front of Mr. Amlani, but mostly when he was in the shower or was napping or busy losing money in his leather business. Mr. Shamsu Amlani was proud of what he did; he viewed himself as an international businessman but his relatives, his friends (even the close ones), his neighbors and his in-laws found it absurd that he thought there was money to be made with cheap stinky leather.

"I'll believe when I see the money," Mrs. Amlani said.

A month before Ashiq's tenth birthday, Mr. Amlani found him in a pair of ripped jeans. He explained to his father that it was Fun Friday, and they could wear whatever they wanted at school. "It's a way to bring his creativity out. It's self-expression," Mrs. Roshan Amlani had said when Mr. Amlani demanded that Ashiq take the "piece of rubbish" off. "What creativity? This is complete and utter nonsense." Mr. Amlani tossed the jeans into the back alley of their house, and a stray cow stepped on it, covering it with its shit.

That image stayed in Ashiq's head for years. When he refused to go for prayers that evening, Mr. Amlani cancelled his upcoming birthday party and called his school to tell the principal that Ashiq would not be going to TSOAE anymore because they decided to send him to an all-boys school.

On July 25, 1988, the day Ashiq Amlani turned ten, no one came over, no balloons were blown and hung off the ceiling, no swirls, no strings, and no sparkles could be found. He didn't come out of his bed, and he pretended to be asleep when his mother came into the room to wish him happy birthday — nothing could have made him open his eyes that morning — so she whispered the birthday song in his ear, gave him a kiss, and left the room.

After Mr. Shamsu Amlani left the house, Ashiq entered the living room with a grumpy face, in his *Teenage Mutant Ninja Turtles* pajamas that his Nani gave him the year before. But what he saw in front of his eyes made his world bright and colorful: a blue bicycle with a red horn, a yellow leather seat, and a basket in the front.

He ran toward his Nani, wrapped his arms around her, and spent the next four hours riding around the neighborhood. A brand-new bicycle was the best gift for any kid in Karachi in the late eighties, but Ashiq Amlani was not just any kid; he was one of the most spoilt brats who always wanted more. He had asked for a bicycle for his fifth birthday, but his father refused to buy one. He asked the next year and the next, but the bicycle never showed up, so Ashiq continued to steal money from his father's wallet and rented a bicycle every evening after school from a local bike repair shop that rented by the hour. He was happy that his Nani had finally brought him a bicycle, even if it had arrived five years late.

When he returned, Mrs. Amlani brought out Ashiq's favorite: a fresh-cream Black Forest cake with pineapples on the top in one hand, and his little sister in the other. After he blew the candles out, cut the cake, and smiled for the photograph, Mrs. Amlani brought out the other surprise of the day. She told him that he would have to keep it as a secret from his father, and Ashiq promised that he would.

His mother had seen his birthday wish list and knew that there was only one thing that year that could elevate him, galvanize his spirits, and bring true joy in his life. She asked her younger sister, Jahanara Poonja, to send the item all the way from Canada.

Ashiq did not believe his eyes when his mother handed him the parcel. He opened it with great care, compassion, and benevolence. It was a 1988 model of the acclaimed, yellow-colored Sony WM-F45 Stereo Cassette Player Sports Walkman. It came with the black and yellow headphones and spare batteries. He jumped up and down every time he looked at it for the next few weeks. No other gift had the ability to do that, not even a brand-new blue bicycle.

That summer, Ashiq Amlani rode his bicycle around town, listening to his most cherished yellow Walkman that every kid, not only in Karachi, but also in Paris, Sydney, New York, and Osaka, wanted.

The only person who did not wish him well on his tenth birthday was his father, so Ashiq continued to take cash out of his father's wallet. Now that there was no need to rent a bicycle, he had found a new place to spend his father's money: Arshi Music, a new record shop in the neighborhood, run by his neighbor who had mastered the art of ripping tapes off of original records. For Ashiq, it was a place that helped fuel his imagination.

He spent the next eight years with the same yellow Walkman, until his younger sister, Fari, turned ten, and Ashiq wrapped it in the best gift wrap he found and passed it on. Unlike Ashiq, Fari found joy in pre-owned things, especially if they were hand-me-downs from her older brother, whom she loved dearly.

Ash had told Shefrina Hookmani about his yellow Walkman when they went to Lake Louise to ski. She had lent him her Panasonic CD player the night he was hungover. Since then, he had wanted one for himself, but saving money for a new place and paying for school was more important to him at that time. But now things were different; he received student loans, and the plastic wrapped Columbia House Record CDs started to pile up on his desk.

On the third day of the reading week, Ash Amlani finished sorting the mail at Residence Services before lunch. He thought about going to the library to read the chapters assigned in his anthropology class, but he felt lazy and took a nap instead. When he woke up, the room had lost the brightness of the day and the sky had turned pink. He felt guilty but he consoled himself that there was one more day left to study for the midterm exams.

Before starting work that day, he looked up the address for the Sony store downtown in the Yellow Pages and called them to ask about the prices for their best portable CD players. He picked up his jeans from the floor and checked the front pocket. There was enough money from selling the stolen CDs to buy the new Sony portable CD player. He put the jeans on and went to the Dining Center for dinner. The sign at the entrance read, *International Night! Cuisines From Around the World.* However, there were no master chefs at the Dining Center, so although Ash ended up feeling stuffed from his dinner, the experience was unsavory.

When he came out of the elevator, he ran into Jonny who invited him for a drink in Sally's room, which turned into a couple of beer runs, peeing in the park, dancing in the street with strangers, and throwing empty cans at rude drivers. That night, Sally gave him a tight hug, a kiss on the lips, and a wink before passing out in the lounge of their floor. Ash hopped up and down and skipped around the lounge. *She kissed me! Holy shit, she kissed me. On my lips!* He put his arms around Jonny and gave him a broad grin. *I'm sure he's so jealous,* Ash thought.

"Let's put her to bed," Jonny said, untangling Ash's arms from around his shoulders.

Jonny and Ash carried Sally to her room. Jonny placed the garbage can next to her bed and Ash pressed the button at the center of the knob on the door before pulling it shut from outside. Ash saw Jonny stumble a few times on the way to his room, and he thought that, unlike Jonny, he was doing great until he passed the communal bathroom and felt a need to turn around. He spent the next half hour kneeling in front of the commode and witnessed everything from Ethiopian bread to Chinese dim sum to Polish cabbage rolls violently exiting his stomach. He brushed his teeth twice and promised himself that he would never drink again.

When he woke up the following morning, his eyes noticed the thick anthropology textbook that he had left on Ben's bed. He frowned. He closed his eyes and went through last night's series of events in reverse, starting with his barf of shame, and repeated to himself that he would never drink again. He remembered putting Sally in bed, and her kissing him on the lips, and he wondered what it had meant.

I guess she was just drunk, he told himself.

He remembered slipping a mickey of vodka into the back pocket of his jeans while Jonny was paying for the beer. He reached for his jeans on the floor and checked all the pockets, but the vodka was missing.

I don't remember drinking it.

He took the cash out and put it in his wallet, threw the jeans in the laundry basket, popped two Tylenols into his mouth, and took a sip of water from a bottle on his desk. He put his head in his hands and took a deep breath. He remembered his mother had taught him that taking a hot shower helped cure a headache, so he grabbed his towel from the back of the door and went to the bathroom.

That was the first time Ash did not take his clothes with him to the shower. He figured that no one would be around on the last day of the reading break and at that time of the day. He was right, until he returned. The door of his room was wide open, and Sally sat on Ben's bed in a pink tank top and denim shorts.

"Blue looks good on you," she said.

He felt liberated because that was the first time he had stood shirtless in front of a pretty girl who smelled like roses and who had the best pair of legs he had ever seen in his life, even better than Samantha the Sunshine Girl. Ash put his thumb under the knot of his towel for added security and looked away. *What should I do now?* He didn't understand why it was so hard for him to make a move. In all his sexual fantasies, he was a dynamo, but in real life, he was a shy and inexperienced guy.

"How can you look so fresh?" he told her and wondered if he should put on a t-shirt first or his underwear.

"I look horrible," she said, covering her face with her palms.

"What are you talking about?" he said in a hoarse voice and cleared his throat. "You look rested. My head is pounding." He sat on his bed.

"It was fun last night, eh?" She giggled, getting up to sit next to him.

"I'm never drinking again," he said and gave her a smile.

"I've said that a thousand times." She rested her back on the bed and stretched her arms. "It never works. Oh man, I'm so tired."

He got up and put some deodorant on. He couldn't figure out why she came to his room so early. She had never done that before. *Does it have to do with the kiss last night?*

"I was heading to the Dining Center and was wondering if you wanted to come along." She got up and walked to the door.

"I don't think I can eat anything right now. Maybe later, after this headache goes away."

"Hope you feel better." She walked out the door, turned around, and looked at him. "Thanks for last night."

"What do you mean?"

"Putting me in bed." She lowered her eyes. "I must have been a wreck. Did I do something stupid?"

"I don't even remember anything," he said.

"Good." She laughed. "Maybe draw those curtains and get some rest. I'll come check on you later."

He locked the door, threw the towel in the laundry basket, and got under the sheets naked. He wished that she hadn't left his room.

He grabbed the Vaseline from the top drawer and imagined Sally Jacobson under the sheets with him, playing with his penis while he undressed her. The Vaseline did its wonders in no time; he was ready to do the in and out, in and out, and be a virgin no more, at least in his imagination, but there was a knock on the door. He froze. They were a couple more knocks and then it stopped, but he could hear there were some people outside. He knew that it wasn't Sally; she would've tried opening the door or would have called out his name. A part of him wished it was her, coming in to finish him off, but he didn't want to take any risks, so he stayed in that position with his penis in his hand. By the time they left, Ash Amlani wasn't hard anymore.

He opened the curtains to let the light in and sat with his anthropology book, but before he finished the second page, his mind traveled back to Sally, and he thought whether he should take the Vaseline back out or continue reading. He took a glance through the chapters and realized he needed to read twenty more pages, but the font was small, and he knew that it would take him longer than the other books he was used to. He forced himself and read the next five pages, but he didn't understand any of it because in his mind, he was still busy undressing Sally Jacobson.

He couldn't stop thinking about her, so he got up, took the cash, and went to the Sony store to buy his new portable CD player.

CHAPTER TWENTY-THREE

He spent most of the night testing his new Sony D-E700 CD Walkman. Around three in the morning, Ben Holston turned the lights on and asked him to put the volume down because he could hear the sound coming out of the ear buds. Ash apologized, brought the volume to the middle bar, and fell asleep grooving to Michael Jackson.

When he woke up, Ben was gone, his bed was made, and his wet towel was hung on top of his wooden chair. Ash put the CD player on the desk and decided to shower, but his towel was missing. He looked at Ben's wet towel and shivered with disgust at the thought of using it. He picked up the laundry basket and went to the basement. When he emptied the dried clothes onto the bed, he found a pair of black-laced panties stuck to one of his white t-shirts. He couldn't figure out how they got in there, but he didn't care. He picked them up and brought them to his nose, but to his disappointment, they smelled like Bounce Mountain Fresh fabric softener. He folded them and placed them on top of his pillow. He thought he could show it to Ben and tell him how much fun his long weekend was. He wanted to finish folding the rest of the clothes, but he needed to review some chapters before his anthropology midterm exam.

He went for a quick rinse, put on the blue t-shirt that he believed brought him luck, and read his book. When he reached the bottom of the page, he took the earphones off because the music distracted him and made him nervous. The last time he had prepared for a test was during the high school finals of the board examinations in Karachi, but that was a piece of cake because one of his friends had given him a copy of the leaked question paper. His friends knew a few people from the MQM, the notorious political party in Karachi, which was known to control the examination board in ways that were beyond people's imagination. But Ashiq Amlani was in Calgary, and there was no MQM, so he looked at his alarm clock and read more. He thought about making an excuse and asking for an extension, but nothing came to his mind, so he flipped the page, finished the next chapter, and got ready to leave.

When he walked into the Social Sciences building, the doors that led to the elevators were shut and an exam cancellation notice was posted in the middle of the two doors by the Department of Anthropology. There had been an unexpected leak in the basement that had damaged the electrical system. The exams were postponed until further notice.

Ash Amlani was glad he wore the blue t-shirt. *It works every time*, he thought, smiling.

He picked up a copy of *Fast Forward Weekly* magazine, which someone had left by the pop dispenser, took out the CD player from his backpack, and stretched his legs on the patch of grass next to the Social Sciences building. When he reached the middle of the issue, a card fell into his lap. It was from Columbia House Records, and there were pictures of different album covers on it. He looked more closely and saw that it was the same ad. He realized that was how Zahra Dossani, Megan Hopkins, Julie Simmons, and all the others got their brown boxes. Columbia House Records was offering twelve CDs for a penny.

For a penny! He read it twice to make sure it wasn't a mistake. He put the card in his backpack and walked home.

When he reached Rundle Hall's main entrance, he remembered that Molly McKenna had asked him to return the office keys in the morning, but he had forgotten them due to the midterms. He tapped his pockets, and the keys jingled against the coins. He went to the Residence Services office, but the counter was vacant, so he checked his mail. There was the blue aerogram his mother had sent, and he put the letter in his backpack and walked back to the counter of the Residence Services.

Adrianna Saul was looking for a paper clip in the reception drawer. Ash told her that Molly had moved most of the office supplies to the back, near the photocopy machine. She told him that he had done a great job on the weekend and asked him if he wanted two free tickets to the cinema. He took them from her hands and in return gave her his biggest smile.

The first person that came to mind was Sally Jacobson, and he wondered if she would go with him to Eau Claire Market, share popcorn and a large drink, and snuggle during all the turning points of the film and especially during the climax, but when he went to her room, he found Jonny putting things in a banker box. Jonny told him that Sally had received a call that her parents had been in an accident while they drove up north. They had died on the spot. She needed to take care of her two siblings who were in junior high, so she dropped out of the spring and summer semesters and went to Winnipeg.

This is horrible, Ash thought. *How is she going to deal with this? Poor Sally.* He pictured her panicking in her room after hearing the news. *I wonder if I can do something for her.* He walked around her room. He couldn't help but recall the kiss she had just given him the night before. *What fucked up timing, just when things were getting better between us.* He put his hand inside his pocket and touched the movie tickets. *I can't believe it.*

Ash asked if he could help with anything, but Jonny said everything was taken care of. *I wonder how she's doing right now,* Ash thought. *I should call her.*

"Do you have her phone number in Winnipeg?" Ash asked. Jonny shook his head.

Ash went to his room, crashed on the bed, and opened the aerogram. His mother had started the letter with "My Dearest Son." She told him how much she missed him every single day, every time she walked by his room, every time she set the table, every time she looked at his younger sister. She mentioned that his father missed him too, but he knew that was a lie. She told him that his little sister, Fari, received the Best Girl Scout Award and had overheard people saying she was Ashiq Amlani's younger sister, the guy who now studied in Canada, and how proud she was to have such an amazing son. She also wrote that his little sister had started dressing up like him, and that she wanted to be like her older brother. That made Ash laugh, and he turned onto his back to read the rest of the letter. Mrs. Amlani mentioned that the *Fairies Fashions* was going well and that she was getting a lot more clients, and it occurred to Ash that she forgot to mention that Mr. Amlani continued to take money from her to run his so-called successful business. She didn't have to write it, but Ash knew that more money in the boutique meant more money his father could burn. Even as the thought heated his face with anger, he had to remind himself: *at least both my parents are alive — unlike Sally's.*

The last paragraph made him miss his family even more. His mother wrote that she prayed to God that she will get to see her son that summer, and she wished that he could come for a visit, even for a short one.

"If only we were rich," she wrote.

He looked at the calendar. There were two weeks off between the spring and the summer semesters. He had planned to work full time at the Residence Services during that time, but now there was a new thought in his mind: to surprise his mother and visit Karachi.

He went back to Sally's room and asked Jonny if he could use her phone. Jonny didn't see a reason why he couldn't because Sally had already paid for the month of May, and it wasn't like making a local call would cost her any additional money. He pulled out the Yellow Pages from under her desk and turned to the Flight Center section. He found that every place offered a different price but the lowest he found was around $1,300. That was a lot of money, and he knew that he would also have to buy presents for his little sister, Fari, as well as for his mother. He wanted to skip his father, but he thought that would be too obvious, so he added him to the list. Then there was Nani, his cousins, and his favorite uncle. He thought about his friends and his teachers.

That's too much. I don't have that kind of money!

The idea turned out to be ridiculous. The next scheduled class was on Friday, and there was one more day. When he pulled the book out of the backpack, the Columbia House Records card came out with it, and it was like a light bulb lit up inside his head.

He reached for his calculator. If he could sell 300 CDs at five dollars apiece, he could visit his mother that summer. That meant filling out twenty-five Columbia House Records cards with fake names and fake room numbers and sneaking them out of the mailboxes before Molly McKenna or anyone else saw them.

But who would buy them? He recalled the DJ guy Sally introduced him to at the university pub, The Den.

First thing's first, he thought. He ran across the campus to find *Fast Forward Weekly*. The stands at the Dining Center, the Olympic Oval, and the library were all out of the issue, but when he walked into the Engineering building, he found seven copies. He took the cards out and left the magazines on the stand. He came across two more by the C-Train station. He took the train downtown but there were none; one of the guys at a fast-food restaurant told him they usually picked up the old copies on Wednesdays because the new issue came out every Thursday. He knew that Columbia House Records didn't advertise every week, so he needed the copies of that week. After spending a few hours around the city, he returned to his room disappointed. There were only nine cards and without the other sixteen that he needed, the nine looked useless.

He looked at himself in the mirror and wondered if the blue t-shirt he had on was lucky or whether it was just something he had created in his head to make sense of things that usually happened out of the blue. And then his eyes noticed the CD.

It works every time. He touched his blue t-shirt and picked up the U2 album *Pop* from the shelf that he had kept aside to give to Khalid. He paused and looked at the CD and remembered Sally in his room, reading the back cover of the CD. He wondered why Sally had such bad luck. She was caring, affectionate, and full of love. So then why did God take both her parents and leave her all alone with her siblings?

He put his wallet in his back pocket, locked the door behind him, and went to the C-Train station.

✦✦✦

On the train, Ash remembered the last phone call with Farook Hookmani, when he had learned that Uncle Farook's younger brother had found a loophole in the Pakistani legal system and planned to take over the family business. So Farook Hookmani needed to go back to Karachi to claim what rightfully belonged to him. He had told Ash that he was leaving the reins of the Hooks Motel in Khalid's hands, because "he was wasting his summer and needed to be more responsible." Uncle Farook had told Ash that he was aware that Khalid hated the idea of running the motel full-time while he ate kabobs and parathas in Karachi, but that he figured that after a few weeks he would find things to distract him. *Like how you found James Dick to distract you?* Ash thought.

He exited the train station and walked toward the Hooks Motel. He wondered how Uncle Farook was doing, and whether he had managed to save his family business back in Karachi or not. When he passed a bakery, the smell of cheese reminded him of Zarmeen, her gourmet lasagna, and the pink walls of her bedroom. He crossed the main road, turned left on a narrow street, and continued walking until he came across a small flower shop. He went inside, picked the most colorful bouquet, and asked the lady to wrap it up. She tore two center spreads out of the *Entertainment Weekly* magazine, wrapped the flowers in it, and passed it to him. He smiled and paid cash, but when he noticed the cover of the magazine, which featured Jennifer Lopez, he thought about Shefrina and he stopped smiling. He wondered if she ever thought about him, if she ever dreamt about him, if she ever missed him. Then he thought about Sally, their kiss and their friendship, and that's when he realized that even though he was crazy about her, she didn't make him feel the way that Shefrina did. Sally was fun, but Shefrina was still the one.

When Ash arrived at the Hooks Motel, he opened the door and walked in with a big grin on his face. "Khalid bhaijan, what up, what up," he said.

"Look what the cat dragged in," Khalid smiled.

Ash looked around the store but didn't see any cats. He gave Khalid the CD he brought for him for his birthday.

"Thank you. For a second, I thought you brought me flowers." He laughed.

"Oh," Ash smiled and passed the flowers to him. "This is for Farida Aunty."

"Look at you, all grown up. Mom will love them," Khalid said.

They talked about the old days. The last time they had seen each other was three months earlier, during their ski trip to Lake Louise. Khalid offered him a cigarette, but Ash shook his head. He told Khalid about school and his new friends. Khalid told him about his dad's latest proceedings in the legal case in Karachi and about Zarmeen's new job. Ash wanted to ask about Shefrina, but Khalid lit his third cigarette and asked Ash to cover the reception desk for him while he went to the back of the motel to take a dump.

When Khalid left, Ash walked up to the newspaper section and pulled out Columbia House Records cards from all the *Fast Forward Weekly* magazines in the pile. He quickly counted them, folded them in half, and put them in his back pocket. *Mission accomplished,* he smiled.

The front doorbell chimed, and a girl with ruby-red hair that flowed like molten lava over her shoulders walked into the motel. A dragonfly also happened to fly in at that moment, and Ash walked back to the counter. *Let's see if I can still do this,* he smiled.

"Look, a dragonfly," Khalid said as he came out of the backdoor of the motel, and then he followed the dragonfly around. "You know Shefrina loves dragonflies," he said. "When she was a little girl, she would go crazy every time she saw one."

"I hate dragonflies," the girl with ruby-red hair said as she walked toward the counter.

"How is she?" Ash said, looking at Khalid.

"Much happier. I guess when you have something to look forward to, life appears colorful," Khalid smiled.

"New job?" Ash said.

"Bro," Khalid put his hands on his waist. "Didn't you hear she's getting married?" He walked behind the reception desk, took out a wedding card from under the counter, and passed it to Ash. "Now you're officially invited," he said.

"I got this," the girl with ruby-red hair interrupted, raising her voice and her handbag.

Ash and Khalid looked at the girl and then looked at each other.

She slammed her handbag on the glass counter, and the dragonfly's body was suddenly splayed across the glass as if it was a piece of contemporary abstract art.

"You better clean this up," the girl said. She put a set of keys in front of Ash and walked out the door.

"What a retard," Khalid said, picking up the bottle of glass cleaner from under the counter. He tore a few paper towels from the roll and cleaned the glass.

While he cleaned the distorted pieces of the dragonfly's body, Ash examined the wedding invitation:

The Hookmani family and the Hamza family cordially invite you to the wedding of

SHEFRINA HOOKMANI *daughter of FAROOK HOOKMANI*
and
ZAHID HAMZA *son of ZAINUL HAMZA*
On …

Ash stopped reading, folded the card in half, and put it in his back pocket along with the Columbia House Record cards.

Khalid threw the dirty paper towels in the garbage can and looked at Ash. "I'm glad Shefrina isn't here to witness this. She would have been devastated."

That's exactly how I feel, Ash thought. "I don't get it," he said.

"What are you talking about?" Khalid said.

"How can Shefrina be so stupid to marry a man who got his maid pregnant?" Ash threw his hands in the air.

Khalid lit a cigarette.

"And how can all of you support her decision?" Ash glared at Khalid.

Khalid looked away as he said, "It's what she wants, and I'm sure Zahid has learned his lesson."

"What if he cheats again?" Ash said.

"He won't," Khalid said and took a long drag of his cigarette.

"How do you know?" Ash said.

"I know because he wouldn't wanna be locked up again."

"What do you mean?"

"One of my elementary school friends from Karachi is now a cop. I sent him to threaten Zahid, and he locked him up overnight." Khalid blew the smoke out of his nose. "He'll never cheat again for the rest of his life."

Ash imagined the scared look on Zahid's face. He wondered why Shefrina agreed to marrying the dumbass who cheated on her. *Why? She could have called me first,* he thought. *I should have made the move on her when she was single and we were under the same roof, but I was too much of a coward, as usual. It's all my fault, and now I've lost her forever …*

"Hey, let's go to Peter's Drive-In for some burgers and a milkshake," Khalid said.

"No, I'm gonna head out. I'm kinda tired." He gave a hug to Khalid and walked out of the motel. He paused, took out the wedding invitation from his back pocket, and threw it in the recycling box.

The next night was pub night at The Den. Every Thursday, the university pub offered pitchers of cheap beer. It was the night when every other guy walked around with a jug in his hand, spilling half on the dance floor and half on a girl before getting kicked out to the curb. The night started with high school girls (who managed to sneak in before the bouncers arrived) ordering nachos and high balls, freshmen chugging beer on special for $5.25 a pitcher before hitting on the high school girls, and the PhD veterans sipping on their tall rum and Cokes, reminiscing about the days when they looked like the ones eating nachos and drinking gin and tonics.

When Ash Amlani finished his prep for the midterm exam, he packed up at the library and went to MacEwan Hall. He took the back entrance, near The Den. He looked around, took a deep breath, fixed his posture, and introduced himself to a few tables. He offered them music that was "cheaper than a pitcher of beer" and promised to deliver the goods in two weeks if they paid in advance, but every single person said that they would be foolish to fall for the scam. One lady threatened to complain to the manager, so he apologized and went to the dance floor, which was as empty as a church on a Wednesday afternoon. The DJ waved at him. When he went closer, he saw that it was Mickey, a high school friend of Sally's whom she had introduced to Ash the night they went to the Tequila Nightclub. Ash told him about his CD business, but Mickey said he only played records on vinyl.

Ash was beginning to think the plan to surprise his mother that summer was unattainable. He would have to work at the Residence Services office for the two weeks during his time off.

When he woke up on Friday morning, he didn't feel the need to wear his lucky blue t-shirt. He had studied all day on Thursday, and he was confident he'd get a grade not lower than B+. He reached the Social Sciences building fifteen minutes before the start of the class and ran into Professor Lachman who asked him to help him set up for the exam. He ran up and down the lecture hall and placed a blank booklet on every seat. He never realized before that there were eighty-five students in that class, a relatively large class for the spring semester.

Professor Lachman told the class that they would write the exam in the first half of the class, and he planned a lecture for the other half, because they had missed the previous Wednesday class. While Professor Lachman collected the completed exams, most of the students snuck out the back door. Ash was glad he had stayed, because the lecture was not an actual lecture but a screening of *Helmut Newton: Frames from the Edge,* a 1989 documentary film about a prolific German-Australian fashion photographer, and he thoroughly enjoyed it. After the class, Ash helped the professor carry the test booklets to his office and told him how much he loved the film and how he one day would love to do something like that. Professor Lachman told him that he was in the wrong school and that he should have been attending Ryerson, which was in Toronto; Emily Carr, which was in Vancouver; or Concordia University in Montreal that all offered great photography and film production programs.

Oh well, he thought and made his way home.

He stopped by the Dining Center to see if they had anything other than their Friday special (fish and chips with tartar sauce), but they didn't, so Ash went to the gardened area between Rundle and Kananaskis halls. When he saw the wildflowers, he thought of Mrs. Farida Hookmani and their walk, and he wondered how she was doing. The place looked like a desolate prairie to him, except there was a girl under the shade, with her back against the cherry tree and a thick book in her lap. Ash noticed her full lips. *They must taste like honey,* he thought. He noticed her breasts that came out of the scooped neck of her dress. *Farida Aunty was right,* he thought. *I am like a wildflower that was plucked from its root. What she didn't tell me is that I am the kind that can't get a single bee to look in its direction. What the hell is wrong with all the girls in this town?*

He circled the area twice but couldn't think of the right thing to say. She looked up once but not in his direction. He pictured himself on the grass with legs stretched, her head rested in his lap, and his cowboy hat providing shade to her face. He thought about asking her what kind of music she liked listening to, mentioning that he could go up to his room and bring his new Sony CD Walkman, and they could spend the rest of the day in each other's arms grooving to Michael Jackson or the Backstreet Boys. Before he could muster the courage, a guy walked out of the Kananaskis Hall in cargo shorts and a t-shirt that looked like it belonged to his younger brother. It wasn't the pattern or the color, but his humongous muscles that bulged out.

The girl looked up, the boy took his t-shirt off, and Ash cringed.

He placed the t-shirt on the grass and lay down in the sun. She smiled. Ash cringed again.

He couldn't understand why God made everyone so different. It wasn't fair that he was born into a race that was gifted with a hairy body, and then there was this guy who was bestowed with not only a muscular body, but a hairless one.

The girl turned a page in her novel, and the shirtless boy turned over to tan his back. She asked him about something, and he got up and arched his back, proving that there was nothing that he lacked.

That is when Ash Amlani saw his tattoo of a phoenix raising from the ashes, in black ink that covered his whole chest. *This is what I should get,* he thought. The muscular guy climbed the tree and brought back cherries. She rinsed them with water, he threw the pits to the farthest corner of the garden, and she clapped and touched his triceps.

Ash cringed, flinched, and blanched all the way to the sixth floor of Rundle Hall, where couples were making out at every corner. It seemed he was the only person in the entire world that was destined to be alone, companionless, and a virgin.

He went to his room, drew the curtains, and played *Quit Playing Games (With My Heart)* on repeat.

CHAPTER TWENTY-FOUR

Like the season, the spring semester had come to an end. Ash received an A- in Introduction to Anthropology and a B+ in the general studies course. He had expected to work eighty hours in the two weeks before the summer semester started, but Adrianna Saul gave him an average of six hours a day, which he didn't like.

At the end of the first week, he heard that a group from Montreal was coming to stay at Rundle Hall for a month and would arrive in the middle of the night. Molly McKenna was asked to be available for check-ins, but Ash offered to take the shift because he needed the money.

All the Montrealers were given rooms on the third floor of Rundle Hall, except for Lauranie Armitage, who got Sally Jacobson's room because she planned to stay until the end of summer.

"My friend used to live in that room," Ash said as he gave her the rental agreement to sign.

"What *'appened* to *'er*?" Lauranie said.

"She went back home to Winnipeg." He had thought that all Canadians sounded the same, but she was different, and he liked that.

"Nice room?"

"Oh yes. Well, all the rooms are the same." Ash laughed.

He couldn't figure out if it was her accent, the skipping of the *h*, the rolling of the *r*, or her lustrous brunette tresses, her round nose, and her fuller lips that made him look twice. She inquired about the pool, so he offered to take her to the Olympic Oval building in the morning to show her around.

"Where are you from?"

"Um, Vancouver." Ash didn't want her to think of him the same way other people did whenever he mentioned Pakistan.

After he closed the Residence Services office and went up to his room, he couldn't stop thinking about Lauranie Armitage. He kept practicing saying her name the way she had said it.

He repeated the sound in his mind like it was a mantra he received from a Sadhu for his meditative practice. As he was calling her name, his eyelids got heavy, and he fell asleep. He saw her brown eyes turn colors, from deep blue to black to purple, but when they turned hazel and he noticed her irises were encased with thin lines of black, he realized he was dreaming. He shook her and told her that they were in a lucid dream and that they could do anything, but before she could respond, he woke up.

It was his day off, the day he had planned to go swimming with Lauranie. He wondered if she would be awake, and if he should ask her to accompany him to the Dining Center for breakfast, like how Sally once came to his room and asked him to accompany her, but he decided not to rush. He might come off as a stalker or, even worse, a psycho. After having his usual chocolate chip muffin with a tall glass of two percent milk, he came back to his room and planned the rest of the day.

He emptied his backpack and put a fresh towel and a pair of black flip-flops in it. *Shit,* he thought. He pulled everything off the shelves behind his bed to see if there was a pair of shorts that would work. He found a black Adidas pair, but they were mesh, and he pictured himself in them, in water, and he could see everything through them. He looked at his alarm clock; he couldn't go downtown and be back on time. So he went to Market Mall and asked around. The person at the Telus cell phone booth thought he was looking for a Halloween shop, but when the salesperson realized that the "swimming costume" Ash was looking for was not actually a costume but rather trunks for swimming, he directed him to go to the men's swimwear section of The Bay.

He liked the most expensive pair of swim shorts in the store: navy blue, featuring feathers and leaves in yellow and turquoise colors, with a drawstring waist with silver tips on the strings.

"You see these two eyelets at the back?" the salesperson asked. "They allow water to drain and reduce the balloon effect when you emerge from the water." Ash didn't understand what that meant. *Must be something good,* he thought, and he bought the trunks.

When he approached Lauranie's room, he found the door wide open. It was brighter than he remembered when Sally Jacobson lived there. It could have been the light coming in through the window because Sally had always kept her curtains drawn. He noticed the walls, which reflected light off the white paint. Sally had covered her wall with dark posters of musicians he'd never heard of and films he'd never watched. There was a vase with fresh flowers on the ledge and white sheets on the bed, which was moved to the left of the room. Her pillow with a flowery case was fluffier than Sally's. He wondered how she had set up her room like a luxurious hotel in such a short time. *Did she even sleep?* he wondered.

There was a white stepping stool in the corner with eight pairs of shoes for all sorts of occasions, from ballroom dancing to rock climbing to a night out clubbing. There were even purple rain boots and a pair that looked like they had been hand-sewn in Peru. He thought about peeking into her closet like he had done at his Jenny Aunty's place, but he heard the flip-flops coming through the corridor.

"Ai, what are you doing here?" Lauranie said.

"Don't you remember? We're supposed to go swimming," he said.

"Oh, I was with my friends and forgot," she said and slapped her forehead. "I ate half an hour ago, and I don't want to throw up."

Maybe I should ask her if she wants to go tomorrow, he thought. But before he could, she grabbed her purse, locked the door, and said, "Sorry, running late for a meeting."

As he watched her walk away, he felt guilty for spending over fifty dollars on his swimming trunks that he didn't even get to wear — an amount he had made the day before at the Residence Services for working six and a half hours. *Fuck it. I should just go to the pool by myself.*

Over the next few hours on campus, he stood by the window, watching pretty girls with their fit bodies dive into the pool, though his favorite part was when they came out and ran across to get their towels. He thought that it would be a great idea to try out the pool so that he could be better prepared for when Lauranie Armitage would accompany him, and they would swim like two dolphins in love.

He wrapped the towel around his waist, dropped his white briefs, and put on his new trunks. He saw the sign that asked everyone to rinse before entering the pool area but when he turned the shower on, the water was cold. He stood away to muster the courage, which didn't quite appear until he witnessed three guys and one little boy jump in and out.

How bad could it be?

After the shower area became vacant, he stepped in and shrieked loud enough for all the swimmers to hear. He jumped up and down for a few seconds and turned the water off. He felt too cold to go back to his locker to get his flip-flops, so he walked straight to the doors that led into the pool area.

Everyone looked like they were prepping for the Olympics. He was used to people flapping their hands hard in the water and people taking fifteen-minute breaks during laps to celebrate their accomplishments, but the students at the Recreation Center were going back and forth, with no breaks in between. None. He counted their laps. Unlike in Karachi, where pools were dedicated to either men or women and were located one hundred kilometers away from each other on purpose, the pool at the University of Calgary welcomed anyone who brought the courage to dive in. It didn't discriminate as long as the person showered before getting in and controlled their bladder. Shefrina Hookmani had once told Ash that the pool at her high school used a chemical that made the water turn color if someone peed in it, and many students had been embarrassed to the point that they refused to swim for the rest of the semester. The thought made Ash turn around and head back to the changing room to pee.

When he returned, he looked for the shallow part of the pool, stepped in, and stood in a corner. *I should buy goggles.* He tried to recall if he had seen any at The Bay that afternoon. He lowered himself under the water and felt warmer than before. *This is fun,* he thought.

He imagined that he was being looked at by everyone, but no one noticed that he was there, and no one appreciated his brand-new swimming "costume."

Ashiq Amlani grew up in a town where people liked to wing everything. Learning was a concept their ancestors left behind after the last Mughal Emperor had lost everything. His uncle had told him once that he'd learned swimming by watching others, and his father followed by saying that he'd gone to the beach one day and found himself swimming like a fish and that he was born that way. But Ashiq never saw his father swim, so he believed that story since his childhood. If his father could be such a proficient swimmer, he could at least finish one lap without the lessons his Jenny aunty had recommended.

He waited for the second guy to swim away, pushed his legs against the wall, and floated, and when he tried stepping on his feet to stand, he realized he'd floated farther than he wanted to. He panicked for a second, but his hand hit the bar on the side of the pool. He grabbed it hard and called the names of God. While he balanced his floating body with the help of the sidebar, he thanked God for saving him from drowning and apologized for not praying for a long time. There was once a time when he never missed a single prayer, but things had changed since then.

Ashiq Amlani grew up in a religious household. His father had headed a one-hour meditation session at four in the morning at the local mosque. Every day, when Mr. Shamsu Amlani returned home after the morning prayers, everyone was expected to get up and pray. It was something they did before anything else. It was the norm, their way of life. It was tradition.

But since Ash had moved to Canada, things changed. The first day he'd missed the morning prayers was when he was staying with the Poonjas in Vancouver. Jenny Poonja woke him up and saw his boner poking out of the sleeping bag. He felt guilty to say the name of God; a part of him wanted to throw Ricky Poonja off the balcony and make sweet love to his aunty. The second time he'd forgotten was on the trip to Lake Louise when Khalid asked him to accompany him while he smoked his first cigarette of the day, but when they returned to the hotel room, Ash forgot all about his morning prayers. The third time was during the snowstorm when he'd slept in the food court. Since then, he hadn't prayed. He found no need for prayers or for religion. He found freedom, he found booze, and he found the fun in life.

He stood in the corner and watched the others swim. He floated occasionally and tried going to the other end, holding the side bar along the way. For the next seven days he did just that, but most of those days he felt like drowning, because Lauranie stood him up every single time. She'd found better things to do, and better-looking guys than Ash to do them with.

On the following Sunday morning, they ran into each other at the pool. She was with a guy, and Ash thought that he must be one of her friends from Montreal, but when she introduced them, it turned out that the tattooed guy was born and raised in Calgary. She told Ash that they went out the night before and continued partying in Lauranie's room. That explained why she was giggling non-stop and when she came closer to him, he smelled the booze on her breath. He couldn't tell what she drank, but it was alcohol for sure. She hugged him and told him that she missed him, but he knew quite well that it was the vodka or the gin or the rum that was talking. When she kissed him on his cheek and told him that he was cute, the tattooed guy grabbed her from the back and they jumped into the pool. For the next five minutes, they made out in the deep end while Ash wondered how they could stay afloat for so long.

He came out of the pool and approached Lauranie, who was busy examining the guy's tattoos while he did things to her under water that Ash couldn't see. "I'm gonna take off," he said.

She didn't look up, but the guy nodded. "Nice meeting you," Ash said, waving at the guy and turning to leave.

"You are going 'ome?" Lauranie said. He nodded. She looked down to his trunks, pointed at them, and then lowered her eyes further.

"Whoa! You're 'airry!" she said.

The tattooed guy burst out laughing and she joined him.

Ash Amlani stood there shaken, like he didn't have legs. To him, it felt like he was in one of those movies where there's an explosion, but instead of the sound of the blast, you hear silence. He felt like his eardrums had all been pierced.

He went back to the men's changing room, looked at himself in the mirror, and suddenly he knew what he needed to do. He took his backpack and went to London Drugs.

When he returned to school after his trip to London Drugs, he went straight to the Residence Services office and started his shift. It was a busy evening. He hardly got to take any breaks, and when things started to slow down, he looked at the clock and couldn't believe it was ten to midnight. He counted the cash and tallied it with the daily account sheet that went into the register and turned the key twice to lock it up for the night.

Right at midnight, he closed the window shutters and turned the lights off. He went to the back into the kitchen area and turned the small light on. He unzipped his backpack, pulled out a paper bag that read London Drugs on it, and placed it next to the microwave. He took out a small pink bottle of Johnson's baby lotion and placed it on the wooden chair.

The pharmacist at London Drugs had told Ash that the hair-removal wax would need to be heated. That could have been an issue for him, but he'd remembered that he was closing the Residence Services that night and could stay after work to use the microwave there. This was all because of Lauranie and her mean comment — *"whoa, you're 'airry!!"* Her voice echoed in his head. He locked the door from the inside, checked the window shutters one more time, and walked back to the kitchen area. He took out the all-in-one value pack from the paper bag and read the instructions. He unbuckled his belt, dropped the cargo pants, and kicked them to the side.

He heated the wax, applied a layer on his right thigh, and pressed the white cloth strip on top as the box instructed. He felt a burning sensation for a few seconds and then it felt like he was under a hot shower. He took a deep breath, held one corner of the strip with his index and middle fingers on one side and the thumb on the other, and ripped it off his skin. He winced and tensed up his muscles.

That's just one, he thought. There were nineteen more patches to go.

He looked at the first empty patch and wondered if he liked what he saw or was ashamed of such an act that would have gotten him disowned by his father. His mother would have understood his dilemma and would have helped him personally. But his father, Mr. Shamsu Amlani, was a traditional man, a religious man, a man who didn't wear bright colors or experiment with facial hair. He kept the same hairstyle he'd received in one of the barbershops in downtown Chicago in the early seventies. And after twenty-six years, he still combed his hair the same way. He wore a white shirt with beige pants, a brown sweater with brown trousers, and a black belt with brown shoes. He once threw Ash's jeans to the back alley of their house because he couldn't understand the diversity in self-expressions, and to him those jeans were ripped and therefore made his son look like a homeless beggar. If his father knew what he was up to that night in his work kitchen, he would have asked him to remove *Amlani* from his name.

He looked at the clock. It took twenty minutes for him to finish his right leg, including the shins and the calves, and his left thigh. He liked what emerged from underneath. *This is how Michelangelo must have felt when he saw David come out of the block of white marble*, Ash thought. He put all the used strips in a plastic bag, tied the knot, and put it in his backpack to dispose of it in one of the garbage bins outside. He squeezed an ample amount of baby lotion into his palm, rubbed his palms together, and spread it on all the areas of his legs that turned red. He pulled up the cargos, zipped his backpack, and turned the small light off.

When he went to his room, he wanted to see himself in the mirror behind the door, but he heard Ben snoring. So, he undressed and jumped into his bed. He waited for Ben to stop snoring so he could fall asleep, but it appeared that Ben was having a lucid dream of his own. Ash brought his left arm out from under the sheets and reached for the chair in the dark. When he got a solid grip of one of the side rests, he pulled it toward the desk, and it banged. That was enough noise for Ben to jerk in his sleep. He didn't wake up, but the snoring stopped, and Ash fell asleep within the next ten minutes.

At six in the morning, when Ben got up from his chair to leave the room, it touched the desk loudly enough to wake Ash up. Ben apologized but Ash didn't respond. His first thought was to check the placement of his bed sheet to make sure his hairless legs weren't showing. He wasn't ready for the world to see them quite yet. He had a plan, but it needed time.

After Ben left, Ash got up and applied more baby lotion to his legs because they were itchy. The redness had settled down, and the skin had turned a pinkish shade. He covered himself with the sheets and tried falling asleep again, but he thought of Lauranie Armitage at the pool. No tattooed guys were around; it was just them. He reached for the bottle of baby lotion, and he saw Lauranie in her bathing suit and then in her birthday suit.

He wiped himself with his boxers, threw them in the laundry basket, and went back to sleep.

CHAPTER TWENTY-FIVE

On the first day of the summer semester, the weather got hotter, the dresses got shorter, and the parties got wilder. It was also the time when Ash Amlani mastered the art of maintenance and learned to use scissors as a grooming tool. By the time his birthday came, his legs flaunted the perfect amount of hair, and his legs looked like everyone else's.

Jonny told Ash that there was a surprise for him. He knew it wasn't a surprise party, because he was the one who planned his birthday extravaganza with everyone. It was decided during an episode of *The Simpsons*.

"Just tell me. I don't like surprises," he said.

"Well, you'll like this one," Jonny winked at him.

Since moving to Canada, Ash Amlani had realized that the way things were done there were different than from back home. One of those things was celebrating birthdays. In Pakistan, the birthday boy or the birthday girl were expected to treat their friends to a dinner, a night out, a special something on the day of their birth. But he liked how things were done in Canada: if it was your birthday, you didn't have to spend a single penny. Your friends picked up the tab.

So when Jonny proposed that they go out and celebrate his birthday because it fell on a Saturday, he said he wanted to go for a nice dinner before they went out dancing. They asked him to pick any place he wanted, and he proposed the River Café, but Jonny asked him not to pick the most expensive restaurant in town. They settled for a steak dinner at Earls on Stephen Avenue, and Ash requested that they bar hop around the 17th Avenue area after dinner. Everyone loved the idea and decided to meet on the sixth floor of Rundle Hall around 7 p.m.

Lauranie Armitage emerged in a short, tight black dress. When Ash gave her a half-excited, half-puzzled look, she said that her horse-riding competition had been cancelled. *Maybe she'll ride me like a horse tonight,* he thought. The Montreal crowd was gone, and she hung out with people on the sixth floor of Rundle Hall. She came closer, kissed him on the cheek, and held his left hand in hers.

"'*appy* birthday," she said. He liked how she held his hand, how she wished him well on his special day, and how she smelled.

Ash went to the liquor store earlier during the day and bought a two-four of Molson Canadian and a bottle of spiced rum. It was his way of keeping his culture alive; not that booze was legal or socially accepted in Karachi, but he wanted to treat his friends like he would have if he was in Karachi that summer. The guests loved his gesture.

"Pakistanis aren't what they are perceived as," Lauranie said.

"Interesting," Ash said. "What did you think of them initially?"

"You know … like, strict orthodox, that don't drink and make their women cover up," she said.

Jonny shook his head.

"My mom wore whatever she wanted. She never covered herself," Ash said.

Most of the people grabbed a beer and put the second one in their pockets for the C-Train ride downtown. Jonny brought out a few shot glasses and within minutes, the bottle of spiced rum was empty. Ash thought that was the fastest way to feel the booze, because every time Jonny refilled a round, he got a shot. It was his birthday and he loved it.

"That would '*ave* cost two '*undred* dollars at the club," Lauranie said.

"True that, true that. Thanks, A," said Jonny. Ash wasn't sure if Jonny was too lazy to say his full name, or if it was to indicate that they were close.

"Ready for your surprise, bud?" Jonny said.

Ash nodded with a smile and stumbled into the elevator.

When they arrived at Earls restaurant, the hostess took them to the longest table.

"So, what's the surprise?" Ash said.

"Patience, my friend. All in good time," Jonny said.

"What would you like to drink?" the female server asked, standing behind Ash.

There was something familiar about that voice, like he'd heard it before, in his dream or in an alternate universe. Ash turned to look at her, but Jonny pushed the drinks menu in front of his face. "Here you go, bud."

"The first drink is on the house," the server said. Her voice made Ash's heart skip a beat. He put the menu down and turned to look at her.

"Sally! No way!" He got up and hugged her. "I've missed you so much!"

"I know." She smiled. "I've missed you too, bud."

"So." Jonny joined in. "Do you like your surprise?"

"She's been here all this time and now I get to see her?" Ash said.

"Happy birthday," she said, kissed him on the cheek, and hugged him again.

"Thanks, love," Ash said, holding the side of her shoulders and looking into her eyes. "I'm so sorry about your parents."

She nodded. "Not a single day goes by that I don't think about them."

"If you need anything …"

"Thanks, Ash. Don't make me cry, it's your birthday." She wiped her tears and then laughed. "So, what are you gonna drink? The first round is on the house."

"Well, the birthday boy is gonna drink for free the whole night. This is Canada. I love this country," Ash said.

Everyone laughed. A few of his friends suggested that he not mix drinks; it was going to be a long night and a little precaution would pay dividends the next morning. Jonny said to get a lager, and others recommended Sex on the Beach, which got his attention, until he realized it was just a name. Lauranie Armitage waited for everyone to name their favorite drinks then told Ash that he should try red wine because that was the best option to have with a steak.

"We have a great merlot," Sally said.

"Try cabernet sauvignon," Lauranie said, bending down and pointing to the menu under the Chilean wines. He didn't bother looking at what she suggested, because her accent dazzled him. The way that she said, "Cabernet sauvignon" — it was heavenly to him, and her cleavage, in his face, hypnotized him. He wanted to tell her that she smelled like a spring orchard, but Sally cleared her throat and asked for his attention.

"That one." Ash pointed at the wine and put his hand on Lauranie's hips. "Thanks, darling." He smiled.

"*C'est quoi ce bordel*," Lauranie said. She took a few steps backward, rolled her eyes, and went back to her seat.

"And a glass of water, I suppose," Sally said.

"No, no, no," Ash said, waving his hand behind his head.

"Yes, please." Jonny tapped on his shoulder and winked at Sally.

After everyone finished their steaks and salad, another round of drinks was ordered. Jonny excused himself from the table and returned with Sally, who held a small dark chocolate cake with a firecracker candle on the top. They all sang the birthday song and congratulated him. He cut the cake and passed it to Jonny, who removed the candle and sliced the cake into smaller pieces.

They laughed, ordered a few more drinks, and waited for Ash to throw up, but he proved them wrong, continuing to stumble across the restaurant. He hit the kitchen wall twice on his way to the washroom, told one of the waitresses how pretty she was, and kissed Sally Jacobson on the lips.

"You should stay at my place tonight," Ash slurred.

"Actually, I'm renting a room near Brentwood station," Sally said.

"So, I can come to your place?"

"Of course, we'll plan something. Jonny knows where I live."

"No, not Jonny. Just me and you."

"I forgot how much fun you are when you drink." She laughed. "Let me finish the paperwork for my shift and I'll join you guys." She kissed him on the cheek and walked away. Ash reached to grab her buttocks, but Jonny pulled him back and passed him a glass of water.

"What's this nonsense," Ash said and raised his hands in the air.

"It's good for you. Take a sip."

"Jonny, buddy."

"What, my friend?"

"I love her." Ash took a small sip of water and left the glass on the side counter.

"Who?"

"Sally. She's soooo hot."

"Why don't we go outside and get some fresh air," Jonny suggested.

"Do you have a cigarette? I feel like having a smoke," Ash slurred.

"I'm sure we can find one." He helped him open the door.

As soon as they walked out, Ash hurled on the curb and on the hood of a green Mustang. Sally came out with a bottle of water and helped him clean up. She asked if he wanted to throw up more, but he shook his head and emptied the water bottle onto his face.

They called four cabs and headed to 17th Avenue. Ash spit the gum out the window that he had been chewing since Sally put it in his mouth while they had settled the bill at Earls. She had got them a thirty percent discount and one round of drinks for free before she left the restaurant with the rest of the group.

Ash cranked the volume up, but the driver didn't say anything. It was a song no one knew, except, of course, the cab driver and Ashiq.

"Is he from your country?" someone asked.

"I don't think so. He's Sikh," Ash said.

"I'm from Punjab," the driver said as he looked in his rearview mirror.

"I have many friends from Punjab," Ash said.

"It's the Punjab in India, not Pakistan," the driver said, lowering the volume.

"How do you know he's from Pakistan?" Jonny asked.

The driver shrugged his shoulders.

"*Vell*, I *vas* born here," Ash shouted. He had forgotten to pronounce the *w* properly.

"I see. You're one of *them*." The driver's forehead lines popped out.

"Them *who*?" Ash raised his voice.

"Never mind."

The driver stopped at the corner of 8th Street and 17th Avenue. Sally gave him a ten and a five and asked him to keep the change. Ash put his arms around her, and they walked in search of a place to initiate their pub crawl.

"Shouldn't we wait for the others?" Sally said.

"I just want to be with you." Ash put his hands around her.

"Hell, no." She jerked his hands off her buttocks. "That's not gonna happen." She looked him in the eye and then said, "Not even in your dreams."

"But it's my birthday."

"So? Besides, it's only for the next two hours, if you can even last that long."

"Oh, I can go all night long. I'm *not* drunk."

"Of course, you're not."

After the second pub, Ash didn't know where he was. At some point during the night, he found himself in a back alley where he ran into three homeless people having an orgy, or that was what that looked like to him. His senses were elevated. He remembered jumping on top of a brand new 1998 BMW Z3, puked on a cop car while they lined up at Tim Hortons for a double-double, and howled in the middle of 17th Avenue, because he thought that was fun.

The last memory he recalled before things went dark was that he was in Sally's bedroom, and she was shouting at him. And she was naked.

CHAPTER TWENTY-SIX

For the next few days, Ash stayed in his room. He didn't remember the details from Saturday night. Some of it was blurry and the rest was as dark as a forest on a moonless night.

He was embarrassed for making a fool of himself, but his biggest concern was what had happened at Sally's place. He couldn't put the pieces together. All he remembered was that Sally was shouting at him, she was naked, and the floor was wet.

To his surprise, when he finally came out of his room and ran into people from the party, they all told him how hilarious he was throughout the night. They told him about his funky dance moves, his ability to put two shot glasses of tequila in his mouth, and how he chugged a pint of Guinness. So he realized that after two in the morning that night, everyone had gone home, and no one had witnessed what happened at Sally's later that night.

Besides, Ash had even bigger fish to fry. The coming weekend was the Heritage Day long weekend in Alberta. It was also the weekend when his childhood love, Shefrina Hookmani, was going to become Shefrina Hamza, and not Shefrina Amlani. He thought again about all the times he could have made his move, especially during the post-engagement breakup, but Ash was chasing the wrong bees. He'd lost the girl he always wanted and wondered if life could get any worse.

Jonny had told him that every year during the Heritage Day long weekend, he and his friends went camping in the wilderness. He had invited Ash to come along with them, to swim in the lake, to eat barbecued meat, smoke herbs around the bonfire, and drink.

Ash had loved camping since he was a young boy growing up in Karachi. The first time he went camping with his fellow five-year-old

Boy Scouts, it mesmerized him, and he'd talked about the experience for weeks afterward with his parents, his neighbors, and Nani, his favorite grandmother.

Jonny asked him to bring along his swimwear, sunscreen, mosquito repellant, and a bottle of vodka. Ash was thrilled, but now he wasn't sure if he was still invited after what had happened at Sally's place. He thought that if anyone knew, it would be Jonny. He grabbed the bottle of Smirnoff, went to Jonny's door, and knocked.

"What's up, bud?" Jonny greeted him.

"Um, I bought this for the camping trip," Ash said.

"Cool, but you know it's Wednesday today, right? We don't leave until Friday afternoon."

"I know. I just thought I'd ask you if this is the right one."

"Dude, it's booze. It can't be wrong." Jonny laughed. "So you've recovered, I see."

Ash nodded with a smile.

"That was a fucking awesome night, dude," he said, tapping his shoulders. "You were fuckin' hilarious."

"Did you talk to Sally?"

"You'll see her on Friday, she's coming with us. By the way, I didn't invite Lauranie." He moved closer and whispered, "Sally doesn't like her."

"That's cool, man," Ash said. He wondered, *Does this mean Sally is jealous of Lauranie being around me*? Then he smiled and said, "Let me know if you need me to bring anything else."

"For sure." Jonny waved at him and closed his door.

Ash was relieved that Jonny hadn't been present that night, but he wondered why Sally had agreed to the camping trip. Maybe they hadn't spoken since Saturday night. He didn't know how to deal with the situation, because he didn't remember what had happened that night. He thought about apologizing to her, but he didn't know where or how to start.

Jonny asked him to meet downstairs and said that Mickey, the DJ from The Den, would bring his SUV around 11:30 a.m. Ash didn't sleep all night. He thought about what he would tell Sally and how he would say it. By quarter to eleven, he didn't yet have the perfect solution, so he went up to Jonny's room.

Jonny's door was slightly open, enough for the light from the curtainless windows to leak out into the dark corridor, as well as the smell of weed. He knocked on the door, and to his surprise, Sally answered, wrapped in a white towel. Her face was radiant, and her eyes sparkled. It was a look he had never seen before on her face. She smiled, unwrapped the towel on her head, and unfurled her hair.

"When are you gonna get ready?" Jonny said as he licked one end of the rolling paper and rotated the joint between his fingers.

"We still have time and he's a boy. He'll be ready in two minutes," she said.

"Not him. He takes forever. He's worse than you." Jonny winked at Sally.

"Did you stay here overnight?" Ash asked her. He looked into her eyes but lowered them before she could respond. Sally and Jonny both laughed in sync. "What?" Ash looked up.

"I've been living here since I came back from Winnipeg," she said.

"But what about your place?"

"What place?"

"Yeah, what place?" Jonny put all the joints in a ziplock bag and threw it in the top compartment of his backpack.

"Your place in Brentwood." Ash raised his eyebrows.

"Oh …" She put on a tank top and threw her towel on the bed. "I just made that up. You wanted me to sleep in your room, and you were too drunk for me to tell you that Jonny and I were seeing each other, so that's that." She put on a pair of denim shorts, and Ash saw her blue panties.

"But what about your siblings. Weren't you supposed to take care of them?" Ash said.

"They are with my grandparents now." She smiled.

He didn't know what that meant. Was she lying to both of them? Ash had been at her place, in her bathroom; he had felt the wet floor. There was an imitation painting of Picasso hung in her living room. He had seen the dirty panties across her carpeted bedroom floor. He had seen her naked. It was real.

"Dude, go get ready," Jonny said.

"Um, I have to finish an assignment and it's due on Tuesday," Ash lied.

"You're not getting out of this. I even baked brownies for the trip," Sally said.

"I really want to, but you know …"

"That sucks, man." Jonny walked between them and headed to the communal washroom. Sally and Ash looked at each other and stood in silence.

"So, you and Jonny, eh?" Ash said.

She nodded. "I wish you were coming."

"Why?"

"Why? Because I like you. *We* like you." She looked puzzled.

"You can't have everything, Sally."

"What are you talking about?"

"My birthday night? The place in Brentwood? What was that?"

"I have no idea what you're talking about."

"Never mind." He walked out the room.

"Ash, what's going on?" She followed him to his room.

"I thought we had something, and I know I was a jerk that night, but we had *something*, Sally." He paused and turned to look at her. "Something special."

"I didn't know that's how you felt."

"Well, enjoy your trip." He reached for the keys in his pocket and walked toward his room.

"You can't just leave things like that, Ash." She stood outside his room while he walked around in circles.

"Here." He grabbed the bottle of Smirnoff and passed it to her. "I bought this for our trip."

"I think you should come." She took a step forward.

"After what happened at your place?" he asked her.

"What place?"

"Never mind. This is just useless."

"Oh … I know what's bothering you." Her mouth widened.

He looked at her with curiosity.

"It's the shrooms. That's what the fuck you're nagging about," Sally said.

"What?"

"The magic freakin' mushrooms. We all took some after we left one of the bars," she said.

"And that's what we did at your place?" Ash put his hands on his waist.

"Dude, there's no place. You were sitting on Jonny's bed, holding a photograph of me, and telling everyone that the image was talking to you," she laughed. "I guess you did more than just imagine, so tell me: What exactly happened *at my place*?"

"Shut up. And take this bottle with you," Ash said.

"You're coming with us and there's nothing else to it," she said. "Get ready quickly." She didn't take the bottle and left his room.

He sat on his bed and thought about what happened. He wondered how he could have imagined something that seemed so real. A part of him believed that Sally was a liar, but she had given him too much to grasp in such a short time and he didn't know what was true and what wasn't.

But the thing that bugged him the most was her hook up with Jonny. Why did she pick Jonny over him? *Why does this shit always happen to me? First, Shefrina goes for that fucking Zahid Hamza, Lauranie runs around with all kinds of guys, and now Sally goes to Jonny. That's just fucking perfect.* He felt like his heart was broken into pieces. He felt betrayed. There was no way he could go camping with the lovebirds. He walked back to Jonny's room with the vodka. The door was locked. He put the bottle by the door and left.

He thought about what had gone wrong, why Sally rejected him, and why she picked Jonny over him. After all, he had been honest with her and revealed his true identity to her. How did Jonny do more? Yes, he called her every other day, he sent her money because her student loan payments were blocked, and he gave her moral support. Yes, they both came from similar backgrounds, their life stories were the same, and they faced similar challenges. Yes, they were more alike than Ash was to either of them. But still, why not him? Was he doomed? Was it the *juju* fucking things up for him? Was he meant to stay a virgin for the rest of his life?

I have changed. I am different now. I am like a new person. he thought. He was not who he used to be. The months Sally was away, the months she and Jonny had bonded over phone calls, the months Lauranie had explored boys on the sixth floor. Ash Amlani abandoned parts of his existence, his identity, his *true* self, and adopted new ones. When he looked at himself in the mirror, he couldn't recognize who he was looking at. How could he ever have gone so far as to wax his legs, to alter his appearance, to be different, just because a stupid girl had made a mean comment to him? That was not the Ashiq he knew. That was not the boy with morals and values and a strong identity. Now, he was made up of loose rags that carried other people's scents, tattered glasses that reflected someone else's reality, and twisted metals that gave out unfamiliar, unknown, and bizarre sounds, every time they touched one another. He wasn't who he thought he was. He was not Ashiq Amlani. He wasn't even Ash anymore. He was just a silent A, like a forgotten, soundless letter.

CHAPTER TWENTY-SEVEN

Ash kept the spare Residence Services key on him because he wanted to call his mother over the long weekend. The admin didn't know about the high-priced direct international calls Ash logged three times a month, usually on Sundays. He also wanted to call the travel agent to find a cheap flight to Karachi, because he had received his student loans and didn't have to rely on his failed CD business anymore. The amount from the financial aid office was more than he had expected. When he had applied for the student loans, he had thought he would receive a monthly allowance from the government, but when he realized that the deposit in his bank account was for the whole semester, he had access to more money than he needed at the time, so why not spend it on surprising his mother?

After lunch, things got quieter. He went to the office, unlocked the door, and picked the cordless phone. He pressed 9, got the dial tone, then dialed the number, and went to Adrianna Saul's office.

Mrs. Amlani wanted to share the highlights of the last few weeks, and she wanted to hear what her son was up to, but she skipped the formalities and asked him if he had spoken to anyone from the Hookmani clan, because there had been an incident. Ash didn't know anything. Mrs. Amlani said that Shefrina was in shock; she had locked herself in the attic, because her fiancé Zahid Hamza had gotten cold feet on their wedding day. Ash didn't know exactly what to say, so he kept quiet. He wondered why Zahid did what he did and if Khalid had anything to do with that, if perhaps Khalid had sent his cop friend again for a quick reminder not to mess with the Hookmanis. He thought about Shefrina and wished that he was there, to hold her hand, to listen to her, to be with her. He wondered if she had eaten anything since she'd locked herself in the attic, if there was anyone who checked on her, if anyone cared for her. Ash realized that there was nothing else in the world he wanted more than to be with her in that moment, but he was in Calgary, and she was in Karachi, and there were thousands of miles in between.

"Please look after her," he told his mother over the phone.

"She needs time, alone time," Mrs. Amlani said.

"I guess you're right."

He was glad he avoided mentioning to his mother that he planned to visit them soon. *It will be a great surprise*, he thought. He imagined the look on his mother's and his little sister's faces, but he didn't imagine the look on his father's face, because that was something beyond his imagination.

He hung up, called the travel agent, and found a few cheap flights leaving in a few weeks. He reserved one for forty-eight hours, jotted down the details at the back of an empty white envelope, and put it in his back pocket.

He thought about Shefrina again and worried about her. Was there anyone to help her? He wondered if Farook Hookmani was still in Karachi. Were they all there?

He picked up the cordless phone and dialed the Hookmani residence. The phone rang eight times, Ash counted, and the call went to the answering machine. It was her voice, the voice he wanted to hear: "You've reached the Hooks' residence. Please leave a message after the beep, and one of us will get back to you. Have a wonderful day." But how could Ash have a wonderful day? Sally had rejected him, Lauranie had ignored him, the love of his childhood was locked in an attic thousands of miles away, and he was alone with a bottle of Smirnoff.

Music and booze helped Ash deal with sorrow. Vodka and Backstreet Boys always came to his aid, in times of despair, in times of loneliness, in times when girls rolled their eyes at him, brushed his hand off their booties, and called him a *Paki*. But he needed more than just vodka and the sad songs of Nusrat Fateh Ali Khan to face the reality.

He walked through the Dining Center and saw a girl in a white summer dress with long blond locks and dimples on both sides of her face. She sat down and smiled at the guy across from her. Ash could see her light freckles, the shine in her eyes, the way she ran her fingers through her hair. There was something about her. He had never seen her before, but a part of him felt as if he had. The boy across from her caught Ash staring at her. It was Oisin Bolton. He waved at Ash, and Ash waved back. At that moment it hit him that she was the same girl in the black and white photograph he saw the day he dropped the pick-up card in Oisin's mailbox. Ash had thought the girl would have hazel eyes in real life, not deep ocean blue, but he had been right about her blond hair, which had grown longer since the photograph had been taken.

Ash hadn't eaten anything since the morning, so he toasted two slices of white bread, grabbed two packets of peanut butter, two packets of strawberry jam, a white plastic knife, and a few napkins. He filled up a tall blue plastic glass with chocolate milk and found a place by the window. He cut the sandwich diagonally and thought about his Jenny aunty, who taught him the art of cutting sandwiches and avocados. He wondered how she was doing. He thought about the last time he saw her and the way she had hugged him, leaving the warmth of her breasts behind. He realized how much time had passed since then, how much had changed since then, around him and within him. He wasn't the same boy he had been when he'd arrived in Vancouver. The only thing that had stayed the same was his horniness and his virginity, and they weren't going anywhere anytime soon.

"Hey Ash," Oisin called out to him. "Why don't you join us?"

Ash walked up to them, and Oisin moved his chair to make room and introduced his girlfriend, Carmen, to him. Ash smiled, sat down, and took a big bite of his sandwich and chased it with a sip of chocolate milk. He wiped his mouth and told them about his recent tragedies. He said he had had his heart broken three times. Carmen and Oisin looked at each other and nodded. They said he should go to Karachi and rescue Shefrina and that it would be the greatest love story ever.

Ash didn't know what to do. He had always loved Shefrina, but lately he seemed to be interested only in white girls, even though he hadn't met a single girl yet who liked him. Carmen picked up the pizza crust Oisin hadn't eaten, took a bite, and looked at Ash.

"You're a hopeless romantic, and you're royally fucked."

Oisin nodded and said, "You need to get laid."

Carmen agreed and said that one of her friends, Ruby McPhee, was having a party tonight. There would be a lot of white girls, and Ash might hit the jackpot.

Ruby McPhee was gregarious, stylish, and Bahamian. She had moved to Calgary to pursue journalism at Mount Royal College and had met Carmen at a hockey game after she had finished interviewing Oisin Bolton for *The Reflector,* the Mount Royal College's independent newspaper.

Carmen told Ruby that one of the photographs Ash took at the Stampede that year was published on the front page of *The Gauntlet,* the University of Calgary's independent newspaper. Ruby pulled a blue pen out of her dreads, wrote down her number on the back of a white napkin, and gave it to Ash. She told him she was working on a project about underground prostitution in Calgary and was currently recruiting a photographer to do a few portraits.

Ruby poured fruit punch into a red plastic cup, passed it to Ash, and explained how five Bahamians at that party had crafted the infamous fruit punch. They started off with a regular rum punch but somehow it turned into something special.

"Heavenly. A gift from the gods," a girl said and refilled her glass. She wore a summer dress. It was longer than what Carmen wore, and every time someone moved away from the bonfire, the light exposed her long legs.

"This is Alize. She's not only gorgeous but an extremely talented musician," Ruby said. The embers of the bonfire sparkled in Alize's brown eyes. Her black, curled hair reached the base of her breasts, and her tanned skin gleamed through her white dress. Ruby said that she was born and raised in Barbados and moved to Florida when she was seven, and that's why she had an American accent. Ash wished he could speak like her. Alize had performed at the Calgary Folk Music Festival the evening Ash hallucinated seeing Sally Jacobson naked in her shower. Ruby and Alize were best friends. Ruby had asked Alize to spend the rest of the summer with her and had planned a road trip to Nelson, British Columbia in a few weeks.

Ash told Alize he liked her dress and her large silver hoop earrings, but Ruby came up to him and whispered in his ear that he was trying too hard and that Alize didn't like boys who appeared desperate.

Oisin Bolton came out of the house with a bucket of chicken wings, a stack of paper napkins, and a large black garbage bag. While they ate, Ash noticed how Alize held the wings and how she curved her wrist. The silver bangles danced around her hands, and her golden-brown skin glimmered in the firelight. *She looks like a goddess*, Ash thought. There was something about her that reminded him of Shefrina: the same energy and the same charm, but just a different color.

She called out "Maxx!" to Ruby's dearest shih tzu and fed him the bones. Ruby yelled at her and reminded everyone not to feed Maxx anything.

Around 11:30 p.m., more people came and, with them, more drinks. Ash made himself another rum and Coke. He met a guy from Australia who was on the U of C's swim team; a Kenyan with Indian heritage; a girl who was too busy to date; a couple who couldn't keep their hands off each other; and a dancer from the Alberta Ballet School. He spoke to a cute girl in a yellow summer dress, but she said her boyfriend was on the U of C football team, and he was the quarterback. Ash didn't care because he didn't know what that meant. All he cared about was that she was *also* taken, just like everybody else.

He looked for Alize, but she had vanished, and he couldn't find Ruby either. He knew that Oisin went out to find a bottle of wine for Carmen while she roasted marshmallows in the bonfire. He walked up to her, and she handed him her roasted marshmallow and gave him two pieces of graham crackers and a piece of chocolate.

"This is amazing," he said.

"That's s'mores for you." She smiled and prepared another marshmallow to roast.

"S'mores?" he asked.

"Yep. Apparently, it's a contraction of the phrase 'some more,' and I think it was started by the Girl Scouts, or so they say," Carmen said.

He told her about his days as a Boy Scout in Karachi and how he loved going on camping trips. She was impressed that at the age of thirteen, he had traveled across Pakistan with his friends and attended an international jamboree, where he performed a dance choreographed by a notorious artist from Lahore. He told her that was the first time he learned to recognize the scent of alcohol. Every time Titli, the choreographer, came closer to give instructions, his breath gave out musk of *gur,* a South Asian solid brown sugar made from boiling sugar cane juice until dry. He could tell that the drink's base was orange or some sort of a citric acid. He heard the other boys complain about how inappropriate it was for Titli to come drunk every day, but to him, to Ashiq Amlani, Titli appeared excited, passionate, and in the flow.

The music stopped and so did Ash's story. Everyone turned toward the house. Alize came out barefoot with her guitar and a bar stool, followed by Ruby who passed around a few joints. Alize sang three songs, and Ash didn't know if he liked her voice or the music more. He loved how the rhythm of the song spoke to his soul. He asked her if they were her songs and she laughed out loud. She was surprised that he didn't know Bob Marley. She took him to her room and played him *No Woman No Cry,* followed by *Three Little Birds,* and then *Buffalo Soldier.* She stood in front of him like a ballerina, bowing and rolling her hands forward.

"I'm the person who introduced you to Reggae music. I'm the one who told you about Bob Marley. Your life is about to change," she said.

He thought that his life had already changed because he was sitting in her room, listening to *Could You Be Loved* while she moved her fingers through her hair. He wanted to lean over and kiss her, but he knew that the time wasn't right. There were no sparks yet.

They went downstairs, and most of the people had left. Ruby called out to the last few that were sitting on the patio, closed the door, and moved the liquor from the kitchen counter to the living area, where everyone gathered.

"We'll need an empty bottle," Alize said.

"Oh, we got enough of those." Ruby picked one from the side of the stairs and passed it to Alize.

Oisin and Carmen got up to leave, and Ash joined them, but Ruby asked him to stay. She said there were enough people around to give him a ride later.

"We'll take good care of him," Ruby said and put her hand on Ash's shoulder, then waved at Oisin and Carmen. The front door shut, everyone converged around an empty bottle on the floor of the living room, and someone cranked up the music.

CHAPTER TWENTY-EIGHT

Ash made drinks throughout the night for guests, including Ruby, who showed him a few bartending tricks and helped him master the craft. She said, "The first few drinks must satisfy the drinker's thirst, like how the inciting incident of a Federico Fellini film gets the audience hooked. The drinks that follow don't matter that much, because they all taste the same."

The first glass he picked was for Alize. He put his glass next to hers and poured a shot of Appleton Rum in each. The warmth of the rum cracked the ice, and he filled the glasses with Coke. There was one piece of lemon left. He squeezed it into Alize's glass and dropped the dried piece into his, and the leftover juice sizzled between the ice cubes. He passed the glass to Alize and took a sip from his. He made a gin and tonic for Ruby. She reminded him about the extra limes in the fridge, but before he could fetch them, Alize got up and went to the kitchen.

"I think she likes you," Ruby winked at Ash. *Is this really happening?* he wondered as he smiled at Ruby.

The swimmer from the U of C swim team stuck around. He grabbed a beer from the fridge and sat next to Alize on the floor. Ash overheard that she admired his Australian accent and that he admired her exotic looks. Ash thought that was lame and that it wouldn't do anything for her, but a part of him worried that he might lose the Barbadian island girl to him. After all, the guy was tall, white, and could swim 100 meters in a minute, and Ash couldn't even go to the other side of the pool without holding the side bar. The thought made him uneasy, and he raised his glass and took two big gulps.

"This is gonna be fun," Alize said.

"So, we play this game a bit different." Ruby put her hands on the floor in front of the empty bottle of Moosehead. "We spin the bottle to select the person to question, and obviously the person who spins the bottle gets to ask truth or dare."

"You can't pick truth twice in a row." Alize smiled.

"And dares can't be repeated," Ruby said.

"Can I just sit and watch?" the cute girl said and took a sip of her pinot grigio.

"Hell no. This is not a free show. Everyone is playing." The swimmer pulled her hands and brought her down to her knees.

"Why don't you spin?" Ruby passed the green bottle to the swimmer. He kissed the bottle and spun with all his strength.

"It's not about the force, buddy. It's all in the wrist," someone said. Ash chuckled.

Kris spun the bottle, and it stopped in front of a girl. She was quiet and petite, with ash blond hair. There were five buttons on her blouse, and they were all closed, including the top one that touched the base of her neck. She picked truth. Kris asked her if she'd ever had a dirty thought during church. She lowered her head and giggled.

"Oh my. You go, girl!" Ruby said.

For her turn, she asked the swimmer if he'd ever masturbated at a friend's place. He said yes. The swimmer made Alize reveal that she once kissed a girl in junior high. When the bottle stopped in front of Ash Amlani, Alize Millington got happy. She asked him if he'd ever been with someone he wasn't supposed to be with. For his truth, he lied and said yes, and that it was his teacher. Ash spun the bottle, and he wanted it to stop in front of Alize, but it pointed at Ruby. Alize came up to him and whispered in his ear to ask Ruby who she lost her virginity to, but Ruby refused to answer that question and threw her ice cubes at Alize.

"Well, you know what that means." Alize clapped.

"What?" Ash said.

"If someone refuses to give the truth, the spinner of the bottle can ask them to kiss anyone in the circle."

"Awesome! Okay, so Ruby ..." Ash looked around. He knew that he could ask her to kiss one of the girls, ideally Alize, but he wasn't drunk enough to give out such requests. So he asked her to kiss Kris, who popped a mint in his mouth, and everyone laughed.

"Go, Ruby, go," the swimmer said. They kissed in the middle of the circle, and everyone cheered.

"I'll get you," Ruby warned Ash, and then spun the bottle. It stopped in front of Ash.

"Again?" He put his drink down.

Ash picked truth again. Ruby thought for a second, looked up at him, and asked to give details about what he did with his teacher sexually. He refused to tell the truth, as there was no truth to the lie; there was no such story.

"I could easily make you kiss the boys, but I've been wanting to see this since I first saw you two together sitting by the bonfire," Ruby said. Ash had spoken to all the girls present in the circle, earlier by the bonfire, so he didn't know what Ruby was talking about.

"I want you to kiss Alize for one full minute," she said and pointed at Alize with both her hands.

Alize jumped up with joy and her enthusiasm made everyone laugh, except the swimmer. She grabbed Ash's hand and they walked by the patio glass door. She held his face in her hands and they kissed.

"You taste good," Ash whispered.

"You too," she giggled.

They kissed more.

"I said a minute, not forever!" Ruby called out. They laughed and walked back to the circle. The bottle spun, people drank, secrets spilled, friends made out, and Ash Amlani couldn't keep his eyes off Alize, the Barbadian island girl.

At 4:30 a.m., people started leaving. The cute girl in the yellow summer dress went home with the swimmer, Ruby took Kris to her room, and Alize Millington and Ash Amlani made out on the patio. The house got quiet, the embers in the bonfire cooled, and birds started chirping on the clothesline.

CHAPTER TWENTY-NINE

At 4:45 a.m., Alize got up from Ash's lap, walked barefoot on the patio's wooden floor, and peeked inside the living room through the glass window.

"Looks like everyone is gone," she said, turning to look at Ash.

Maybe tonight is the night I'll finally do it, Ash thought.

"Do you wanna stay over?" Alize said. Ash nodded and gave her his biggest grin. She grabbed his hand, pulled him up, and together they went back inside the house.

"Let's be quiet," Alize whispered as they walked up the stairs. Ash stopped her, put his hands around her waist, and kissed her.

"You're so horny," she whispered in his ear.

Finally! It's happening!

When they entered her room, she lit a candle while Ash looked around the room. He noticed a framed photograph of a little girl who stood next to a pink bicycle with a white basket. "Is that your sister?" he asked.

"No, that's me. I was six when I got this bicycle," Alize picked up the frame and looked at it. "I love this photo," she said, then put the frame back on the nightstand.

"Me too," Ash said.

"You know, maybe it's a stupid superstition, but it helps me write new songs." She smiled.

"You mean this photo?" Ash said.

She nodded. "Not always, but when it works, it works," she said.

He walked around her room, looked at her books, and walked back to her bed. "The candle smells nice," he said.

"It's spicy cinnamon," she said and kissed him again.

They sat on her bed and kissed some more. She pulled back and looked at him. "You're so damn irresistible."

She took off her white summer dress, threw it on the floor, and laid on her back in her red panties and black lace bra. *She's so hot*, he thought. He looked at her, but he didn't know what to do.

"Are you just gonna stare at me?" she said.

He swallowed his saliva and moved closer to her.

"Come here," she said, pulling him toward her. "Take your clothes off."

She got up and helped him undress. He wanted to enjoy every moment, but he couldn't stop thinking about the possibility that she would find out he was a virgin, an unmapped, unexplored, immaculate virgin.

She took her bra off and placed his hands on her breasts. He couldn't believe he was touching the naked body of a girl for the first time in his life. He played with her breasts like he was molding dough.

"Suck on them," she said. He put his mouth on her right breast and put his left hand under her panties. He expected it to be a smooth area, but his fingers touched hair and he moved them around. She took her panties off, pushed his hands between her legs, and his fingers got wet. He did the in and out with his fingers, and the more he sucked on her breasts, the wetter she got. *This is amazing*, he thought.

When he moved his fingers further down, she objected and pushed his hand away. "I want you in." She pulled his penis and it got harder. He didn't know what to do next. He thought about the girl in *Deep Throat* and wondered if he should open her mouth and do what Dr. Young did to Linda Lovelace, or if he should wait for her to get on her knees like how Justine Jones did it in *The Devil in Miss Jones*. But she stayed there, opened her legs, and he went for it.

"Wait," she held his hands. "Do you have a condom?"

He shook his head.

"Shit." She sat up and covered her face and said, "I'm so sorry."

"Why?" He pulled her hands away from her face.

"We *have* to use protection," she said. "Let me see if there are any here."

She got up and opened the drawers. "Can't believe you don't have condoms on you," she said.

Why would I have condoms? He didn't know if he should help her find the condom or let her do her thing. "Did you find any?" he asked.

She turned and stared at him. "What do you think?"

"You can get one from Ruby," he said.

"No, it's too late to knock on her door." She went to bed and put her panties on. "She's probably doing it with Kris."

He picked up his clothes from the floor and looked around the room. He didn't know if he was supposed to get dressed and go buy a pack of condoms from one of the 24-hour convenience stores or go home. *Maybe I can call Khalid, and he can get me some from the motel,* he thought.

"Get back in bed. We cannot have sex, but at least I can sleep in your arms," she smiled.

I don't want to sleep. I want to have sex, he thought.

"It's like a blessing in disguise," she said. But he didn't see how that could be true; he didn't see any grace in this moment, the moment that had left him a virgin yet again.

She got up, blew out the candle, pulled out a baggy nightshirt from the drawer, and put it on. It read, *SLEEP LESS. DREAM MORE.*

The morning breeze blew in, the white curtains fluttered, and Ash Amlani smelled coffee.

The previous night played in his head: the room was dark, one candle burned, and it was spicy cinnamon. Her lips were soft, and every time she gave him her tongue, he got a mouthful of a flavor, and it was pleasant. He thought to himself that if Alize was a coffee, she would be a full, smooth delicious brew, with a very subtle roasted flavor added to it.

When he woke up, Alize's arm was around him, the room was dark, and he needed to pee. He carefully moved her and walked on his tiptoes to the bathroom. The seat was up; he peed and put it down.

He touched his temple with his index and middle fingers together. He opened the small white cabinet, took two Tylenols, and chased them with tap water. When he put the bottle of Tylenol back in the cabinet, his eyes widened. *No way!*

He picked up a single condom and examined the edges. He saw that it was expired, but whatever.

I have the perfect luck, he shook his head and left the condom on the sink, flushed the toilet, and went back to bed.

"Are you okay?" she asked.

"Yeah, just needed to pee."

"Me too." She got out of bed and walked to the bathroom. The room was dark, but when the wind blew through the curtains of the open window behind the bed, he saw the roundness of her buttocks, and he got excited.

He heard the toilet flush, the bathroom door opened, and Alize hopped back to bed. He saw the reflection of the moon light in her widened eyes.

"You will not believe this," she said.

"What?" he said, sitting up. She pulled his hand into hers and placed the foil-wrapped packet in his palm. "This was just sitting there, on the sink, all this time. Can you believe it?"

"That's crazy," he said, hesitating.

"Wanna play?" She brought his hand to her breast and grabbed his penis, and it sprang up with all its might.

What about the expiry date? He wondered if he should tell her or just go with the flow.

"Umm," he said as he held the condom in his hand.

"What's wrong?" she said.

"It says August 1997."

"Oh, that means nothing. It's just a trick to boost sales," she said.

Thank God this is not a dream, he thought, smiling.

"I'm so wet for you," she said as she moved his hands between her legs. He ripped open the package and pulled out the condom. He examined each side with his finger, but it was dark, and he couldn't tell right way from wrong.

"What are you doing?" She took the condom from him, pushed her thumb in, and brought it to the tip of his penis.

"I can do this," he said and snatched it back from her. He kissed her on the lips and pushed her on the bed.

"I want you to fuck me hard," she moaned.

"Yes, as soon as I put this damn thing on." He tried to roll the wrong side of the condom on his penis. It popped off and flew out the window.

"FUCK!"

"What happened?"

"I lost it." He drew the curtains, but it was too late.

"No, you didn't," she said, sitting up.

"But who cares? We can just pretend it's a dream." He pulled on her legs.

"You wish it was a dream," she said.

"Now what?" He looked at her.

"I don't know," she said. "You messed up, so forget it. Let's get some more sleep."

He frowned and noticed that she didn't look for her nightshirt or her panties. She stayed in bed with him naked.

"This is not too bad, though," she said as she put her head on his chest. He smelled Wella shampoo. The neurons in his mind jumped around and made him think of Jenny Poonja and the ferry ride to Vancouver. Her voice echoed in his head: "If you didn't do the in and out, in and out, then you're still a virgin."

He closed his eyes and fell asleep.

CHAPTER THIRTY

Two weeks after the Heritage Day long weekend party, Ash met with Ruby a few times to help her on a feature story she had written about the underground prostitution in Calgary for *The Reflector,* the Mount Royal College's independent newspaper. He shot portraits of three girls, individually, on the roof of one of the strip clubs on 3rd Avenue. He didn't have access to the university darkroom, so he developed the film in his own secret after-hours darkroom, Adrianna Saul's office in the Residence Services. Ruby loved his black and white portraits and so did the editor-in-chief. One of his photographs made the cover, the editorial team said.

During that time, he also spoke to the Hookmani clan, who told him that Shefrina had moved from the attic to a room on the second floor. Ash pictured her on the veranda, sunlight falling on her face, children playing in the streets, and pigeons shitting on the clothesline. He called her a few times, but her family said she needed her privacy. He sent her flowers, and the family said that she received them. He thought about flying to Karachi, showing up on her doorstep, and bringing her back home with him, but he hesitated. He didn't know if she would accept him. He wasn't the Ashiq she preferred; he was Ash now. He was different. He was not like the other brown immigrants that swarmed around their own kind. He avoided them, and instead he hung out with white friends, Canadian friends that took him out dancing, gave him drugs, and accepted him the way he was. He doubted if Shefrina would want to see Ash. She only liked Ashiq, the boy who was proud of his culture, his blood, and his own skin. Ash was a fake persona; he lived in his own world, where fiction imitated reality. Shefrina was the only person in Canada who called him Ashiq; everyone else called him Ash. She was the only person who kept him connected to his true self. She was the link, she was the connection, she was the one.

Ruby and Alize planned to go to Nelson, British Columbia. Ruby invited Kris to come along, so Alize called Ash to see if he wanted to join them. Ash was surprised that Alize called, because two weeks earlier, after the Heritage Day long weekend party, Ruby told Ash that Alize had waited for him to call to ask her out, but he didn't. At first, he wanted to but, after he spoke with his mom, something changed in him.

During their regular weekend call, Mrs. Amlani told Ash that she ran into Shefrina at the fruit and vegetable market, where Shefrina was getting ingredients for her newly established restaurant. His mom said that Shefrina wanted to do something for the underprivileged and at-risk youth in Karachi, so she established a vocational program to help them pursue careers in hospitality.

"She's happy now," Mrs. Amlani said. "By the way, I wanted to ask you something."

"What?"

"This morning I read a feature about her in the newspaper, and your name was in it," Mrs. Amlani said.

"What do you mean?"

"Shefrina told the reporter that when she was young, she used to play some sort of a game, pretending to cook at home with you and some other kids. Do you remember that?"

"I do." Ash smiled.

"I should send you a copy of this. Shefrina looks so elegant in the feature photo, and I also love the title."

"What does it say?"

Mrs. Amlani read the title: "*Ghar Ghar, the Karachi Restaurant Where Empowerment Is on the Menu.*"

Ash thought about *Ghar Ghar*, the pretentious game he had played with little Shefrina when they were ten years old, when they made chicken biryani and baked birthday cakes in imaginary pots and pans. The more he reminisced, the more it made him change his mind about asking Alize out on a date.

Ash spent days thinking about Shefrina, how to get her back, and if he should get her back. It was a struggle, going back and forth from Ashiq to Ash, from Ash to Ashiq.

So when Alize called Ash to see if he wanted to join them on their trip to Nelson, British Columbia, he wasn't sure.

"I would have loved to, but I'm going to Karachi, to see my family," Ash said on the phone.

"Can you change your ticket?" Alize said. "I'll make it worth your while."

"What do you mean?"

"You're so stupid," Alize said.

Ash didn't understand what Alize was referring to, so he stayed quiet.

"Oh God, Ash. I mean, we'll make sure we have enough condoms this time." She laughed.

He imagined himself naked with Alize under the waterfall, surrounded by the lush green wilderness of beautiful British Columbia.

"Let me call the travel agent," he said and hung up the phone.

He reached for the Yellow Pages, looked up the travel agency's phone number, and dialed. The travel agent told him that there was a flight available the following weekend and he could make the changes for a small fee, but later if Ash wanted the original flight back, he would have to pay twice the price. Ash thought about it for a few seconds, but Alize's naked body occupied his mind.

"Let's do it," he told the travel agent, hung up, and called Alize to pick him up.

✦✦.

Ash put his toiletries, a set of fresh clothes, underwear, and a small notebook in a weekend bag, and hopped in Ruby's car to go to beautiful British Columbia, in hopes of losing either his virginity or his dignity.

Ruby drove. Kris called shotgun. Ash and Alize sat in the back of the Jeep. Their hands touched twice, and she rolled her fingers into his.

Ruby pulled the Jeep up to a gas station to fill the tank. Ash came out from the back seat and offered to do a candy run. Ruby asked for a popsicle, Kris wanted a pack of Du Maurier Extra Light, and Alize wanted Skittles.

He got the popsicle from the cooler, grabbed Skittles for Alize and a box of condoms for himself, and stood in line to pay. He noticed a calling card poster that hung nearby, which read, *IT'S NEVER TOO LATE TO CALL.*

He thought about Shefrina. He wondered, why now? Why was he thinking about her again when there was a hot girl outside waiting for him? When he held a box full of extra lubricated condoms? He came prepared, it was his time, it was his day, and it was his moment to conquer. There was no need to reminisce about Shefrina. She was gone. She was history. She was his past. *Ghar Ghar* was just an imaginary game that they had played years and years ago. Yet, there was something that kept bringing her back to his mind, to his heart, to his soul. He made his purchases and returned to the car.

The Jeep made its way through the prairie wilderness. On the radio, Bob Marley sang *Is This Love,* and Alize Millington and Ash Amlani pulled a sarong over themselves. The sun shone high in the sky, and the wind blew across the prairies.

He looked out the window, and the warm breeze on his face reminded him of the drive he had taken from the Vancouver International Airport to the Poonjas' residence in Yaletown. *So much has changed since then*, he thought. The boy with a thick accent who came to Canada with an expectation of living a privileged life, a life where he was accepted, as an equal, as a friend, as a fellow Canadian, was now on the other side of reality. Who was he now? Was he the Ash who Jenny Poonja wanted, was he the Ash who Sally desired, or was he the Ash who sat in the backseat of the Jeep, waiting for the moment of glory? Or was he someone else entirely?

Alize held his hand under the sarong, and he opened his eyes and looked at her. Her skin glowed in the sun, her hair blew in the wind, and she looked stunning to him. *I am a lucky guy,* he thought.

She put a Skittle in his mouth, and he spit it out. "Eww! Why would you eat that?" he asked. She raised her eyebrows and wrinkles formed on her forehead. He couldn't believe that, for a moment, she looked old.

Ruby cranked up the music, Kris put his right hand on Ruby's legs, Alize put her sunglasses on, and Ash looked out the horizon through the dirty glass on the window, as if it would tell him what the future held for him.

The car sped along the open road and, suddenly, a dragonfly hit the windshield and exploded across the glass.

"Where did you come from?" Ruby said.

"Turn the wipers on," Kris said and looked at Ruby.

"I hate dragonflies," Alize said, putting her head on Ash's shoulders.

She loves dragonflies, Ash thought. He remembered the day he'd visited Khalid at the Hooks Motel, when a dragonfly came into the motel and Khalid told Ash that Shefrina had loved dragonflies since she was a little girl.

Ruby turned the wipers on, the disassembled pieces of the dragonfly's colorful body dispersed across the windshield, and Ash wondered how Shefrina would have felt at that moment if she was next to him instead of Alize.

It's easy to ignore a plethora of bugs around you, except the ones that vex you, Ash thought, *the ones that sting you, the ones that eat your food, the ones that splat on your windshield.* He let go of Alize's hand and pulled the notebook out of his bag. She lifted her head and looked away. He pulled the cap of the felt pen with his mouth and wrote:

"What about the ones that fly far from you, yet they make your life colorful and joyful, the ones that help you see the world with a different lens, the ones whose sting forces you to wake up and see your true self?"

As they drove along the prairie wilderness, Ash saw a field full of wildflowers, and he recalled what Mrs. Hookmani once told him that he himself was a wildflower. He thought about all the threats he had faced, the habitat loss when he had left home, the difference in the weather when he'd shoveled snow, and the intimidation of the white invasive bugs who'd wanted the Paki gone, back to his natural habitat. He would have been extinct, but he overcame those threats. He fought, he survived, he persevered.

"I totally forgot," Ruby said and pulled out a copy of *The Reflector*, passing it to Ash. The vertical black and white photograph he had taken covered half of the front page. It was a powerful portrait of identity. Underneath the title, it read:

Photographs by Ashiq Amlani (guest photographer)

"Why does it say Ashiq?" Alize asked. "I think Ash sounds better."

Ashiq does not replace Ash, because Ash never really replaced Ashiq. Both exist at the same time. He heard Shefrina's voice saying those words in his head, in his heart, in his soul.

"I'll always be Ashiq," he said.

"Well, duh. But you're Ash now," Alize said.

"Sometimes you're the windshield, sometimes you're the bug," Ash said.

"What?" Ruby looked at Ash in the rearview mirror.

"Can you drop me at the bus station?" Ash said. "It's time for me to go home."

Two days later

Karachi, Pakistan

At the end of summer and the beginning of fall, pink and burgundy Sapium leaves twirled for the first time; pomegranate, pear, and papaya blossomed; and Ashiq Amlani arrived at the *Ghar Ghar* restaurant, holding his breath, his large blue suitcase, and a bouquet of red roses.

He put a mint in his mouth, walked up to the entrance of the restaurant, and passed the flowers to the host. "I'm here to see the most beautiful girl in the whole universe," he said.

The sunlight fell on Shefrina's face, the children played in the streets, and Nusrat Fateh Ali Khan sang *Afreen Afreen* on the radio.

She took the bouquet, kissed him on his cheek, and said, "What took you so long, you dumbass?"

ACKNOWLEDGMENTS

This book wouldn't exist if it wasn't for my brother, Faisal, who inspired me to write my first novel. I still remember the day when I was depressed and clueless about what I wanted to do with my life, and he said, "You should write a novel. Isn't that what you always wanted to do?" So, I did. And I'm grateful to him for being there for me when I needed him the most. Writing this book saved me and changed my life, forever.

I would also like to thank my wonderful editor, Annie Tucker, who taught me everything I know about writing. You know the saying: when the student is ready, the teacher will appear. That's how I feel about Annie. She is a Godsend.

An enormous thank you to my dear friend, Natasha Fracchiolla, for rekindling my soul. She picked me up, held my hand, and touched my heart.

A huge thank you to all my first readers, especially Donna Serafinus, who helped fill the gaps and made this book a thousand times better.

Initially, this novel was part of a transmedia project, which failed. Since then, I learned that making mistakes was good; the process was what mattered the most. I met some amazing people on that journey, people who shared their creativity and their insights with me. I believe that everything happens for a reason, and now I know what I had to go through to get where I am now. I would like to thank everyone on that team, especially Ambreen Hooda, who spent months on the content edit. Saqib Khan, for his creative vision. And Farhan Shah, for his incredible music. I would also like to thank all the people that supported that project financially, who believed in me and my creativity. Thank you all from the bottom of my heart.

www.ingramcontent.com/pod-product-compliance
Lightning Source LLC
Chambersburg PA
CBHW020601030726
47497CB00007B/2039